MOLASSES
MURDER
IN A
NUTSHELL

MOLASSES MURDER
IN A
NUTSHELL

A Nutshell Murder Mystery

Frances McNamara

Frances McNamara

First published by Level Best Books/Historia 2022

First edition

ISBN: 978-1-68512-250-8

Cover art by Level Best Designs

This book was professionally typeset on Reedsy.
Find out more at reedsy.com

For Frances Glessner Lee and Dr. George Burgess Magrath in recognition of their contributions to Legal Medicine and Forensic Science.

The purpose of a forensic investigation is said to be "convict the guilty, clear the innocent, and find the truth in a nutshell."

Praise for Frances McNamara's Previous Novels

"Historical mystery readers who enjoy female sleuths and action firmly centered in realistic portraits of the past will find *Death in a Time of Spanish Flu* a compelling story... With so many facets and conflicts emerging from the start, it takes a deft writer to draw readers into a scenario which juxtaposes social issues, political strife, home life, and solving murders. Frances McNamara is such a writer, capturing the personal observations, lives, and approaches of believable (and likeable) characters who find themselves caught up in situations beyond their ken or control... The action is nicely paced, the premise and mystery are unpredictable, and the historical backdrop of the times is so realistically integrated into the plot that readers will find it a snap to absorb its atmosphere, principles, and the sense of changing times... Although it's the 9th book in the Emily Cabot series, newcomers to Emily and her times will find *Death in a Time of Spanish Flu* stands nicely alone as a solid introduction to her life, world, and approach to problem-solving. Libraries looking for powerful blends of history and mystery which present a sense of place that feels familiar and is engrossing to modern readers (even those who normally don't read books from either genre) will relish the realistic and personal portrait that makes *Death in a Time of Spanish Flu* hard to put down."—*Midwest Book Review*

"Set in 1918 Chicago, McNamara's excellent ninth Emily Cabot mystery (after 2020's *Death on the Home Front*) finds Emily's physician husband, Stephen, serving on the front lines of the Spanish Influenza epidemic... The real-life characters mingle seamlessly with the fictional ones to capture the

i

myriad contradictions of Chicago, from the dirty politicians and gangsters who run the city to the idealists, intellectuals, and revolutionaries who are committed to social change. This timely novel informs as much as it entertains."—*Publisher's Weekly*

"McNamara's suspenseful third Emily Cabot mystery...convincingly recreates a pivotal moment in American labor history...Laurie King and Rhys Bowen fans will be delighted."— *Publishers Weekly*

"McNamara...proves, if anyone was asking, that librarians make great historical mystery writers... I'd follow Emily to any location."—*Historical Novels Review*

Chapter One

Boston North End, January 15, 1919 12:30 PM

Theresa Ryan marched along Commercial Street, skirting patches of wet ice. The frigid temperatures had suddenly let up, but it was much too early for spring. Clouds hung low on a day that was unexpectedly close and warm for January. Streetcars rumbled overhead on the elevated tracks rounding the jumble of tenements that squatted on Copp's Hill.

She was in search of her sister, Maggie. She hadn't called or visited for more than a week. Since leaving her husband, Maggie's moods swung between bubbling optimism and dark dread. Theresa had skipped the midday meal to search for her sister. She didn't like leaving her new housekeeping job in the middle of the day. Luckily, if she was late getting back, she was sure Mrs. Lee would forgive her. The lady from Chicago was a fair employer and Theresa was grateful for the job on Beacon Hill. Housekeeper was a step up from her last position. But something was wrong with her only living sibling, and she needed to find out what.

Reaching the door of her sister's boarding house, Theresa shouldered it open and yelled, "Maggie!" No answer. "Maggie, where are you? Why didn't you come to dinner yesterday?"

She clambered up the narrow stairway. The door to Maggie's room stood open. Theresa sniffed. Alcohol. The bed was mussed but empty. There were two chairs pulled up to the foot of the bed and dirty glasses on the floor. The bathroom door was ajar, and she heard water. Pushing the door open, she saw black stockinged legs sticking up from the tub. "Maggie, what are you doing?" Two steps forward, and she tripped on something that caught her ankle. An empty bottle rolled on the floor. She saved herself by grabbing the edge of the wooden surround that encased the tub. One of the faucets was running, pouring water into Maggie's open blue eyes.

Theresa jumped backwards, slamming into the sink behind her.

Suddenly the floor rattled. There was a sharp, splatting sound like the rat-ta-tat-tat of a rumbling train that was close and getting closer. That wasn't right. The wooden building shook as the rumbling continued. Theresa grabbed the sink. The floor cracked beneath her, and she felt herself falling. She threw an arm over her head as the room flew apart, and she felt as if she were being shoved by a hand on her back into a thick liquid smelling of gingerbread or baked beans. Before she could react, a heavy black wave pushed her down, filling her mouth, nose, and ears. The sink leaned against her.

She wanted to yell for help but if she opened her mouth, she'd drown. Squirming, she pushed the sink away. Keeping her eyes shut, she tried to swim through the sludge that forced her into the bathtub. She got a foot braced against the edge and tried to climb up, finally getting her head out when the great shoving motion against her back stopped. Desperate, she wriggled a hand out to scrape the muddy substance from her eyes and mouth. Then she gasped for air. Treading the heavy liquid, she realized it must be molasses. A big tank of the stuff stood across the street from the boarding house. It had to be from that. After coughing out more of the sodden muck, she breathed in a lungful of fresh air.

Where was Maggie?

Chapter Two

Mrs. Frances Glessner Lee envied Jake Magrath his profession, even if it required cutting into dead bodies with a scalpel. She'd waited a month, settling into her new city, before contacting him. Dr. George Burgess Magrath was a friend from her past. A big man with unruly salt and pepper hair, he was medical examiner for Suffolk County. He had gone to Harvard with her brother, and she had known him when she was a young girl in her parents' home. She still thought of herself as "Fanny" even though she was forty-one and had three children. As if she had never quite reached adulthood. And she remembered him as "Jake" who visited her brother in Chicago. Her father and brother admired him for his accomplishments. So did Fanny. She was determined to recruit him as an ally in the face of her family's disapproval of the upheavals in her life.

When she finally invited him to lunch at the Parker House, Fanny explained to him why she'd moved East to manage a home for returning soldiers on Beacon Hill. "Even before the divorce, I realized what a lonely and rather terrifying life I was living," she told him. "I never went to school. I have no letters after my name, and I'm seen as 'a rich woman who doesn't have enough to do.' I couldn't live like that anymore. I want to do *something* in my lifetime that has *some* value to society." Sharing this confidence might make Jake uneasy, but she wanted him to understand. Even in the short time she'd been in the city, she'd heard people talk about him and seen his name in the papers. He was recognized by his flowing black Windsor tie and fedora hat. Fanny admired the way he forged his own idiosyncratic trail through the world. Why couldn't she do that?

Before Jake could answer, a young boy appeared beside the table. "Sorry to interrupt, Dr. Magrath, but there's been an accident on the waterfront. They need you." He struggled for breath. "The morgue people told me to say you should come. Mr. O'Connell said he'll bring the motor. You're to go straight to Commercial Street by the docks."

"What happened?" Jake asked. Fanny realized that *whenever* something happened involving deaths in the city, he would be consulted. She'd always longed to study medicine. Of course, it was her own fault that she hadn't.

"It's awful, sir. The tank burst on Commercial Street, and there's *molasses* everywhere." The boy flapped his open hands by his sides. "It exploded—covering everything. People are *stuck!*"

Fanny had an awful vision of people waist-deep in melted candy. How absurd.

Jake beckoned to the waiter and stood, dropping his napkin. "I'm sorry, Fanny, I have to go."

She grabbed his sleeve. "Can't I help, Jake? Can't I do *something?* Anything?"

He looked down at her, and she sensed exasperation. He probably thought she was useless in her lace-edged blouse and velvet jacket. What did she know about the people who lived in the crowded streets of the North End? How could she be anything but a hindrance? She bit her lip and willed him to overcome that view of her. She knew Jake believed it was a mistake to repress a person just because she was a woman. It was why she wanted him as an ally. Years ago, when she'd visited Magrath's family, they took her to see Radcliffe College, but when Fanny returned to Chicago, she forgot all about her desire for an education. She regretted that choice now.

Jake pursed his lips and peered at her through his eyeglasses. Expelling a gust of air, he shook his head. "All right, then. Come along quickly. I'll get us a cab."

While the maître d' helped her into her coat, Jake was already at the door calling for a taxi. If she didn't hurry, he'd leave without her. She liked that about him. Too many men of her acquaintance treated her with an unwelcome solicitude that made her feel like an invalid. She hurried out behind him.

On the way, she asked why there would be molasses in the middle of the city. "It's used to make industrial alcohol for ammunitions," Jake explained. "They ship it up from the Caribbean, then pump it into a huge tank beside the harbor. It gets trucked over to a refinery in Cambridge, from there to munitions factories. All part of the war effort." He concentrated his dark gaze on her face. She felt like she was being examined under a microscope. She clenched her jaw, determined to show him her interest was serious. "As medical examiner I'll have to take charge of the fatalities. Death from this type of accident is an 'unexpected death,' and it's my responsibility to investigate it. If any deaths are caused by the tank failure, the owners will be held liable. I need to see the circumstances of the accident at the site before I examine the bodies in detail. Unexplained death must be explained. That's the point of having a medical examiner."

Fanny suppressed a cringe at the thought of dead bodies sunk in molasses. This was no time to appear delicate. Even with her sheltered background, she'd seen death before. Between the war and the flu epidemic, they'd all seen death. Everyone had grown toughened hides. Fanny stiffened her back. Jake had thought well of her once. She hadn't lived up to his expectations then, but she wanted to earn his respect now.

Chapter Three

The cab stopped, and Jake stepped out and waved to a young man. While he pushed through the crowd to reach them, Fanny took Jake's hand to climb down. When he withdrew it, she nearly tripped. "Good Lord," he exclaimed, looking up.

Above them hung a huge metal web of elevated train tracks that ran down the middle of Commercial Street. Fanny had studied maps of her new city in the past month, so she had a picture in her mind of where they were. Industrial yards extended out to harbor wharves on the right while brick and clapboard tenements climbed Copp's Hill on the left. Directly ahead of them, the elevated platform was crushed as if some clumsy child had stepped on a toy train track. Beneath the tracks that remained was a huge pile of rubble. She could see that molasses must have come in a wave from the wharf side, swept under the elevated, engulfed a rickety tenement, and pulled it apart as the wave receded again, like the ocean. It left a mountain of pieces of walls, broken shutters, wooden floors, shattered furniture, and splinters of wood. In the distance, beyond the hole, the track curved left toward North Station.

"Look at that." Jake pointed. Overhead a train had stopped a few yards short of the drop into oblivion. "It's a wonder they weren't all killed."

"Dr. Magrath, I've got boots for you," the young man said when he reached them. He kept talking while he held out the long rubber boots. "They're looking for survivors. There are five dead already. We put them on the walkway over there. All the transports are taking the injured to the Haymarket Relief Station right now."

Jake grunted as he pulled off a natty pair of loafers, handed them to his assistant, and stepped into the hip boots. "Fanny, this is my assistant, Edwin O'Connell. Edwin, this is Mrs. Lee, an old friend. We were dining when I got your message."

The young man nodded to Fanny as he packed Jake's shoes into a satchel. Burn scars marred the right side of his face. His right hand was scarred and withered as well. She assumed he'd been wounded in the trenches.

Both legs encased in rubber, Jake stood tall and snapped the suspenders on his shoulders. "We'll need to take a look at where it happened. The tank was over there behind the paving yards, wasn't it?" He pointed toward a pile of brick and planks some distance from the broken train tracks.

"That's right, sir. See that piece of twisted metal under the El there? That was the side of the tank. The whole top is intact over there." He pointed toward some wharves. "The sides must have exploded, and the molasses flowed out, then the top just fell down where it stood."

There was a heavy sweet smell in the air and a brown slick on the ground. Men used their hands to dig into the mound of brick, glass, and broken slats of wood under the elevated track. In some places, they stood knee-deep in the dark molasses. Above their shouts, horrible animal squeals and snorts came from the yard on their right. A shot rang through the air, and Fanny flinched. The squealing became more frantic until another shot rang out. Then it was quiet.

"It's the horses," Edwin O'Connell said. "Some of them were buried in molasses. The police are putting them down."

Fanny thought of the coal-black stallion she kept for riding at her family's New Hampshire estate. Her stomach lurched. She took a big breath.

Jake Magrath looked at her and huffed. "I've got to go look at the damage. Will you be all right, Fan?" There was impatience in his stance and a challenge in his eyes.

"Yes, of course. I'll be fine." She waved her hands in a shooing motion. "You go on. Don't worry about me." She was the one who'd insisted on coming, and he had duties to fulfill. He glanced around and seemed reluctant to leave her. "I'm fine," she told him. "I can take care of myself."

Jake frowned, but he shrugged and grabbed Edwin's arm to pull him along through the crowd of men. Fanny stepped out of the way as two young sailors lifted an injured man into a taxicab. The poor soul groaned, and the slop of sticky brown molasses coated him. Only his eyes, nose, and mouth had been wiped.

Chapter Four

Fanny walked toward the mound of debris and saw that the men clambering over the ruins included young sailors, firemen in oilskins with wide heavy hats, and other men in boots and jackets who must be dock workers.

Her left foot sank down in the slick muck just as she heard someone yell, "Up here. She's alive." The young sailors took up their stretcher and the crowd parted to let them through. Fanny tried to take a step back but felt the tug of the sucking molasses on her foot. How ridiculous. She'd insisted on coming along to help, and now she was going to need help herself. She was mortified. Her right foot was sinking. She struggled, near panic, until she felt a hand under her elbow lift her up.

"Mrs. Lee, what are you doing here? Can I help you?"

It was Lt. Matthew Bradley, a broad-shouldered young man who was one of the first residents to move into the home for returning soldiers that she managed. Injured in the war, he usually walked with a cane. Even without it today, he was steadier on his feet than she was. Fanny regretted that he was seeing her in such a helpless state, but she clutched his arm for balance. After asking, "May I?" he reached down and grabbed her ankle to pull her foot out of the muck. She leaned on him as they walked a few yards back to where the molasses had hardened.

Above them, a brown-streaked woman on the side of the mountain of debris yelled and struggled against two men who tried to lift her down to the sailors with the stretcher. Dripping and stumbling, she resisted their help.

"Maggie, Maggie's down there," she yelled, weeping with rage. When she doubled over in a spasm of coughing, the men picked her up and handed her down to the sailors. She was coated with molasses, and her overcoat was torn to shreds in places.

Fanny recognized her voice. She clutched Lt. Bradley's arm. "I think that's Mrs. Ryan." Theresa Ryan was a diligent young woman Fanny had hired as housekeeper at the home. How had she come to be here?

Fanny let go of the lieutenant and groped her way through the crowd. "Mrs. Ryan?" she called when she got within a yard of the stretcher.

"Mrs. Lee." Theresa Ryan pulled away from the young men trying to make her lie down. "Please, Mrs. Lee, please help me. My sister's in there." She waved at the pile of planks and bricks behind her.

She grabbed Fanny's sleeve. Brown liquid oozed over the silver fox on the cuff. It occurred to Fanny that she must look foolish to them all with her fur collar and cuffs and her stylish helmet of a hat. She took for granted that her position in life demanded courtesy and deference from people like the rough men around her, and she got it automatically. When she saw them move apart for her now, it was clear to her that deference was a veneer over the hard facts of life for people like these. It was Theresa Ryan who needed help. What good was Fanny to her?

Fanny gulped and stood her slippery ground. "Is she alive? Do they need to dig her out? Should we tell them?" Putting an arm around Theresa's molasses-coated shoulders, she hoped she wouldn't become stuck to her. How silly, but she needed to comfort the poor woman however she could.

Theresa was crying. "No, no. She's gone. She was gone already when it happened. She was in the tub underwater. Dead."

Fanny had an awful thought. Would the poor girl be found naked by this crowd of strangers? "Was she bathing when she died?"

"No. She was dressed. She must have fallen in...or someone pushed her." Theresa clutched her employer's hand. "They'll think it was the molasses, but it wasn't. She was dead already."

One of the young sailors hovered over her. "Ma'am, please, we need to get you to the relief station."

Lt. Bradley moved closer. Above them, the search for survivors continued. Men threw planks out of their way as they worked.

"Found one," one of them yelled down. "She's gone already, though."

Theresa looked up, tears streaming down her face, making brown tracks. "My sister, Maggie," she said.

Two big firemen elbowed their way through the crowd then, clanking with tools, their huge helmets showing above the heads of civilian bystanders. "Clear the way, please, folks. There's still people alive, and we need to search for them. I need a couple of you men to come with me. We've got men trapped in the firehouse, and we need help moving debris to get to them. You, and you." The older of the two firemen chose a couple of the sailors who were standing around and led them away.

The other fireman began to move away, then stopped to look at Theresa. He squinted at her features through the molasses caked on her face. "Is that you, Mrs. Ryan? You're Thomas's wife, aren't you? I thought I heard someone yell your name out." He stopped to remove his helmet. Then, glancing after his fellow fireman who was disappearing into the crowd with his recruits, he cleared his throat. "We've just taken Tom to the relief station. He's in a bad way, ma'am. He and some others were in the fire station on the wharf when it collapsed. There's still men stuck there, and we've got to get back." He pointed to the sailors. "You men, get Mrs. Ryan to the Haymarket Relief Station and help her find her husband." He turned back to the stunned woman. "I'm sorry, but I have to go." He forced his way through the crowd to catch up with the others.

"Tom," Theresa moaned. "Oh, no, Tom."

Even through the molasses, Fanny could see she'd blanched at the news, all blood gone from her face. She tottered. Fanny held her under the shoulders and lowered her to a plank. "Tom," Theresa said. "I must go to him." But when she tried to rise, she tumbled back.

"You need to sit for a moment," Fanny said.

Theresa trembled with shock. Her shoulders heaved, and she sat for a while, weeping. When she tried to rise, Fanny helped her. "I must go to Tom."

Lt. Bradley stepped up. "Come, Mrs. Ryan, Mrs. Lee and I will go with you, help you find your husband." Fanny was grateful for the young man's presence.

Theresa pulled away when he tried to take her elbow, and she appealed to Fanny. "I can't leave Maggie. They'll think the molasses took her. Oh my god, Tom." She broke down again, put her dirty hands to her face, and bent over double at the waist. Lt. Bradley looked on helplessly.

Stooping to pat the woman's back, Fanny gently got her to stand up again. "You let Lt. Bradley take you to your husband. I'll stay here and make sure they get your sister out. They've had to move on to look for other survivors," Fanny pointed up at the pile of rubble. "But they left a marker where they found her. See it up there? I promise I'll make sure they take her to the morgue. I'm so very sorry, my dear."

Theresa straightened, looked her in the eyes, and gulped. "You'll make sure they dig her out? I can't leave her there under all that." She waved at the pile of broken planks and pieces of walls.

Fanny imagined the young woman buried beneath all that rubbish. It might be better to spare Theresa the sight of her sister's damaged body. "I promise. And I'll come to you at the relief station and tell you all about it. You go now. Go to your husband."

The weeping woman turned back to Lt. Bradley. She leaned on him as he helped her to a waiting ambulance. He looked back over his shoulder, but Fanny shooed him away. Two young sailors stomped away with their stretcher in search of other living victims. Fanny moved her feet, trying to make sure she didn't get stuck again as she watched the men sift through a mound of splintered wood. She'd wait for Jake to return, then she'd follow the corpse of Theresa's sister. It would go to Jake's morgue, and he would know what to do. At least she could do that much for Theresa.

Chapter Five

Fanny waited under the elevated tracks. An hour later, Jake Magrath returned to arrange for transportation of the dead. Fanny watched as he organized the placement of the bodies in a row along the edge of the street. All the transports were still being used to take the injured to the relief station, and only after that was done would the dead be taken to the North Grove Street Mortuary next to Massachusetts General Hospital.

"I have to go back and get things ready," he told Fanny as he removed the hip boots. "Edwin will stay here. He'll help you find the woman you're looking for."

Fanny stood with Jake's assistant as the medical examiner drove off in an old model T outfitted with police bells, gongs, sirens, and lights. "What a peculiar machine," she commented.

"He calls it Suffolk Sue," Edwin told her as they watched it pull from the curb and heard the roar and clang it made.

"Where in the world did he find it?"

"It's a 1907 model he got when he was first made medical examiner. For what he pays to keep it running, he could have bought a new one years ago. But he's got it all set up the way he likes. He can throw beams of light on the scene of an accident and make his way through any traffic with the bells and gongs. I've never seen anyone so dedicated to his job." Fanny could imagine Jake roaring up to a crime scene and flashing lights into everyone's eyes. Full of energy, he'd take command of the situation and boss everyone around.

Turning to Edwin, Fanny noticed he placed himself so she wouldn't see the damaged side of his face. Even so, he was solicitous in a way that made her feel elderly. Pulling out a crate, he sat her down near the row of shrouded bodies while he went off to oversee the extrication of Maggie's body from the rubble by a couple of sailors he'd persuaded to help. Fanny resigned herself to wait while they worked to free Maggie's body from the wreckage. *What a grim day.*

Finally, an ambulance stopped at the line of shrouds. There were eight now, and men began loading them. By then, Edwin had laid Theresa's sister down with the others. Covered by a canvas shroud, she made an oddly shaped bundle. When Fanny stood, intending to straighten the body, Edwin stopped her. He explained that rigor mortis had set in with the woman's legs splayed out in an awkward pose. When he saw the repulsion on Fanny's face, he reassured her that the body would eventually relax. Fanny felt like she was failing Theresa. She had promised to take care of the woman's sister. But there was nothing she could do to restore dignity to the poor dead soul.

While she rode with the driver of one of the transports, Fanny thought of what a strange way it was to learn about the body in death. If she'd studied medicine, as she wished she had, perhaps she would have learned about rigor from a book. Instead, she had the unforgettable experience of this day to imprint that knowledge on her mind. "Rigor mortis" would be forever set in her mind attached to the image of the dead woman's shrouded body.

The mortuary was in a side street off Cambridge Street very near Charles Street, at the bottom of Beacon Hill. Fanny realized it was not far from the home where she lived with her returning soldiers on Mt. Vernon Street, at the top of the hill behind the state house. Jake's place of business was a brick building that stood in the shadow of the huge gray stone block that was Massachusetts General Hospital. Two wide doors were used for ambulances and hearses to deliver or take away the dead. Despite the gloom, she could see the dank garages already held one corpse. Perhaps they needed to wait for space inside the building for more bodies. She felt a strong resistance to entering this place of death, as if the air itself pushed back at her, but she told herself not to be a coward.

Edwin led her inside, where she blinked at the brightly lit industrial-sized rooms. Medical instruments, scales, and glass jars on metal shelves lined the walls. Everything was streaked with brown molasses, and water ran over two tabled corpses to wash off the sticky mess. Two other corpses were covered in sodden sheets.

Jake was waiting to take her arm and lead her to an office stuffed with bound volumes, notebooks, and loose papers. A long wooden paddle leaned incongruously against the wall. He

sat her down in a metal chair and removed a blood-and molasses-stained apron that he hung on a coat rack before perching on the end of the wooden desk. "Now, what's this all about?"

Fanny told him how worried Theresa Ryan had been that no one would know that her sister Maggie was already dead when the flood hit. Fanny admitted that she didn't know the dead woman's surname or history or whether Theresa thought she'd died in an accident or if someone had harmed her. Jake frowned impatiently at her ignorance, then he got up and told her to wait while he looked at Maggie's corpse.

Fanny was annoyed with herself for failing to ask the questions Jake wanted answered. Yet, remembering how Theresa had looked, she couldn't imagine trying to extract names and addresses from her when she needed to go to the side of her injured husband so desperately. Theresa must be at the relief station now.

Fanny looked around the office. It was messy but organized. So much information in dozens of bound volumes and reports. She hungered for that knowledge. What was it like to be Jake Magrath and do investigations and come to conclusions on how people had died? He must have a sense of power and satisfaction such as she had never felt. Ignorance was a trial. Her ignorance made her feel as if she were trying to climb the side of a slippery hill, never getting any purchase. She envied Jake the competence he had from the knowledge he'd gained from all those books. But she was a divorced woman with children, far too old to become a student now.

Jake returned with a thoughtful expression. "There are some curious elements. I've set Maggie aside for a thorough examination and a complete autopsy. That's all I can promise. We have our hands full trying to identify the bodies and notify kin. Meanwhile, I need you to find out more about

'Maggie.' What's her full name? Where did she live? Who's her next of kin? What was she doing in that building? We need to know all of that."

Fanny stared at him. He had an assignment for her. She was grateful and surprised.

"You don't have to do it tonight." Jake took in her disheveled appearance and frowned. "You should go home to recover. It's been a trying experience for you."

Fanny's hackles rose. He thought she was too weak to experience the sights and sounds of the day. "Not at all. I promised Mrs. Ryan I'd let her know what happened. I'll be off to the Haymarket Relief Station. Her husband's a fireman. He was injured so she went to him there. I need to tell her that her sister's body was found, and I'll ask about her background." She stood up, only a little shaken on her feet. She dreaded what she might see at the relief station—so many injured people. But she truly didn't want to go home to Mt. Vernon Street, where the cook would be ladling out hot soup and serving meatloaf and potatoes. She would feel empty if she returned to the safety of the home without seeing this thing through.

"All right." He stood up. "If you insist. Edwin can take you. He needs to pick up a couple more deceased from the relief station. But you can wait until tomorrow to let me know what you find out. You may be willing to keep on into the night, but I've got enough to do here as it is, and I won't be able to get back to Maggie until tomorrow…afternoon." There was a hint of weariness in the way he stood, but Jake never gave in to weakness. Fanny knew that about him. He prided himself on his heartiness, preaching physical fitness and exercising by rowing and swimming. It gave her a secret feeling of relief to see him flag, even for a moment. He was human, after all.

"I'm off then," she said, trying to sound as jaunty as he would be if he were in her molasses-soaked shoes. But she was glad to get a lift from Edwin, even if it meant riding in a hearse.

Chapter Six

Magrath waited until Fanny left before he took down his dirty apron and dropped it over his head again. He wasn't quite sure what to make of Mrs. Lee's inserting herself into the day's disaster. She was driven by an ambition he didn't understand. He'd known her when they were both young but, in recent years, he'd kept in closer touch with her brother. It was a good sign that she took no notice of the ruin of her fur-trimmed coat and leather shoes. At least she wasn't out for the kind of attention he often saw Beacon Hill matrons seeking—the "I'm a poor little woman" act. Managing a home for soldiers returning from the war suited her, and he was sure her father and brother approved. But rushing off to the scene of a disaster in the slums of a city she hardly knew—that was unexpected and probably would not be approved by her family. Jake was well aware of the prominence of the Glessner family compared to his own humble origins. He never minded the difference, but it was always there. The family's wealth and position were a barrier between them. Curious that she seemed to want to break that down.

He stepped out into the white-tiled space that was his laboratory. Metal tables held sheet-covered bodies, all still clothed. Earlier, Edwin had pulled back the sheets on a few so that water from a faucet could flow over them in an attempt to remove the sticky coating of molasses. The brown stuff clung to everything and streaked everywhere. It would make examination of so many corpses difficult, and Magrath knew there were more bodies in the garage. Soon they'd need to be able to allow relatives in to view and identify the victims. He had a lot of work to do before he could rest.

Still, the molasses flood wasn't as bad as the influenza epidemic. Last autumn, they'd had to release hundreds of bodies without even a cursory look. Jake was lucky the flu spared him, but three of his workers succumbed, and only after the nightmare was over had he found Edwin O'Connell. Since then, the young medic had become indispensable.

He hoped today's tragedy wouldn't be as bad as the streetcar disaster in 1916. Forty-six died that night after a streetcar plunged over the edge of an opening drawbridge into Fort Point Channel. Families had clamored at the doors that night, looking for loved ones. He could still remember the grief-stricken cries that haunted his building for days.

Despite the need to start examining bodies, Jake found himself in the operating theater used for the Harvard Medical School classes he taught each week. Edwin had put Fanny's Maggie beside an unidentified young soldier who had died from a head wound the previous week. His was the lone body in the morgue before the molasses disaster.

He pulled the brown stained sheet down and saw the open blue eyes of the dead woman as she lay on her side, with her legs bent up and splayed wide where they had leaned against the side of the tub. If she'd been alive when the molasses encased her, she would have closed her eyes. The gooey coating was thinner on the face and the back of the body. It lay thick on the legs and the folds of the dress between her thighs. Fanny had mentioned the bathtub. If Maggie had been partly underwater, it could explain the difference in the thickness of the molasses. He could picture the whole tub being shoved forward and down by the wave of thick liquid.

Fanny wanted him to examine the body because she believed the woman had died before the molasses disaster. He wondered why she was so anxious about it. Did she assume someone had purposely killed the woman? Surely it was some kind of accident.

He touched the extended legs. They were encased in roughly knitted stockings under the skirt, and they were stiff, very stiff, and very cold. Puzzled, he stepped into the other room and pulled the sheet off the corpse of an older man. Taking a wet towel, he washed away some of the molasses and felt around the head. It was just beginning to stiffen, and the flesh was still warm as room temperature. That told him the man had been dead from three to eight hours. The flood had happened before one o'clock in the afternoon, and it was now around five. Rigor was just starting on this corpse. Replacing the sheet, he went back to Maggie in the other room, checking that she was as cold and solidly stiff as he had noticed before. It was true. The woman had been dead for more than eight hours and not more than thirty-six. Fanny was right. This was a death that could not be explained by the molasses flood. It was a puzzle, but it was one that would have to wait until after the many other corpses were identified. He turned away with a huff. He needed to get a start on the night's work. They already knew who this woman was, and her sister knew that she was dead. There were others whose families didn't even know yet that they were gone. They were the first priority.

Returning to the main room, he began examining the bodies for identification. He placed a chart at the foot of each table, and for each body filled a bag with any identifying jewelry, papers, and money. He had called in additional staff, and they would arrive soon. They'd help when the relatives came looking for missing family members. While he moved from corpse to corpse with automatic motions, his mind wandered to memories of Fanny Glessner.

Jake had been deeply impressed by the Glessner family ever since his Harvard classmate George Glessner had taken him home to Chicago for a visit so many years ago. It was a wealthy, cultured family very different from his own. Later, he'd been invited to the family's New Hampshire estate, where he remembered how the enthusiastic young girl had served breakfast to two hungover undergraduates in the cottage out back. Over the years, Jake had kept up his friendship with the family, visiting them in Chicago or New Hampshire. Today, Jake had seen a spark in Fanny's eyes that had been absent ever since her huge wedding. He hoped it wouldn't die out again. He missed the impulsive, generous young girl who'd followed him around, lapping up information about his time at Harvard. He'd been disappointed in her when she didn't attend college, but surely that was true for most young women of her station. More than most, she had the resources to get a degree if she wanted it, but she hadn't. Fanny might bemoan that now, but she had little enough to complain of, really. Did she know how much better off she was than the working women who ended up in his morgue?

He looked down at the wrinkled face of such a woman on the next table. Probably she was no older than Fanny, but there would be white hair under the brown caked molasses, and her hands would be red with the stains of the heavy detergents she used. He knew she was a laundress. He recognized the signs. He could categorize the bodies so easily after all this time in the job. Hers was an unexpected death, but he was sure he knew how it happened. This poor woman had been hurrying to deliver packages of clean shirts or sheets when the tidal wave of molasses swept her to oblivion. If he cut through the heavily patched coat and skirt, he'd find gray woolen undergarments, so different from the silk lingerie he was sure Fanny wore.

He shook his head, carefully replacing the sheet over the woman's tortured face. He'd find molasses in her throat and lungs, he knew. Straightening up, he looked around. So many bodies, and there would be more to come. People would want to know who to blame. Everyone would remember the bombing back in December 1916 at the Salutation Street Police Station, not far from the tank, and assume this was another explosion. That earlier bombing was the work of anarchists. He closed his eyes and pictured the scene on Commercial Street. Yes, he had noticed that windows in the upper floors of the buildings were intact. You'd expect them to be blown out by the concussion of a bomb...if a bomb had been responsible for the collapse of the tank.

What if anarchists weren't to blame here? Was the company at fault? Could it be their negligence that caused the disaster? It was his job to do everything in his power to bring justice to the souls of these poor corpses. If the deaths were due to negligence rather than criminal actions, he would need to say so in his report. It was his responsibility to identify what had caused these deaths.

And yet, his highest duty was to be objective. On the first page of every one of his field notebooks, he wrote a quotation from Dr. Paul Brouardel, a noted French pioneer in legal medicine: "If the law has made you a witness, remain a man of science: you have no victim to avenge, no guilty or innocent person to ruin or save. You must bear testimony within the limits of science." Besides living by this principle himself, Jake tried to instill it in the medical students who came to his operating theater once a week.

As he continued examining the corpses, he wondered. Did Fanny envy him his work? He'd gotten that impression when they talked at lunch. He wondered if she was sincere in this quest for meaning in her life. He'd believed her once, a long time ago, when she told him she wanted to break free of her place at home. He'd been inspired then, to help her.

He remembered the trip to Chicago when, unbeknownst to his friend George, he'd plotted to free the girl from her home so she could explore the streets of Cambridge. But Jake never unpacked the chemistry textbook and Radcliffe application he brought. As soon as he entered the mansion, he was asked to toast Fanny's engagement to Blewett Lee, the slow-talking southern lawyer she'd chosen. Obviously, Jake had misunderstood. And he'd thought himself barely saved from a serious blunder as he watched Fanny become locked into a dance of social engagements as if she were a figure carved into the frieze of a tomb.

After all, the strictures Fanny complained of applied to most women of her station. Certainly, he knew some women who turned their backs on the expectations of society and sought a career, but it was never easy. Nonetheless, Jake believed a person should exploit the possibilities of their situation, whatever that was. He himself had worked his way through Roxbury Latin to graduate with a scholarship to Harvard, where he met young men like Fanny's brother. Yes, they had many more advantages than he did, but that was irrelevant. Their situation had nothing to do with his own. After graduation, he worked in pathology laboratories, attended medical school, and eventually became medical examiner. At the same time, he rowed with the Boston clubs and sang with the Handel and Haydn society. He had a full life. Jake had never aspired to the wealth or social position of the Glessners. He was in a different station in life, and he always knew it. He felt sorry that Fanny couldn't reconcile herself to her own place, which, after all, was so much better than that of many women he saw in the working classes. He was skeptical about what she thought she could accomplish here, in a city that was not her own. He hesitated to jump in and try to help her again. If she truly had a passion for a profession of some kind, she'd have to prove it to herself and the world.

Chapter Seven

In the hearse, Fanny sensed that Edwin O'Connell hated sitting with the damaged side of his face toward her, but there was nothing she could do about it. His right hand, curled like a claw, moved the gear shift between them.

"The relief station is a last resort for the poor," he told her. They drove through crowded streets to Haymarket Square, where he stopped before a three-story brick building with a white portico entrance. "I need to go around to the back," he said. "If you go to the front desk, they'll help you."

Fanny climbed out. There were people gathered on the sidewalk, but she excused her way through the crowd. They gave way to her sex and the wealth they could see in her clothing. Inside it seemed as if some huge brush had swept a layer of brown molasses across the place, like a watercolor on white paper. It ran in stains down the jackets and aprons of the medical staff and swirled in muddy circles along the linoleum floor. A janitor with a pail of steaming water swabbed the sticky entranceway as wheels on stretchers jammed to a halt. When she asked for Fireman Ryan, the nurse at the desk directed her to the second floor.

In the corridor upstairs, Lt. Bradley leaned against a wall. He came to attention when he saw her. His handsome face looked drawn above the khaki of his uniform. His Adam's apple rose and fell before he got out the words. "Mrs. Ryan is in there." He pointed to a closed door with a panel of frosted glass. "Her husband's very bad. I'm not sure what to do."

Fanny patted his arm. Despite having seen combat, he was too young to know how to deal with someone else's tragedy. She hushed him and approached the door. Inside, she could hear a steady murmuring. Pulling off her stained gloves, she turned the handle. Gently opening the door, she heard women's voices, prayers punctuated by a clicking noise. Theresa Ryan and another woman sat beside the bed with rosary beads in their hands, tears running down their faces. The figure on the bed was a great bear of a man who groaned and mumbled, turning his bearded face from side to side. An effort had been made to wash away the molasses, but it matted his hair and beard, and dark lines of it outlined his features. The odor of sweetness mixed with a sharp anesthetic smell. "Oh, Tess," the man moaned in agony. "I'm bad, Tess. It's really bad now." His hands scratched at the sheets, and he rocked his large body. "I can't stand it anymore. It's crushing me. The pain, the pain."

Gulping a sob, Theresa stood and put a hand on her husband's cheek. It seemed to calm him for a moment. She looked up at Fanny and Lt. Bradley in the doorway. "I'll be back, Tom. It's Maggie. Her building's destroyed, and she's dead. I have to see what happened to her."

He squeezed his eyes shut. "I'm so thirsty," he whispered. Theresa's face reflected his agony. She clearly wished she could do something to take away the pain. The older woman rose and poured water into a glass. She gently waved Theresa away as she put an arm behind the man's head and helped him to drink.

Theresa took Fanny into the corridor. "He was in the fire station on the wharf when it collapsed. They're still trying to get some of the other men out. Did you find Maggie?"

Fanny looked at Lt. Bradley, who beckoned them to a bench down the hall. After seeing them seated, he hovered a step away, as if to prevent anyone from interrupting. Fanny was grateful.

"We found her body, and I went with her to the morgue. Dr. Magrath is the medical examiner. He's an old family friend, and he'll take care of her." Even though Maggie was dead, Theresa would want someone to watch over her sister. Fanny took the woman's hands in her own. "I'm so sorry, my dear, about your husband and your sister. But Dr. Magrath needs to know some things about Maggie. What is her full name? Where does she live? Is she married? Are you her next of kin? What was she doing in that building, do you know? And what did you see before the molasses knocked the building down?"

"Oh, Maggie." Theresa sniffed and wiped her eyes with the back of her hands. "My sister is… was Margaret Timilty McKenna. Her husband is William McKenna. He's a police detective." She frowned as she said it. "They live at 225 D Street in South Boston. But Maggie moved out a few months ago." Theresa looked around. Fanny could see she worried they might be overheard. Lt. Bradley sensed her discomfort and moved a few more steps down the hallway.

Theresa swallowed. "Billy McKenna can be a hard man, and she'd had enough of it. I tried to help her, but she felt she had to leave him. Maggie worked in the office at the place that owned the molasses tank, so she found a room near there. She was supposed to come to dinner at our house yesterday, but she never came. That's what made me go look for her." Tears brimmed in her eyes. "She wasn't in her room, and it looked as if she'd had people in there with her last night. She drank, you see." Theresa bowed her head. "She said if *he* could do it, so could she." She looked Fanny in the eye. "I told her that rooming house was a bad place for her. It was too near the bars in Scollay Square. I'm afraid she was drinking last night. I found her in the bathroom. There was a bottle on the floor, and her legs were sticking up from the tub. She was dressed, but her slippers were on the floor, and her head was under the water. I could see she was dead. Poor Maggie."

"I'm so sorry." Fanny patted her back.

Theresa wiped her eyes. "I don't think she just fell down. She could have been drunk, that's what Billy will say. But I don't think so. I think someone did this to her." She wrapped her hands around her waist and hugged herself. "She was getting away from Billy." She groaned and shook her head. She didn't look at Fanny. "I'm so ashamed for her. There was another man, a soldier. She said he was going to take her away, but I didn't believe her. She was always wishing for more. Maggie wouldn't ever be satisfied. She mocked me for being happy with too little. She had such ambitions. She didn't think my Tom was good enough. He's the kindest, best of men, not like that Billy McKenna. And now see what's happened. He doesn't deserve to suffer like this, poor Tom."

Fanny felt a pain in her heart. She wished she could say something to Theresa that would soothe her like cool water on burning flesh. But there was nothing. The woman's sister was on a table in Magrath's morgue, and her husband was dying in agony in the next room. Fanny felt ashamed of her own situation. She'd divorced her husband a few years earlier and left her children behind in Chicago to relieve the pain she felt at her own emptiness. How could she claim to sympathize with Theresa? Like the dead sister, Maggie, Fanny had ambitions beyond the circumstances where she found herself and, like Maggie, she had attempted to escape. Her children were older now, and away at schools, but hadn't she abandoned them just as much as Maggie had abandoned her husband?

Fanny heard a man's deep voice and the sound of boots at the far end of the corridor. She turned to see two large men coming toward them. One wore a gold badge on the pocket of his wool overcoat and a bowler hat on his head. He had a dark brown mustache that covered his upper lip, heavy eyebrows, and a thick waist. Behind him was a taller, younger man in a gray overcoat with brown pants tucked into rubber boots. He had a small brush mustache on his square face, and no hat on his thinning reddish hair. They came barreling down the hallway, calling out to Theresa, who appeared to know them.

Fanny and Theresa stood at their approach, and Lt. Bradley moved out of the way with a look of doubt on his face. They didn't seem to notice him as they bore down on the women.

"My brother-in-law…Maggie's husband," Theresa whispered. She stepped forward. "Mrs. Lee," she said loudly. "Here are my brothers-in-law, Patrick Ryan and Detective William McKenna of the police department. This is Mrs. Lee, my employer. She's come to comfort me."

Theresa gripped Fanny's hand.

"Where's Tommy?" the taller man asked.

Theresa pointed at the door. "Your mother's with him. He's in a bad way, Patrick." She gulped back a sob. "They don't think he'll live the night. He was in the fire station when it collapsed."

His face white from the impact of the bad news, Patrick Ryan went into the room where Theresa's husband was groaning.

"What about Maggie?" Detective McKenna asked. "That house she was living in was destroyed. Is she here somewhere? Have you seen her?" Theresa stiffened but, before she could reply, McKenna noticed Lt. Bradley. His face became red with a vicious scowl. "You," he said. "What're you doing here?" He flung himself at the soldier, pinning him to the wall with one arm across his throat.

Theresa tried to pull him off. "What are you doing, Billy? He's just a resident from the home Mrs. Lee runs. He helped me find Tommy." She pulled at the policeman's back, but he stood hard as a rock.

Fanny was astonished. What should she do? She was helpless in the face of this kind of physical confrontation.

"Get off me, Tess." McKenna shoved Theresa away with one arm and pressed against the soldier's body. Fanny caught Theresa before she fell. "You stay away from my wife, you hear, soldier? I see you with her again, and I'll make you wish you'd never left the trenches. You get it?" He straightened up and shoved Lt. Bradley away, turning back to the women. "Where's Maggie? I want to see her now."

Fanny was afraid. He looked like a horse gone mad. He took a step toward her. She put an arm around Theresa, who huddled at her side. With all the backbone her mother had ironed into her for use in social occasions, Fanny looked the angry man directly in the eye. "I am so sorry to have to tell you, Detective McKenna, your wife is dead. Her body is at the morgue."

With a wail, the detective launched himself at Lt. Bradley again.

Chapter Eight

Fanny was paralyzed with fear. She looked around for help. Two firemen hurried down the corridor. They must have come to visit Theresa's husband. When they saw the fight, they pulled McKenna off Lt. Bradley. Fanny stepped back to the wall, keeping her arm around Theresa. The commotion drew Patrick Ryan from his brother's room, and he was the one who finally talked the incensed police detective into a calmer state. Fanny tightened her hand on Theresa's shoulder. She steeled herself to keep from cringing. She'd never felt such roaring emotion so physically close to her before. The arguments she'd had with her own husband were cutting and cold, nothing like this.

"Pat, Maggie's dead. Her body's at the morgue," Theresa said.

Patrick looked around at Theresa as he held the angry detective by his upper arms. "Maggie? Oh, no." He enveloped McKenna in a tight hug then, and the detective finally broke down with wracking sobs. The display of grief shocked Fanny even more than the violence.

She stepped forward and took Lt. Bradley by the arm. Theresa nodded and motioned for them to leave. The lieutenant was reluctant. He looked back and forth between the men and Theresa as if worried for her safety. "Come," Fanny whispered. "We need to let them grieve." When Bradley saw all the fight had drained from the police detective, he responded to the pressure of Fanny's hand.

Outside, she found a cab to deliver them to the soldier's home. Lt. Bradley seemed in shock. He kept saying "I don't know what he means. I didn't know his wife. Why did he say that?" Fanny had no idea, but she tried to soothe

28

him as the driver drove up the steep hill.

Wendell House consisted of two buildings connected by a walled garden. The larger, five-story brick dormitory was on Mt. Vernon Street, while the second, a brownstone, was behind it, around the corner on Hancock Street. Both stood in the shadow of the gilt-domed state house. About a hundred enlisted men were housed in the big building, which had parlors and a large dining area. She felt like the principal of a school when she walked through those spaces. Today, she entered by the door of the smaller four-story house on Hancock that housed a few officers and a suite for Fanny herself. She could relax a bit more in the brownstone. She didn't have to project authority as much as she felt she had to in the larger building.

The tall wooden door had a graceful lily outlined in the frosted glass window. As Fanny unlocked it, she felt chilled. She hurried to step out of the falling darkness into the warmth of the brownstone. Inside, she sighed with relief to be home.

The air was tangy with smells of meatloaf, and she could hear the tapping of silverware against porcelain coming from the dining room on the left, where the officers dined. After she and Lt. Bradley removed their coats and soiled boots and chose slippers from the tangle of footwear by the coatrack, she led the way into the drawing room on the right.

Fanny let out a breath as she looked around at the dark wood panels that glowed in the firelight. The smell of burning wood and the crackling noise from the fireplace reassured her. Not only clean and warm, compared to the scenes she had witnessed that day, the room was quite handsome. Even her mother would approve of the leather padded chairs and sofas, the Tiffany glass reading lights, and the Japanese prints on the walls. Fanny had made this home for the young men coming back from the trenches, and she felt proud of it. She wanted them to feel as safe as she had felt growing up in just such a carefully maintained household. After the chaos of the streets that day, she was a little surprised to find it still so peaceful.

As she stood now in her own home, the molasses-filled streets of the North End seemed like a bad dream. She may have been useless at the scene of that disaster, but at least here, she'd created a place of rest for her officers, and she'd taken equal care in the larger Mt. Vernon Street building.

Lt. Bradley moved in shocked silence as he followed her. He sank into one of the armchairs, dropping his head into his hands. Fanny clutched her own hands at her waist. "I hope you weren't hurt, Lt. Bradley. I'm afraid Detective McKenna was out of his mind with worry about his wife. When he comes to his senses, he'll realize he's mistaken." Fanny believed Lt. Bradley's denial of McKenna's accusations. How could he have known the dead woman? He'd only been in Boston a few weeks.

"Why did the tank explode like that?" Bradley asked. Leaning his face in his hand, he shut his eyes. "It reminded me of the trenches. Men buried alive after an explosion." He sat up. "I promise you, Mrs. Lee, I didn't know Mrs. Ryan's sister. I suppose all men in uniform must look alike to civilians but it wasn't me. I swear it."

Fanny felt a pang of sympathy. He looked so young and yet so haggard. A police detective ought to be able to distinguish one soldier from another, she thought, but perhaps McKenna had seen Lt. Bradley through the eyes of a jealous husband rather than a police detective. "From what Mrs. Ryan told me, her sister was living apart from her husband." She didn't like to betray Theresa's confidence, but the young man deserved to know about the strained relations. After all, the jealous husband had attacked him.

"I see," he said. "That's why he was so angry. And then to find out she died in the molasses flood—that must have been shocking. I've never seen anything like that—molasses flowing in the streets, have you?"

"No. I was dining with Dr. Magrath. He's the medical examiner. When he was called to the scene, I thought I could help." She let out a short laugh. "I was embarrassed to find myself stuck in the molasses. It's a good thing you came along at the very moment I needed you, or I might still be stuck there."

"I was on my way to meet a man from my squad when I heard the sounds and saw people running that way. They said a tank burst. Somebody said there was a bomb."

"A bomb? I didn't know that."

"I thought we'd seen the last of bombs when we left France." He shivered, and she could see him trying to stop himself from shaking.

30

"Are you all right?" she asked, moving toward him.

He held up a hand to stop her. "Yes. It's just the shock, I suppose." He took a deep breath, and she saw beads of sweat on his forehead. "You've no idea how something like that can bring you right back. It's as if you were still there in the trenches with the guns going all the time." He paused. "Poor Mrs. Ryan. One of the nurses told me they don't expect her husband to make it through the night. I guess there wasn't much they could do for him."

"Yes, that's what Theresa said. So sad." Fanny lowered herself onto one of the sofas. "Her sister and her husband all in one blow," she murmured. She wanted to do something for her housekeeper, but it would be intrusive to return to the relief station. Theresa Ryan was with her family, and the best thing Fanny could do was to tell Jake what she'd learned about Maggie. But not until the following day. He'd been quite clear about that.

She wished Lt. Bradley had family to help him. She hadn't found his relatives back in Chicago yet. "Lieutenant, I'm sorry it's taking so long to locate your parents. There were disruptions everywhere while you were away. My contacts promised to get back to me later this week." The lack of news worried Fanny. She hoped she wouldn't need to comfort the soldier as well as poor Theresa. So many had passed suddenly when the flu hit in the fall, Lt. Bradley would be lucky if there were any relatives still waiting for him back in Chicago. The young man certainly needed that support. "You have a fiancée, too, don't you? A Miss Ballard? You were going to give me her address, weren't you?" If the worst happened, she would find the young woman to console him.

He sat up, clutching the arms of his chair. "Yes. I know you asked me for her address." She watched his prominent Adam's apple as he swallowed several times. What had she said to distress him? "The truth is, Mrs. Lee, I'm a bit anxious about facing Sophie…Miss Ballard. We got engaged in a hurry before I left but so much has changed since then. I don't know what to say to her."

A silence fell on the room like a sodden blanket thrown on the last embers of a fire to snuff it out. For the first time, Fanny wondered if the basic plan for the soldier's home had been a good idea. The Special Aid Society for

American Preparedness that founded the home wanted to locate the families and connections for these young soldiers before sending them back. Perhaps not all of the old ties could or should be re-established. Perhaps men like Lt. Bradley would need more time in Boston to prepare them to pick up those ties again, even if the people were still alive and waiting for them.

"Your feelings have changed?" she asked quietly.

"It's not that…or maybe it is. I don't know. But what I've seen and done… it's nothing Sophie could understand. I wouldn't want her to. But looking back on the vows we made then…we were such children."

Inside, Fanny recognized the feeling. She didn't know how to tell him that even without a war, the vows made before marriage could seem childish when you looked back. She shouldn't let her own experience infect a young man like Lt. Bradley, but she longed to agree with him. Instead, she asked, "You worry you've outgrown Miss Ballard? I'm quite sure Miss Ballard has had her own experiences that you don't know about." She remembered the piles of coffins lining roads, the closed schools, and cancelled events—all due to the influenza epidemic. There had been so many funerals, one after another, people had become practiced mourners. These young men had no idea how many empty places there would be at the tables they returned to. How could she prepare them for that?

Her duty was to help her soldiers find the way back to their old lives. She needed to make sure they had time to heal and a stable environment before transitioning back to the wounded world they'd left behind. Time was what they all needed. "You mustn't worry too much, Matt." Of course, she knew all their first names, and she was beginning to realize she needed to reach out to them more firmly, perhaps as if they were sons. "There's plenty of time to come to terms with Miss Ballard and anything else that haunts you. Come." She rose. "I can hear them all still in the dining room. I'll go down and have cook send up plates for us. She'll forgive us for being late when she hears about the molasses flood."

Lt. Bradley rose. He looked a bit shaken still. A hot supper was what he needed. As she led the way out, he said, "Please, let me know if there's anything I can do to help Mrs. Ryan."

"Yes. I'll find out how she is." Rather than joining him, Fanny headed down the steep stairs to the kitchen. Behind her, she heard deep voices greet Lt. Bradley in the dining room.

She was gratified that they needed her. Of course, she loved and missed her own son, John. But he was well taken care of in his preparatory school and in their house on Prairie Avenue, a mere block from her parents' mansion. In fact, rather than John needing her, she had come to depend on him since the divorce. How many times was she forced to ask him to intercede on her behalf with her father? It was humiliating to have to send her son to his grandfather to beg for money, and she hated it. John didn't need her, but her soldiers did. And so did her housekeeper. Fanny was determined to help Theresa find out how her sister had died. She would go to Jake tomorrow with what she had found out, and she would make him help them.

Chapter Nine

By nine o'clock that evening half the victims in the morgue had been claimed. Jake told his staff to close the doors and go home. He cleaned up the laboratory, thinking about a rare steak at a nearby restaurant that was open late. He should invite Edwin to join him. His assistant rented a room in a house full of ex-soldiers. Too bad he wasn't in Wendell House. Jake suspected the home Fanny offered her men would be quite opulent compared to Edwin's rooming house.

A knock on the door frame made him turn. Edwin was pushed aside by a whirlwind of solid male presence, a squat man in a bowler hat followed by a taller man with thinning red hair.

"Dr. Magrath, Detective McKenna of the Boston Police Department, and Mr. Patrick Ryan want to see you," Edwin said. He looked apologetic about the intrusion.

"Can't it wait, gentlemen? I was about to go in search of a juicy piece of beef. We've been at it all day." Unlike his gentle assistant, Jake was in no mood to be bullied by these men.

The police detective swept forward, ignoring Jake's words, until he was inches from the medical examiner's face. McKenna's dark eyes were buried between round cheeks and wiry brows. Hate, anger, and alcohol radiated from him. Jake took a measured step back. Not the first drunk he'd dealt with. But he prided himself on being able to calm all kinds of people in the extreme situations in which he met them. Like a wrangler known for laying hands on nervous thoroughbreds, Jake Magrath was known for being able to gain the trust of hysterical souls even at the scenes of the most atrocious crimes. The trick was to not allow anyone to provoke you. Keep calm. McKenna wore rubber boots layered with molasses. "You have my wife," he said in a voice that could have scraped cement. "Where is she?" He was shorter than Jake, and he shook a fist in the medical examiner's face. Jake could tell he was the kind of man who got angry when he had to look up at anyone's face.

The taller man, who must be Patrick Ryan, put a large hand with reddened knuckles on the detective's shoulder. "Billy, man, slow down, would ya?" McKenna shrugged him off violently.

Still in his shirt sleeves, Jake took another step back to get a better look at them. The medical examiner knew most of the homicide detectives but didn't recognize McKenna. He must be assigned to robberies or vice or the special flying squad that did undercover work. "I'm sorry for your loss, Detective McKenna. We do have a number of victims who haven't been identified yet. Mr. O'Connell here will help you to locate your wife among them."

McKenna's dark little eyes glared and, pulling off his bowler hat, he gripped it in both hands as if he would crush it. The taller man stepped forward. "I'm Patrick Ryan, Dr. Magrath. My sister-in-law is Theresa Ryan. She said you found Mrs. McKenna...who is her sister, Margaret, Maggie McKenna."

They were here for the body Fanny had brought him. Jake looked beyond the men to Edwin. He could see his assistant understood this was going to be difficult. "Detective McKenna, I can show you your wife's body. Please come with me," Jake said. He brushed past the angry man and headed for the operating theater where the bodies of Maggie and the unidentified soldier lay.

In the room, Edwin removed the sheet from Maggie's corpse. She was still bent into an awkward shape, so Jake began to explain about the stiffening that followed death.

"Maggie." McKenna ignored him and stooped to look in the open eyes of the dead face. Patrick Ryan hung back.

Jake felt sorry for the poor woman posed in such an undignified position. He wasn't an imaginative man, but he prided himself on being a scientist.

As such, he tried to ignore the shadows that seemed to flit just outside his vision when he worked on a recently dead body. He sensed them now, after this catastrophe. It was a sort of presence, but it wasn't real. He knew the sensation came from the weight of the knowledge of lost lives represented on his dissection tables.

Watching the white-faced husband stare at his dead wife, Jake thought Maggie McKenna would hate to be seen bent in half as she was. He took a breath and stood straight, as if he could somehow compensate for her.

Patrick pulled a chair over to the distraught McKenna and pushed him into it. McKenna hunched over, his shoulders shaking. When he finally sat up, tears flew to the side. "It's them anarchists that done it. They blew that tank. We'll get them." He squeezed his eyes closed while he shook with sobs.

Jake cleared his throat. He might as well get this out of the way. "Detective McKenna, we haven't done the autopsy yet, but we have reason to believe your wife may have been dead before molasses destroyed the building she was in." Jake took advantage of technical vocabulary to describe why they thought she was already dead when the wave hit. He hoped the lengthy digression would bring the emotional temperature down a notch. "We'll know more after the postmortem, of course." Unfortunately, the language only made the scene more vivid for Jake himself. He repressed a shudder at a vision of the woman held under water to drown in the tub, eyes wide with disbelief. He'd know for sure by what he found in her lungs, but he feared the worst based on what Fanny had told him. Apparently, her sister was sure Maggie was dead before the molasses flood. No need to burden the husband with that now, though, so he obscured the nightmarish vision by the language he used to describe it.

The shaggy detective wasn't going to be soothed. His eyes opened wide, and he jumped up. "You mean she was killed? Somebody killed her? One of those wops she was hanging around with killed her. I knew they were no good. I told her so."

"Now, Detective, I didn't say she was murdered. It could have been an accident," Jake said. He didn't approve of the policeman's use of "wop" to describe his wife's Italian friends, but he wasn't surprised by it. There was a lot of prejudice against the more recent immigrants, even by the Irish, who had suffered from a similar stigma not that long before. Magrath knew it was a dog-eat-dog world out there on the streets of the city. He hoped he could temper the policeman's wrath.

"She was drinking with them wops," McKenna yelled. "Those fucking anarchist bastards. Them and that Galleani. We knew they was planning something." He pounded his knees with his fists. Jake recognized the name of Galleani, who was a well-known anarchist sought by the police.

Patrick squeezed his shoulder. "Billy here is on the special force of the police," he told Jake. "They've been after the anarchists and the strikers."

"Luigi Spinelli and Tony DeCarlo. She was seeing them." McKenna looked up at them with bloodshot eyes. "Those fucking wops. I warned her about them."

His face was bright red in a way that made Jake worry the man would drop dead of a stroke. There were broken veins in his nose, and his round cheeks bulged. Looking at his clenched fists, Jake could picture them raining blows on his wife's body. He thought the man was barely restraining himself from venting his anger on the stiffened corpse as it was. Jake's neck muscles tightened. He'd examined too many female victims of marital violence. Always, by the time he saw the results of such misplaced passion, it was too late. He longed to see the men who did it beaten to a comparable state of hurt. But that was not possible, and he had to live within the realm of the possible. It was a deadlock that drove him to a brandy bottle on many a night.

He accepted now, as he had accepted so many times before, that there was nothing he could do for the dead, stiff Maggie except to identify the cause and manner of death so that those whose responsibility it was could find whoever had killed her and see him convicted. McKenna was a brute, but he seemed sincere in his grief. Not that Jake hadn't seen other wife beaters weep when they finally smashed the fragile sack of bones beyond repair.

McKenna gulped air, blinking back tears. Seeing him calmer, Jake asked, "These men you named, Spinelli and DeCarlo, you think your wife knew them?"

"They worked for USIA, the company that owns the tank. Maggie worked in the office there."

"I see. But apparently, your wife was not at work today. Do you know why?"

McKenna hunched over his knees. Patrick spoke up. "Maggie should have been at work. She moved out on Billy more than three months back. She was drinking some. She came to my pub some nights. I didn't like to see her there. She'd buy a bottle sometimes and take it back to her room. I think she'd have them up there, just to drink, you know. They wouldn't be welcome at my place, her a woman and them Eyeties." He was looking at Jake but keeping a wary eye on McKenna as if expecting him to erupt any minute.

"Did you see her last night?" Jake asked.

Patrick moved his mouth around as if he tasted something sour, then grimaced, squinting his eyes. "Oh, dear, now, it's like I said. She bought a bottle of whiskey, and I saw Luigi and Tony outside waiting on her."

McKenna groaned, but he didn't protest. Jake could see that the private party must have been a common occurrence for the dead woman. It would have been taboo in South Boston for a woman to carry on in such a way. But on Commercial Street, closer to the heart of town and closer to the blighted depths of Scollay Square, no one would take any notice. No doubt that was what drew the tired, beaten wife to that part of town. Still, she was a secretary for the company with the blown tank and familiar with the two Italians. Maggie's death seemed rather too coincidental with the disaster. Jake wondered if she could have known anything about the cause of the tank's failure.

McKenna was staring into space now, his grim visage stuck on his rumpled body. "If it wasn't them wops it was that soldier boy that killed her. Come back all wild and crazy from war but promising her a good life. As if you could believe a half of what these fellas say. She was a stupid bitch was Maggie when it came to men. She thought she could do better than me, and look where that got her." He reached a hand across to her thigh and stroked it. "You poor stupid bitch. I tried to tell you. Why you wanna get yourself kilt like this?" He pulled his hand back to hug himself and rocked back and forth, keening.

Patrick looked distressed. Jake looked at him quizzically, wondering who this "soldier boy" was. Patrick frowned, then spoke softly. "Rumor was Maggie was running around with some soldier. She never brought him to my place. Probably she didn't want Billy to know who he was. For fear of what he'd do. Like I said, that was the rumor. I don't know if it's true."

So, besides the two male Italian friends, the dead woman had a soldier as a lover. If he even existed. Any one of them might have killed her. Or her angry husband might have found her and done it. Or perhaps she'd slipped and fallen, and it was an accident after all. In his heart, Jake despaired of finding a killer. How could they find out what happened when the whole crime scene had been swept away in the torrent of molasses? The police would jump on the first explanation that suited their prejudices. He saw it all the time, and it angered him. He dearly wanted to explain the death of the poor woman lying there in such an undignified pose, but he wasn't confident at all that he would be able to do her justice.

Chapter Ten

Fanny gulped for air, drowning in a heavy sludge of molasses with her ex-husband and brother looking on from above...then she heard a yell followed by whimpering. She clawed her way to consciousness. She must go to Martha. Her youngest daughter had bad dreams sometimes, and she needed her mother. Fanny forced her eyes open. A strange room. It wasn't home. No, and the sound came from above, footsteps, more moans, a stifled yell.

She was in Boston, in the Wendell House brownstone. She was safe in her own large bedroom suite on the second floor. Martha had grown out of her night terrors and was safe at her boarding school. Fanny heard men's voices above her. The officers. They were moving around above her. She clutched the linen pillowcase and closed her eyes. There were big men upstairs. Whatever was causing the disturbance, they could take care of it. She should stay asleep, surely. They were men back from violent battlefields, having suffered terrors she couldn't know. How would her getting up help them?

She calmed down with the realization that she could pretend to sleep and hear about it in the morning. But then she pictured her father's face wrinkled with scorn for her. She had volunteered to come and look after these men until their homes were ready for them. She couldn't just ignore a commotion in her own home. She had invited them here, and she was responsible for them. She felt ashamed to be shirking in her bed.

She found her long woolen dressing gown and cinched it over her nightgown. She had nothing to fear from the young men above. She had no more concern for propriety than if she were going to her own son. She certainly had no thought that her presence could be provocative. She was bitterly aware that any allure she might have had when younger was long gone. It was a long time since she had inspired lust, if she ever had.

With a sigh, she overcame her reluctance, lit a little oil lamp, and climbed the stairs. The men were quartered on the third and fourth floors, two men to a room, with a bathroom on each floor. At the landing, she saw a door close on the left. Down the corridor, light streamed from a front room, and there was the sound of low voices. Men's voices. She followed them to the doorway.

Lt. Bradley was kneeling by the bed of a man still wrestling in wrinkled sheets and blankets. Eyes wide open, the man thrashed back and forth. Bradley looked up. "I'm sorry we woke you, Mrs. Lee. It's Hammond Stillman here. He suffers from bad dreams. I try to wake him, but he thinks he's still in the trenches." Bradley's hair was mussed, and he was alarmed. "Hush," he said, putting a hand on the man's arm to try to stop him from moving.

"No, no, no," the man mumbled.

Fanny stepped forward and, reaching out, she shook the man by the shoulder. "Wake up, Mr. Stillman. It's Mrs. Lee. Wake up."

The man's eyes popped open. He was breathing harshly, and he stared at her.

"It's quite all right, Mr. Stillman. You're here in Boston with us now. There are no more Germans, no more bombs."

The man raised his hands to his face. Bradley moved back to let Fanny perch on the edge of the bed. Stillman mumbled apologies. She could see he was mortified to have disturbed her.

"You mustn't feel bad, you know," she told him as she pulled at his bed covers, straightening them up as she might have done for one of her children. "We all have bad dreams. But we can't have you waking everyone, can we?" She pursed her lips. "I think I have something to help you with this. Lt. Bradley will stay with you. I'll be back in a moment."

At the door, two other men in dressing gowns stood, looking worried. She sent them back to their beds and hurried to her own room. From the bottom drawer of a dresser, she pulled out a leather box. Inside were stoppered bottles.

Before she left Chicago, her mother sat her down and helped her gather supplies and medicines for common ailments. Fanny's hand trembled as she pulled one out. Laudanum. She remembered her mother's warnings about its use. It could help to calm and bring on sleep, but in the past, it had been misused. Her mother had told Fanny about a friend from her youth, and the story had stayed in Fanny's mind like a lump of clay. When the woman of her mother's generation found herself in an unhappy marriage, she had been dosed with laudanum to stop her arguing with her husband. Discord wasn't acceptable. She took the medicine as she had taken the instructions to act like a lady all her life. It had stopped the arguments for a while, wrapping her in a dense fog of utter misery. Fanny's mother had tried to help her friend, but in the end, she had taken too much of the drug and died from it. The story gave Fanny a glimpse of the perils women of her mother's age had faced. She shivered.

Only use it in an emergency, her mother had warned. Fanny wasn't sure it was right to give the drug to the anguished soldier, but she reasoned that if it had numbed her mother's friend so effectively, it would work against the imagined threats the young man couldn't escape. Wraiths of memories haunted the ex-soldier. You couldn't fight the past, only the future. She thought the laudanum would serve to quiet the man and let him sleep without dreams for the night, and she could consult a doctor the next day. Jake would know if it was the right thing for the disturbed soldier.

When she returned to the bedside and fed laudanum to the man with a spoon, he was as obedient as a child to his nanny. She pretended to be quite sure the medicine would chase away the bad dreams, and he believed her. She shooed Bradley away. He shook a little before climbing back into his bed. "He's not the only one. We all have bad dreams," he told her.

"No need to here. You're all safe here," she said. She returned to her own room, not nearly as certain as she appeared for the men. But, even if her own uneasiness prevented sleep for the rest of the night, she hoped the men would be able to find some rest.

Chapter Eleven

Thursday, January 16, 1919

T he next day, Jake found himself invited to the St. Botolph Club on Newbury Street by Jeremy Wrentham, manager of the U.S. Industrial Alcohol Company of New York. A long-time member of the club himself, Jake was a little surprised the man had been nominated. Wrentham was obviously a New Yorker, and the Botolph was popular with locals. Jake was fond of the club, which was a convenient stop on his walk home from the morgue. A well-known local institution, the Botolph held monthly art exhibitions and served a juicy sirloin steak.

The dining room smelled of mutton during luncheon hours, and Jake noted the usual tables segregated by profession. Some young bankers with pretensions to art appreciation took a large round table near the windows overlooking Newbury Street. They tended to snap their white linen napkins as they sat down. The real money was in the corners where tables were occupied by gentlemen who took annual trips to Europe to purchase art. They nursed grudges and rivalries and clumped at the smaller tables to shelter information about planned purchases. After all, someone might try to outbid them at auction, and that wouldn't do.

The artists themselves sat at a long table near the kitchen door. The club had been established with them in mind, but there were never more than twenty who could afford the dues. Jake had gotten himself on the board and helped establish some paid memberships for upcoming young artists. There were no women. Women were allowed admittance to certain functions when accompanied by a member. It was a fact that would infuriate Fanny if she knew. Magrath himself had joined after viewing the club's exhibition of Mary Cassatt's works in 1909. They hung women artists, they just only fed them on special occasions.

Jeremy Wrentham fit right in. He wore a three-piece suit of soft worsted wool in a smudgy gray that reminded Jake of charcoal drawings. He had flat dark hair parted in the middle with a short fringe hanging over his forehead and a small mustache just carpeting his upper lip. Jake sensed immediately that the man's lithe grace and the dimples in his cheeks would attract women. The medical examiner also had a more scientific view. He couldn't help imagining how the man's body would look on his table, naked and cold. Wrentham would have well-articulated muscles and a flat stomach. Later in life, he'd gain more fat.

"Dr. Magrath, I'm so glad you could join me."

"You were quite insistent."

Wrentham motioned to the maître d' to seat them. Demanding in his attitude toward the staff, he made ushering movements to urge Jake on—as if the long-time member needed help navigating his own club. "Thanks, Benson," Jake told the maître d'. "How's Mrs. Benson? Recovered from the holidays, has she?" Having made his point, he sat himself down.

Wrentham ran a finger around his collar while they ordered from the day's offering. When the waiter left, he cleared his throat. "I was glad to be able to join St. Botolph. I see you're a member. I didn't know. I find it a good place to bring business colleagues. And there wasn't a great waiting period. Some of the other clubs make you wait for years."

Jake was amused to hear his own club put down so innocently.

Wrentham's face clouded over. "I do wish I could find something comparable for my wife. She belonged to several of the women's clubs in Albany. They're so difficult to join here, though."

Jake chuckled. "The ladies are very selective. It's not a case of time, from what I hear, more a matter of pedigree. But I'm sure you didn't invite me to discuss the local clubs. I'll need to get back to the morgue in a timely manner. We're still dealing with corpses from the tragedy yesterday."

"Oh, yes, it was a terrible, terrible thing that happened. That's why I asked you here. I wanted to let you know U.S. Industrial Alcohol will support you and the local authorities in any way we can. In fact, we have an expert team of engineers examining the site at this moment. They'll give us a written report in no time, and we'll make it available to you and other authorities immediately."

The waiter arrived with steaming plates. Before cutting into his steak, Jake said, "Of course, we'll be grateful for any help you can offer, but you can expect a full and fair investigation from us."

"Oh, yes, yes, I know. I understand, as medical examiner, you'll make a determination of the cause of death for any of the poor souls who were lost."

"The cause and circumstances," Jake said. "I also need to recommend any criminal proceedings against responsible parties."

"I know, I know. We wouldn't hinder that in any way, but I can tell you that our experts are among the most distinguished men in the country."

"Mmm," Jake said. He was relishing a mouthful of the tender meat. The gravy was fulsome without being too thick, and the roasted potatoes dripped butter.

Wrentham had not cut into his sirloin. "We did want to let you know that *we* believe the tank was blown apart by an external device."

Jake chewed, watching the USIA executive with raised eyebrows. When he could, he commented, "You think it was a bomb?"

The company man looked uncomfortable. "Yes, we do. As you probably know, there's a problem with anarchists in this town."

Jake's appetite was diminished. He could see where this was going. He eyed the juicy meat regretfully, figuring it was meant as an inducement, if not a bribe. They must think him a complete bumpkin. Didn't they know he could afford his own meal? He wiped his mouth with the linen napkin and sat back. "Mr. Wrentham, I don't know what your 'experts' have to say. I'm sure the police will be happy to review their conclusions. However, I must tell you that, so far, I have seen nothing to support the idea that there was an explosion."

"I can assure you the tank was sound. We have specifications and test results to prove it."

"I'm sure you do. But I've seen no sign of concussive injury in any of the bodies I've examined. I'd be happy to show you autopsy results and allow you to examine some of the bodies yourself if you'd like."

Jake saw the executive swallow and drop his knife and fork at the suggestion. "But perhaps the people were injured by the flow of molasses, after the explosion," Wrentham said. "Just because you haven't seen injuries caused by the explosion doesn't mean it didn't happen. The tank was sound, and it would take a substantial explosion to cause it to fail like that."

"So you say. We also observed that windows in nearby buildings were not damaged by the blast. Lower stories were damaged by the molasses, but you would expect the upper stories to have windows broken by the force of a bomb. They were not."

Wrentham's jaw was slack. He wasn't expecting his experts to be contradicted like this.

"You were lucky to be spared injury yourself," Jake continued. "Your offices were demolished, were they not?"

"Yes. I was lucky. I met my wife for lunch, so was out of the building. Otherwise, I would have been killed."

"And what of your staff? Do you know what happened to your secretary, Mrs. Margaret McKenna?"

Wrentham frowned. "Luckily, Mrs. McKenna did not show up for work that morning. Several of our workmen were injured, but none were killed."

"I'm sorry to tell you Mrs. McKenna was not so lucky. Her body lies in my morgue."

The man looked surprised. He pursed his lips for a moment without speaking, then said, "Oh, my. Of course. Her building was in the way of the flood. How terrible. Was that the one that was completely destroyed? And she was there when it happened?"

Jake tried to judge if he believed the surprise of the man. He couldn't be sure. "She was in the building, yes. But she was dead before the tank burst. I have yet to complete an autopsy, but she was found dead by her sister before the molasses flood hit the building."

"How awful. I'm so sorry for her. How did she die?"

"We don't know yet. It might have been accidental, or it might have been homicide."

"Homicide? You mean someone killed her?" Wrentham asked.

"It's possible. Why? Do you know of anyone who would want to kill the woman?"

"No, but she was estranged from her husband. I know she had moved from her home some months ago. I don't concern myself with the personal lives of our employees, but I had heard that her husband beat her. He's a policeman, you know, so she couldn't call the police on him. A brutal man by all accounts."

"You've met him?"

"No, no, of course not."

"Is there anyone else who might have reason to harm her?"

"I don't know. I'm sorry to say she was known for drinking after she moved to that part of town. Never on the job. It never caused her problems at work." He seemed to feel the need to explain why he'd hired her. "It's a very male shop, so it's not easy to find clerical help, most of our workers are laborers, and most women don't want to work there. But she didn't mind."

"Do you think her drinking companions could have harmed her?"

"How would I know?" His meal completely forgotten, Wrentham frowned and stared into space as Jake went back to his own steak. The medical examiner needed to finish so he could go back to work. He had no doubt Fanny would come looking for him as soon as she thought he was back.

Wrentham fingered his fork without lifting it. "She was somewhat friendly with a couple of our Italian workers. I believe she socialized with them outside of work. Luigi Spinelli in particular."

Jake wondered if Wrentham had some reason for mentioning the man. Perhaps the Italian was a thorn in his side. How much did Wrentham know about his secretary? "Did you ever hear Mrs. McKenna mention an ex-soldier? Some people believed she had been seeing a soldier since leaving her husband."

Wrentham looked up as if startled. "What? A soldier? No, never. I never heard such a thing. Someone said she was seeing a soldier? Who would blacken the poor woman's reputation when she's died in such a terrible fashion? That's awful."

Jake was puzzled by the reaction. A moment before Wrentham had seemed to have no qualms about blackening the woman's reputation. Now he seemed to be worried that someone else was spreading gossip about her. He certainly was adamant about there being no soldier in Maggie's life. How would he know that if he was really as ignorant of his employees' personal lives as he claimed? Curious.

"Was Maggie McKenna at work the day before the molasses flood?" Jake asked.

"Yes."

"Did she mention where she was going or who she was meeting after work that night?"

Wrentham's eyes widened. "No, of course not. I wouldn't know. I live out in Arlington, so I get the train promptly after work. I don't have time to dally with the employees."

Jake hadn't mentioned "dallying." He wondered why the USIA manager was so touchy. He didn't really care, although he was curious. With a feeling of self-satisfaction, he thought of a way to satisfy his curiosity. Dropping his napkin on the table, he said, "Well, I have to get back. We'll look forward to seeing this report of your experts. Oh, and another thing, I think I know someone who could help your wife with her problem."

Wrentham frowned. "What?"

"The ladies' clubs. I believe I know someone who could help your wife get membership in one or more of them." Jake could see the man was disappointed. He'd come to recruit the medical examiner to his company's side in any future dispute over their disaster, but he'd leave with no such agreement. Jake didn't want him to complain that a local official was set against him, and he saw a way to get some gossip from the female in the family. He figured the offer to help the man's wife would at least endear him to the lady who would hear no wrong about him in the future. Despite being single, Jake understood the dynamics of marriage. A wife's influence could stifle complaints and might satisfy his curiosity as well.

Besides, it would be a good task for Fanny. As the daughter of a prominent, wealthy family in Chicago, he had no doubt the ladies of Beacon Hill were after her to join their clubs. While those groups might represent the world she was trying to escape, Jake believed everyone needed to take full advantage of whatever opportunities were open to them. It was a lesson he thought Fanny would do well to learn. He took a printed business card proffered by the USIA manager. "I'll be in touch if something can be arranged."

Chapter Twelve

F anny was tempted to peruse one of the thick tomes balanced on Jake's desk while she waited for him. Of course, she was early. She should have known he'd be eating a midday meal, but she had waited in her coat and gloves in the parlor until noon chimed on the mantel clock, and only then had she walked to the morgue on North Grove Street. Edwin had taken her to Jake's office.

She pulled out one leather-bound volume. It was in French, by someone named Locard. Just then, Jake came in. He wasn't surprised to see her but seemed a bit exasperated. She told him what she had learned about Maggie.

"Yes, Detective McKenna came here last night. So, I already know all of that." Seeing her disappointment, he said, "I'll do a full autopsy as soon as I get time. You should be satisfied. You told your housekeeper her sister's death would be investigated, and it will."

Fanny frowned.

"What's the matter, don't you believe me?" Jake asked.

"It's just that, with her husband a policeman, I can't help being concerned. He's a violent man. I could see that by the way he acted at the hospital." She didn't want to tell him exactly how McKenna had attacked Lt. Bradley. She was sure the detective was mistaken when he accused the young soldier of having known his wife, but she hesitated to put the idea in Jake's head. "He was so jealous, he might have killed her himself. But he's a policeman. I'm afraid he'd get away with it."

"Fanny, are you accusing McKenna of killing his wife?" Jake leaned forward with wide eyes. "That's one very serious accusation."

"I saw what he was like. Wild, and he'd been drinking. Theresa told me how Maggie moved out of their house. It's obvious he was beating her. Is he going to get away with killing her, too?" She needed to press the point. Someone needed to speak for the poor dead woman.

"You assume McKenna killed her. Well, let me tell you, he assumes she was killed by an Italian anarchist."

"He's lying to protect himself. Jake, can't you do something? Don't let him get away with this. You must find the truth. It's your duty." Surprised at her own vehemence, she realized she had taken a sharp dislike to Maggie's husband after a single meeting.

Jake sat back, crossing his arms. "Yes, indeed, my duty is to find the truth. More specifically, it is the duty of the medical examiner to determine the cause of death and the manner of death, and the circumstances surrounding the death of an individual. But you don't find the truth by jumping to conclusions based on the first thought that comes into your head, or, even worse, based on dislike for a person involved. That's no way to find truth. All too often, that's just what's done. The police decide the husband did it, pull him in, and never even look at the facts of what happened. I have to fight this kind of assumption all the time."

"But how else can you find out who did this to her?" Fanny asked. "You can't ignore the fact that she moved out to get away from her husband, and then she was found dead."

He leaned forward. "Yes, that's one fact, but only one of many." His eyes narrowed, and she felt as if he were judging her. "Here, you want to see what I'm talking about? Come along."

She followed him out through the big room where sheet-covered corpses lay on tables. On her way in, she'd seen a line of hearses come for bodies. Jake ushered her into the operating theater, where two corpses were laid out. From the doorway, he beckoned to Edwin. Pulling down the sheet from one of the bodies, Jake exposed the head and shoulders of a young man. It was cold in the room, but Fanny could smell the corruption of flesh.

"This young soldier was found at the bottom of a flight of stairs in a local bordello," Jake said. She could tell he was trying to shock her, so she pulled her breath into her chest, hardening her surface. She wouldn't be shaken by him. "His uniform was soaked with gin. Police officers brought me the body, saying he had fallen down the stairs because he was drunk. They prejudged the situation. It was a brothel. They smelled the gin, they saw the staircase, so they assumed it was an accident. The approach was all wrong. Backwards."

He waited for comment, so she stirred herself. "It seems like a logical explanation."

"Hah, logic. There's nothing logical about it because it starts with the conclusion, instead of using facts to come to that conclusion. There was no objectivity at all, as I told Edwin here. The fact is, this man was not drunk. He had gin on his clothing, but when we tested his blood, there was no alcohol. When we examined the blow on the top of his head, the blow that killed him, we saw it was from a round object. Right on the top of the head, here." He pointed, and she stepped around to see the wound.

"Even if he wasn't drunk, he could have fallen down the stairs," she said.

"Right, so Edwin and I went to the place. The *brothel*," he emphasized. To shock her, she thought, but she refused to be shocked. "At the scene, what did we find, Edwin?"

The young man cleared his throat. "It was a steep staircase, with sharp edges to each stair, and a metal railing with equally sharp edges."

"Nothing round about it," Jake said. "Furthermore, a discussion with the women of the house elicited the information that the young man had not been seeing any of them. He'd rented a room from the madam in which to meet someone. She didn't know him, but she saw his money. He had plenty. More than a soldier ought to have. So, he took the room and was served a bottle of gin which was empty by the end of night when he was found at the bottom of the backstairs. And what do you conclude from that, Mrs. Lee?"

"You don't think he fell because he was drunk?"

"It's not what I think, it's what the facts tell us. Facts have a way of telling the real story. If you go in and theorize as the police did, you make up your own story. If you wait and just accumulate the facts, they will build up a story all their own, without prejudice, so that sooner or later the truth will crystallize out of the facts."

"Do you know who killed him then?" she asked.

Jake carefully pulled the sheet back over the man's head. "We still don't even know his name, poor boy. But we know he didn't die by getting drunk and falling down the stairs of a brothel. He was knocked on the head with something round, and thrown down the stairs, his body doused in gin to make it look like it was an accident of his own making. We don't know the whole truth, but if we didn't pay attention to the facts, we'd still believe it was an accident." He turned to his assistant. "We've finished with our soldier for now, Edwin. You'd better put him back in the cold."

"The cold?" Fanny asked.

"Yes, to slow corruption of the flesh. We use an icebox to refrigerate the cadavers. We brought this body out for the medical students, but I had to cancel the class because of all the work we need to do today. We haven't put poor Maggie in the freezer because we're letting her rigor thaw out," Jake said. Edwin wheeled the body away. "The point is, we will *not* look at Mrs. McKenna's body with the idea already in our heads that she was killed by her husband or by Italian anarchists. We *will* approach her with minds that have a clean slate to let her tell us what happened. We have to have faith that the facts will tell the story."

"I see," Fanny said. It occurred to her that Jake was used to having students to impress. Curious about his work, she was happy enough to act the student. It must be lonely for him in this cold building, working on the shells of former lives. Edwin was a quiet man, but at least he had a heart that still beat. She was glad Jake had him there to hear his lectures when there were no students present. She pulled her coat closer.

"It's too bad we can't revisit the room where Maggie was found," Jake said as he gently pulled the sheet from the woman's body. "It might have told us more. Did you say Mrs. Ryan was in the room before the molasses destroyed the building?"

"She barely saw her sister's body in the tub before it was all swept away," Fanny said.

"Perhaps we could talk to her—see what she remembers."

"Her husband died last night. She's taken his body home to hold a wake for him."

"We'll have to wait then. The family will want to bury Maggie, too, but we'll need to have a closer look before we can release the body." He sighed. Edwin slipped back into the room. "Is there anything more we can do for you today, Mrs. Lee?" Jake asked.

"There is one thing I wanted to ask you about. It's one of my soldiers. He's having bad dreams in the night and waking the rest of the residents. It happened last night, and I gave him some laudanum. Was that all right? And if so, can you help me get more for him?"

Jake looked at her for a long moment. She wondered if he would tell her she'd made a mistake giving the disturbed soldier the drug. But, instead, he expanded his chest with a large breath and said, "I think we need a drink to discuss bad dreams. Edwin, what do you say? Will you join Mrs. Lee and me?"

Fanny wondered at the idea of drinking in the middle of the afternoon. What was Jake thinking?

"Consider it medicinal," he said, noticing her hesitation. "It's a cold day, and I'd say we can all use something to warm us up. Come along. I think the hotel down the street serves ladies. A little brandy after the shocks of yesterday won't hurt you. If you think that was bad, I should warn you that delving into the battlefield memories of these young men is harrowing. Trust me."

Fanny agreed to join them. She understood that Jake faced the consequences of death every day of his working life. That he could be shaken by the accounts of the returning veterans of the war was notable. She wanted to understand the history of her young soldiers, otherwise, how could she help them? She sensed that Jake was inviting Edwin along so he could share some of his own experiences. Jake must think his scarred assistant could help her understand.

Chapter Thirteen

I t took a bit of persuading to get Edwin to accompany them. Fanny was glad to see the Beacon Hill Hotel was on her way home. They entered a small formal lobby and followed Jake through a doorway to an elegant bar room paneled in dark wood with Oriental rugs on the floors.

Jake led them to a velvet-lined booth in the back. "Take advantage while we still can," he said after ordering brandy for them all. "Prohibition's just around the corner. They expect the last required state to ratify before the end of the month. A plague on all these temperance women who'll put the poor pub keepers out of a job," he said.

Most men that Fanny knew scoffed at the idea of Prohibition and were taken by surprise when it passed. She didn't feel strongly about it. She enjoyed a small glass of wine with a meal but no more than that. It seemed to her that the female reformers gloated about how they'd bested their male relatives by insisting that alcohol damaged society. They blamed poverty on the drunkenness of working men. They forced wealthy men to agree, even while the men believed there was no need to stop drinking themselves. She was sure the only reason the measure had passed was that the rich were confident in their ability to ignore the law.

Jake bantered with the barman who brought the drinks. The man was morose looking, and he spoke gloomily about the future. When he left, Jake said softly, "Don't worry about him. I've heard they're already planning how to deliver the stuff illegally for twice the price." He raised his glass. "To dry days ahead."

Fanny felt the liquid burn as it slid down her throat. She seldom drank brandy.

"So, Fanny, one of your young men is having bad dreams?"

She told them about the disturbance the night before.

"One or two doses of laudanum will do him no harm," Jake said. "It's not recommended as much as it used to be. It was overused for a long time, especially on women patients." Fanny remembered the story of her mother's friend. She wondered how many women had used the drug and then struggled to escape it. As examiner of the dead, Jake learned all their secrets.

Jake noticed her dismay. "It won't hurt him to use for a short time. I can give you a prescription, but it won't make the nightmares go away for long. Eventually, he'll build a resistance to it, and it won't work anymore." Fanny decided she'd abandon the plan to offer more laudanum to the soldier. But she felt she needed to do something.

"He must have seen awful things to be so disturbed in his sleep," Fanny said. "But now he's safe. What can I do to help him forget?"

"I defer to Edwin on that," Jake said. "He's seen the horrors they can't forget. Edwin?"

The quiet young man looked on from a spot he had chosen in the shadows. The scars on his face seemed to dictate every move and choice he made. After a gulp of his brandy, he said, "There's not much you can do for them. I don't know if time or other activities or new memories will ever replace what was seared into our brains over there." He stopped, looking at Jake with doubt on his face.

"It's all right, Edwin. You should tell her what you can. If she wants to help the soldiers in her home, Mrs. Lee needs to understand something of the horrors they can't speak about," Jake told him.

Edwin seemed to have a hard time deciding where to begin.

"I do want to know whatever might help them," Fanny said.

"I see that, Mrs. Lee. It's just that sitting here now, with you, in the light of a warm fire with brandy to warm my insides, everything is a nice dull gray to me." He looked around the room. There was a fireplace cheerfully crackling in the corner. He held her eyes with a steady gaze. She felt afraid.

"Then, all of a sudden, a door will bang, or a log on the fire will pop, and everything, all of this, is gone in a second, and I'm back on the battlefield with shells falling and mud splashing, gunfire ahead of me and barbed wire behind. And I'm all in a sweat, scared as I've ever been. Rationally, I know I'm safe here with you. But, in that moment, I can't believe that. I think I'm back there, trapped, and I can't get out."

Jake nodded in agreement. Fanny gritted her teeth at the thought that the man before her could be so easily transported back into the horrors he'd escaped. "How awful," she said. "How do you stop it?"

"You don't, Mrs. Lee."

Jake tried to explain. "There's some hope that, in time, this kind of vivid memory of the battlefield will appear less frequently, that, eventually, Edwin and the young men of his generation will be able to hear a door slam without slipping back in time. But no one knows how long it will take."

"So, laudanum won't cure him," Fanny said.

"No, and it could do harm. He could become dependent on it and need more as it becomes less effective. An overdose could kill him."

Fanny sighed. "I think I understand." The memories must be like a whirlpool pulling the men into the past over and over again.

"Man's inhumanity to man," Jake said

Silence descended like a door closing. Fanny took another sip of the burning liquid.

"They aren't all bad memories, you know," Edwin said after a while. "There were incredibly brave acts by men who are gone. You probably wouldn't believe me if I told you about some of them." He shook his head. "Civilians can't understand."

Jake and Fanny didn't contradict him.

"It's like this one story a friend of mine told me," Edwin said. He seemed to be encouraged by their silence, the fact that they didn't try to say they understood. "His squad got hit by a shell, and just as it went off, an officer threw himself on an enlisted man to try to shield him. It was incredibly brave. He grabbed the man and fell on top of him. But they were buried in the mud, and there was more fighting, so it was hours and hours before it let up enough for their comrades to dig them out. When they found them, the enlisted man was still alive, but the officer was dead, wrapped around the other man. And, by then, the officer was stiff, with the stiffness of the dead." He looked at Jake, who squeezed his eyes closed. Fanny shivered at the thought of the live man embraced by a dead one. "They couldn't get them apart. They had to send them to the medics still wound together. When they finally did, the live man was still talking to the dead one, telling him it would be all right."

Edwin drank the last of his brandy, then put the glass down firmly. "Sometimes, it's like we all came out of the war with the men who didn't make it still wrapped around us, in rigor. Just like that corpse in the mud. We're here, and we're walking around…but, really, they're with us, all the time. *You* can't see them, but *we* can."

Fanny declined another glass of brandy and, after thanking them for their advice, left the men there drinking. They had both worked overtime that week and Jake had announced they were done for the day when he'd ordered another drink. He waved her off home.

As she climbed the hill on Mt. Vernon Street, she wondered if, when she saw her men from now on, she would picture them with a stiff corpse wrapped around each and every one. She understood her task was to make it easier for them to bear that burden until it grew lighter and faded away as she hoped it must at some point.

Chapter Fourteen

Friday, January 17, 1919

The next day, Fanny attended the funeral for Thomas Ryan. Lt. Bradley asked to accompany her, and she was glad to have his arm. She noticed that he was limping but still didn't carry a cane. When he admitted he'd lost it in the chaos of the molasses flood, she felt guilty. The need to help her must have distracted him. She worried that was how he lost it his cane.

On the way, their cab was stopped twice by other funeral processions. The city churches would be crowded with mourners of various denominations in the coming week. When they arrived, they slowly climbed the steps to the Catholic church. Inside, the pews were filled with sturdy men and their black veiled wives. The services were murmured in Latin, so Fanny couldn't understand a word of it. She didn't think the other mourners could either, but they seemed unbothered by that fact. It was strange to her to stand by and listen as prayers were sent to heaven like incense, floating up in murmurs like magic spells.

After the mass, six pallbearers carried the coffin down the aisle. McKenna was one of them. Fanny bit her lip when she saw him recognize Lt. Bradley. An unhealthy wash of ruddy color rose in the police detective's cheeks. Only the weight of the coffin kept him from confronting the soldier. Patrick Ryan was also a pallbearer, and he whispered to McKenna to move him along. Fanny silently blamed herself for bringing the young soldier. Of course,

McKenna would attend the funeral for his brother-in-law. She took a deep breath when the coffin was carried away with the sweep of the procession. Theresa followed, wearing a long black veil and supported by a white-haired man. Behind them, the weeping mother was practically carried by two men who must have been other sons.

Fanny refused to budge from the pew until the church had emptied out. She couldn't face another confrontation between McKenna and Lt. Bradley. When she finally allowed the soldier to lead her out, she insisted they stay at the back of the crowd as the dead fireman was lowered into his grave in the small cemetery beside the church. The wreath she'd sent was displayed prominently. As the crowd dispersed, she wondered whether she could speak to Theresa without seeing McKenna. She saw the widow and Patrick send the police detective away in the care of several large men who must be firemen, friends of the dead man. Only then did she dare to step forward to console Theresa.

The widow came to Fanny herself, followed by Patrick. "Mrs. Lee, thank you for the flowers. It's good of you to come." She'd folded back the long veil, and her face was white as snow.

"I am so very sorry, Theresa. You mustn't worry about the home. Take as much time as you need. Your place will be waiting for you when you're ready." Fanny knew the position was necessary for the young woman's survival, and she'd be worried about losing it. With her husband's salary gone, she would need it even more.

Theresa's brow smoothed at that reassurance, and she was choked up with relief, but she got ahold of herself. "It will be a blessing to have work to do," she said. "I'll return tomorrow, if that's all right with you. There's naught to do at home but weep, and weeping will not bring Thomas back." She looked ready to weep at that moment.

Fanny patted her arm. "Of course. Whatever you want. We'll be blessed to have you back." She knew Theresa lived with her in-laws and imagined it would be a tearful place with the mourning going on.

Theresa clutched Fanny's hand in both her own. "Thank you for that. Have you heard any more about Maggie?"

"Dr. Magrath will be seeing to her today," Fanny said, trying to suppress the picture of the dead woman's staring eyes from her mind. "He promised to let me know as soon as he determines the cause of death. I'm so sorry that you have to mourn your sister as well as your husband."

"There's nothing to be done except to find justice for her," Theresa said. She glanced at Lt. Bradley. His face showed a raw grief, as if he was restraining himself with a huge effort from reaching out to the young widow. Fanny sensed that he wanted to comfort her. She remembered the talk of how the men returning from the trenches could not shake off their guilt and sorrow over the deaths of their comrades. That must make them especially sensitive to grief in others.

"I'm sure Dr. Magrath will find the truth," Fanny said.

"I'm worried about Maggie's husband," Theresa said. Beside her, Patrick moved as if he felt a stone in his shoe, but he kept quiet. "Billy McKenna is going around claiming he found the soldier who was seeing Maggie and that he'll have him arrested before the week is out."

"He's grieving, Tess," Patrick said.

"He's wild," she said, looking up at the barman. It was cold, and wisps of smoke seemed to come from their mouths as the air froze the words they spoke. "He's a bully of a man, and he made Maggie's life hell. If my Tom were here, he'd not put up with him and his ravings." She looked as if she would burst into tears, but she held herself in, grimacing with the effort.

Lt. Bradley took a step forward. "Mrs. Ryan, I know McKenna says I knew his wife but it's not true. I swear to you, it wasn't me." He raised his hands in a gesture of helplessness.

Patrick frowned. He looked like he would step between the soldier and the widow, but Theresa spoke first. "I know that, Lieutenant. And I know it can't be true. No, Patrick, Maggie *was* seeing a soldier. She told me months ago, in October, but she wouldn't say who it was. Lt. Bradley, here, never even got back from the war until December. Isn't that true, Mrs. Lee? You tell him."

"That's right. Lt. Bradley and the rest of the men didn't arrive until after Christmas."

"So, it couldn't be him." Theresa looked up at her brother-in-law. "You know what Billy McKenna is like. It's him who scared Maggie so much she left him. It's him who's wild with jealousy. He claims he saw her with a soldier because he's guilty, Pat. He did it, I'm sure of it. You know he's capable of it. He's a brute." She trembled.

Patrick stooped to put an arm around her. "It's all right, Tess. They'll find out who did it. Billy's got a temper, sure. But he loved Maggie, you know he did. Come on, now. There'll be people back at the place, and Ma and Pa will be worried about ya. I told them to go ahead, and I'd bring you along. Come now, will ya?"

Fanny felt, rather than saw, Lt. Bradley move forward, but she grabbed his arm and held him back. "You go along home, Theresa. I promise I'll talk to Dr. Magrath tomorrow about Maggie. Lt. Bradley and I will go home now. I don't want to cause you any trouble with Detective McKenna. If he did hurt Maggie, I promise you I'll get Dr. Magrath to make sure the truth comes out." Fanny hoped she wasn't going too far in promising cooperation from Jake. She believed he was sincere and incorruptible. She had to hope that even if the husband was a policeman, Jake would see him convicted if he was guilty.

Chapter Fifteen

Saturday, January 18, 1919

Saturday morning, Fanny received terrible news from Chicago. It was after breakfast when the post was brought to her little office at the back of the first floor in the brownstone. Reading the letter was not enough. She put through a telephone call to her brother in Chicago, and he confirmed the bad news. The young officers had all gone out on various errands, but she expected them back for a meal at noon. Anxious about breaking the news, she dressed herself warmly and walked to Charles Street, where she had seen a store that carried men's scarves and canes.

She consulted the salesman and had picked out a plain but sturdy cane for Lt. Bradley, when she saw a more elaborate one with a wolf's head in silver at the top. She decided to purchase that one, even though she knew a wolf's head cane would not go far in comforting the young man.

Back at Wendell house, Theresa had arrived and was busy in the big Mt. Vernon Street building working with the cook and laundress to plan the week. Fanny was glad she was too busy to ask about Dr. Magrath's findings. Before she could consult with him, Fanny had an unpleasant task to complete.

When she saw Lt. Bradley return to the brownstone, she led him to her office and sat him down. He was full of gratitude for the cane she gave him, but he noticed her tenseness. He watched closely as she sat down behind her desk.

"I'm so very sorry. I finally heard from Chicago, and the news is not good.

Both your father and your mother passed away during the flu epidemic. I'm doubly sorry to tell you that your fiancée, Miss Ballard, also succumbed to the flu. I feel terrible to bring you such awful news."

Lt. Bradley sank back in his chair, covering his face with his hands. Fanny looked away. She heard him breathe heavily. When she thought he'd had time to compose himself, she turned back. He rubbed his eyes with a handkerchief.

"I am so sad for you," she said. "But I want you to know that my brother is willing to act in your place for any business that must be done. Your parents' home is empty and waiting for you but will need to be opened up. Your inheritance is waiting, and my brother can assist in making it available to you, and he can help with any other legal issues that need attention. We're all so very sorry for your loss."

Lt. Bradley, a blank look on his face, collapsed back in the chair. His eyes swam in a sudden rise of tears. "Thank you for telling me," he said, standing up. "You must excuse me." He limped from the room, leaving the new cane behind. Fanny heard his steps on the stairs.

Theresa Ryan came to the door. "Mrs. Lee, is Lt. Bradley all right?"

"Come in, Theresa, and shut the door." She did as she was told. "I'm afraid Lt. Bradley's parents and his fiancée in Chicago are all dead from the flu epidemic. He has nothing to return to."

"Oh, that is so sad," Theresa said.

"And you want to know about your sister, I'm sure. I haven't had time to talk to Dr. Magrath yet today, but I promise I will."

"Thank you. I'm so sorry about Lt. Bradley. He'll not want to eat with the others. Should I ask cook to make him a tray and take it up to him?"

"That's a good idea. Thank you so much, Mrs. Ryan."

They heard a loud banging at the front door knocker.

"Good Lord, they don't have to break the thing down," Fanny said.

"I'll go," Theresa said. Fanny followed her out.

When Theresa opened the front door, a red-faced Detective McKenna plunged into the hallway. "Where's Bradley? We're here for Matthew Bradley." He was followed by three large, uniformed policemen wearing long double-breasted coats, thick leather belts, and tall helmets. They filled the hallway and loomed above the women. "Search the place," McKenna said. "Find him."

"Billy McKenna, what do you think you're doing?" Theresa asked. She stood nose to nose with him, arms akimbo. Fanny thought Theresa would never have stood for the bullying her sister had taken from her husband.

"Out of the way, woman, we're the law."

Young officers started piling in from the dining room where they had congregated for luncheon. Fanny thought they looked only too ready for a brawl. *Not in my foyer*, she thought, stepping forward. "I'm Mrs. Lee, I run Wendell House. What is your business here?" She found the police detective frightening, but she was determined to hide any fear. She remembered her mother and drew herself up to her full height to stare the angry man in the face. His mustache was shivering with rage as he pulled the bowler from his head. The men behind him stopped in their tracks, uncertain how to proceed when faced with a Beacon Hill matron. Fanny could tell they were used to showing deference to someone like her. She raised her eyebrows as if in disdain, although she was really cowering inside. *Just don't show it*, she thought.

"Exactly what do you want, Detective McKenna?"

"We're here to take in Matthew Bradley for questioning in the death of my wife, Margaret McKenna. The medical examiner has ruled the death a homicide, and Bradley is under suspicion. I saw him with my wife. He killed her, and he's going to pay for it. So get out of my way."

Fanny saw Theresa stiffen at the news that the medical examiner had pronounced Maggie's death a homicide. Fanny wished she'd spoken to Jake that morning instead of shopping for the useless cane. Still, she was sure McKenna was wrong about Lt. Bradley. She just didn't know what she could do about it. She needed to talk to Jake.

She heard footsteps on the stairs above her. "I'm Matthew Bradley." He came down the steps awkwardly.

McKenna pointed. "Get him."

Two of the policemen rushed up and took Bradley by the arms, carrying him down the stairs.

66

"Where are you taking him?" Fanny asked as the policemen dragged their prisoner through the crowd of soldiers to the doorway. She remained calm as she didn't want her young men to get into a fight with the police. What a day for poor Matt Bradley, first hearing of the deaths of his family and then having the police take him away. She wanted to shout down McKenna, but there was too much tension in the air.

"Station One," McKenna said.

Theresa rushed up and grabbed his coat lapels. "Billy, you're wrong. He wasn't Maggie's soldier. He wasn't even here in Boston till a few weeks ago. She was seeing someone for months, Billy, for months. But it can't have been Lt. Bradley."

He pulled her hands away. "Get off me, woman." He seethed with a fury that made his eyes bulge. "I saw him with her. D'ya hear me? I saw him. He'll hang if it's the last thing I do." Pushing her away, he flung himself out the door and down the stairs to the paddy wagon waiting outside.

Theresa turned back to Fanny. "What are we going to do, Mrs. Lee?"

Chapter Sixteen

Fanny sent the young men back to their luncheon. She put up a good front, authoritatively assuring them all would be taken care of. It wasn't until she slumped behind the desk that she let down her guard. Theresa followed, shutting the office door behind her. "Billy McKenna won't listen, he's blinded by jealousy," she said.

Fanny bit her lip. She couldn't let Theresa know she was beaten by this. If she were in Chicago, she would turn to her father. He'd know someone who could stop the arrest. He'd call the mayor. But the need to beg favors from her father or husband was exactly what she'd run away from. She hated being so dependent. She wanted to stand on her own. That was why she came here.

Yet now, she felt alone, tottering over an abyss…helpless. How could she let poor Matthew Bradley down like this?

* * *

"Jake, why didn't you let me know that you'd determined that Maggie was murdered? And why did you tell Detective McKenna it was murder without warning me?" Fanny arrived at the morgue, angry and distressed.

"Of course, I had to tell the police!" Jake sat behind his desk in shirt sleeves, spectacles sliding down his nose. "This is official business, Fanny. I don't know where you got the idea you were owed some sort of private communication about the matter."

That put her in her place. "You and the police wouldn't have known she

68

wasn't killed by the molasses if her sister and I hadn't told you." Fanny moved to reveal Theresa Ryan behind her. Jake sighed at the sight of the young widow. "Besides, you said Detective McKenna is not a homicide detective. He's just wildly jealous of Lt. Bradley, and he won't *listen*. Lt. Bradley wasn't *in* Boston when Maggie was seeing that soldier. Mrs. Ryan says it was months before our soldiers had even arrived."

Jake stood and waved the women to chairs. "I'm sorry for your loss," he told Theresa, then he frowned at her employer. "Listen, Fanny. Just because you think of these young men as *your* soldiers doesn't mean they get special treatment. Maybe you could get away with that in Chicago, but not here. If the man they arrested—"

"Lt. Matthew Bradley. He's not just some ruffian off the streets. He served in the army, and he comes from a prominent family in Chicago."

"Fine, if Lt. Bradley isn't the soldier that Mrs. McKenna was see-ing—whether he's from a prominent family or not—the police will find that out. Let them do their jobs."

"But they're wasting their time. Can't you at least make them listen? He wasn't here. He wasn't Maggie's soldier."

"The police don't cut into the bodies of murder victims, and I don't look into the alibis of suspects," Jake said, removing his spectacles to look Fanny in the eye. The office door opened. "It's all right, Edwin. I'm just explaining to Mrs. Lee that when we completed the autopsy of Maggie McKenna, we were obliged to inform the police that there was water in her lungs, not molasses, and she was dead before the tank burst. Furthermore," he looked at Fanny, "there were definite indications of a struggle. It's certain that the woman was held down against her will and drowned in that tub. And if Detective McKenna was angry when he arrested the soldier, it may well be because he learned that his wife was with child at the time of her death." Jake huffed at her. Then he remembered Theresa. "I'm sorry to tell you that so bluntly, Mrs. Ryan."

Fanny was horrified. Maggie was carrying a child when she died. She had left her husband's house months before, so it wasn't his child. She was carrying an illegitimate child conceived out of wedlock. Such things happened, but they were hinted at, never, ever spoken of in Fanny's world.

"Do you know how far along she was?" Theresa asked.

While Fanny gulped for air, Theresa never flinched. In her housekeeper's world, nothing was unspeakable. Fanny felt lost and a little dizzy, but she clenched a fist to force herself to listen. This was the real world that she was determined to breach. If Theresa could hear about her sister's condition, Fanny would face it. She thought how, in her own circles, being with child was called a "delicate condition." From experience, she knew it was anything but delicate. She forced her attention back to Jake.

"About three months," he was saying.

"Then you see, it couldn't have been Lt. Bradley. He was still in France three months ago," Fanny jumped in.

"Who's to say the man who killed her was the father, Fanny? You claim the husband is jealous. A lover could be just as enraged if he found out she was having a child by another man. Did you ever think of that?"

Fanny flinched. Jake was flaunting her naïveté in her face, and she had to sit there and take it. Men acted so superior when it came to physical relationships. As if she, who had carried three children herself, had no knowledge of carnal relations.

"It wasn't Billy's," Theresa said. "She'd moved out of their house more than three months ago. I knew Maggie was keeping something from me, but I didn't think she was so far gone as that."

"What about the men she was drinking with that night?" Fanny asked. Theresa had told her about the dirty glasses in her sister's room, and she'd admitted Maggie drank with some of the men who worked with her. That a young married woman would do such a thing shocked Fanny, but she was determined to examine the facts with an open mind. "What if one of *them* was the father and was jealous of her? Or what if they feared she would tell her husband? What if it wasn't about her love affairs at all?" It was as if Fanny had opened the gate in her mind that stopped her from imagining forbidden things. Ideas flooded out. Why did men always assume if a woman was involved, it was about a love affair? "She worked for the company that owned the molasses tank. What if she knew something about the explosion?

Or something else? And even if it was a love affair, what if her husband found out she was pregnant by another man? Don't you think he would be mad enough to attack her?"

Jake's eyes had narrowed during her tirade. Now he said, "I saw his face when I told him she was pregnant. He didn't know."

"How can you be sure?"

"If Billy suspected, he'd be wild, sure enough," Theresa said. "He's not one for keeping his feelings hidden. He'd have torn the place apart looking for her."

"Perhaps he knew and killed her in a rage but then the molasses flood gave him time to think about it and pretend he didn't do it," Fanny said.

"That's all in your imagination," Jake said. "Where are your facts to back it up?"

"There are no facts to back up arresting Lt. Bradley," Fanny retorted.

"Fanny, there's nothing you can do to help that young man except to find him a lawyer. I don't know what you expect to accomplish by coming to me. You must let the official investigation uncover the truth."

Once more, the thick oak doors of male supremacy slammed shut in her face, and she hated it. She felt sure Jake himself would have done more than find a lawyer. Lt. Bradley had been captured and taken into the legal jungle where there were no paths a woman in her situation could follow. She had to recruit some male relative, friend, or employee to act as her agent. It pained her that Jake refused to help.

"Don't look to me," he said. "I'm just the medical examiner. I've given the police the information that the death was a homicide. I can't tell them to release a suspect." He put up a hand as if to stop her questions. "Listen, just get the boy a lawyer. But if you want to help me with the flood investigation, there's something you could do for me."

He picked up a pen, dipped it in ink, and wrote on a slip of paper. "This is the name of the wife of the manager of the company that owned the molasses tank—where Mrs. McKenna worked. This woman is desperate to be accepted by some of the ladies' groups on Beacon Hill. I'm sure, with your connections, you could help her." He blew on the scrap to dry the ink

71

and rose when Fanny abruptly stood.

She was angry. Invite some social climbing woman to a Beacon Hill sewing circle—that was how she was expected to help? She stared at him.

"Come, come, Fanny. You say you want to help. This man, Jeremy Wrentham was Mrs. McKenna's employer. He knows more than he's telling me about the flood. You could befriend his wife and find out what she knows. A man confides in his wife." When she still didn't move to take the slip, his hand dropped. "It's more than I could do. Don't you realize there are things you *can* do that I—or even the police—can't? Why won't you use your advantages instead of spurning them?" He was slightly red in the face. It was unattractive and made him look older. Her heart sank like a cold stone. Jake wasn't the man she remembered him to be.

She held out a gloved hand, and he gave her the paper. She managed a polite goodbye and brushed past Theresa and Edwin to the door.

Hearing murmurs behind her, she ignored them and made her way out of the morgue and onto North Grove Street. Her teeth were clenched as she marched along Cambridge to Hancock Street, up the hill, and through the door with the frosted pane of glass.

Trembling when she reached her desk, she pulled out her diary and found the name she had been given when she left Chicago. Henry Cabot Lodge was a senator whose son did business with Fanny's father, and she'd been instructed to turn to him in time of need. She hated doing that. Uncapping a new bottle of ink, she carefully laid out stationery. After two drafts spoiled by inkblots and holes from the nib of her pen stuck too forcibly into the paper, she had a finished letter. In it, she explained her need for help and requested an appointment as soon as possible. In the street, she found a boy to hand deliver the letter and, finally, she collapsed into her chair with a pounding headache.

Chapter Seventeen

When Fanny left his office without another word, Jake swore, then excused himself to Theresa, who stood watching her employer's proud figure retreat.

"I'm sorry there's nothing more I can tell you about your sister's death, Mrs. Ryan," Jake said. He was still standing behind his desk in deference to the widow.

"No. I thank you for what you've done already. It's a sad end for poor Maggie. But Mrs. Lee is right that Billy McKenna was acting wild when he took Lt. Bradley." She looked back and forth between the doctor and his assistant, Edwin.

Jake dropped into his chair. Theresa Ryan looked like she was barely more than a child herself. He knew she wore the unrelieved black of widow's weeds for her fireman husband as well as her sister. Her skin looked gray, and the bones of her wrists were prominent in a way that bespoke a limited diet. No doubt she would benefit from the meals in Fanny's household. The girl needed the job badly. She showed no signs of the alcohol use her sister's battered body had displayed. He motioned her to a chair.

"No, thank you, I'll be going. It's just that what Mrs. Lee said is right. Maggie's been seeing a soldier. She said he'd be taking her away from all this, although I never saw that her soldier had any money. She borrowed from me to get him new boots in December. But she talked like she'd have money and be living high soon. Of course, I never believed it. And I couldn't tell Billy McKenna that. It'd be too much disgrace for him. But she was expecting something—a windfall like. Money, not a child. I had no notion about that."

"Did she ever suggest there was trouble at her job?" Jake asked. He wouldn't step a foot into the murder investigation, no matter what Fanny wanted. But he had questions about the molasses flood. As medical examiner he needed to investigate the circumstances surrounding the deaths that had occurred when the tank exploded. Was it a bomb? Was it an accident, intentional malice, or negligence that caused those deaths? He was fully justified in following up on those questions.

He noticed Edwin scrutinizing the young widow. Jake felt sorry for him. Edwin had no family or friends, and no young woman to look out for him. Fanny had her soldiers, but Jake had his own damaged young man to protect.

Theresa bowed her head. "She didn't speak about her job much," she said. "In fact, she avoided my questions about it. She was too friendly with some of the men, and she knew I didn't approve." She looked up. "I hoped Maggie and her husband would reconcile. I hoped he'd change his ways to get her back."

It was sad. Jake knew women like Maggie had few options in the world. If they left their husbands, they were labelled fallen women and often had no choice but to live up to the label. If they stayed with the abusive husband, they'd be dead before their time, and what an example for their children. He sighed.

Theresa moved to the door.

"Mrs. Ryan, your brother-in-law, Patrick. He owns a pub. Where is it?"

"The Jug of Punch on West Broadway," she said.

South Boston. "Thank you. Edwin, show Mrs. Ryan out, would you?"

Jake sat back. Fanny was exasperating. Maybe he should be flattered by her assumption that he could cure all ills and solve all problems but knight in shining armor he was not, and he resented her attempts to throw responsibility onto his shoulders. He knew it was something women were taught to do, but he believed it was wrong to encourage such delusions. He wouldn't do it. If he took her whole messy pile of romantic assumptions and dumped them back into her lap, it would do her more good in the long run.

Fanny was an attractive woman, and he recognized his early affection for her was still buried somewhere in his aging heart. But she was too hell bent on fighting shadows to tempt him. In recent years, he'd found solace in the company of widows. He'd come to realize that when women lost their husbands and found themselves responsible for their own lives, at last, they either remarried immediately, because they couldn't stand the burden, or they sat back and relished independence. He had several good friends who were widows of the independent type, and he enjoyed time spent with them. He thought that Fanny would be happier if she developed a love for independence like those women. Perhaps shedding a husband by divorce was not as liberating as becoming a widow. He didn't know any other divorced women. Still, breaking the bonds of her upbringing was something Fanny would have to do by herself.

Nonetheless, her accusations against him stung. He itched at the thought that the wrong man might have been arrested for the death of the girl in his operating theater. Fanny claimed the accused soldier couldn't have done it. If she was right, someone who had knocked Maggie down and held her face underwater was walking around the city. But he could do nothing about that. It wasn't his responsibility.

His responsibility was to determine the cause of death for the other twenty-one bodies that had passed through his morgue. He placed his hand on a stack of typed forms that were the death certificates for the victims of the flood. Most of the bodies had been released to their families for burial, except for two found after several days of cleanup. One little boy was so badly crushed he could only be identified by the red sweater his mother had knitted for him.

Jake knew the authorities wanted to accuse anarchists of causing the tank explosion. Like Jeremy Wrentham of USIA, most officials, including police, assumed a bomb had been set off. No anarchist group had claimed responsibility as they had for the bombing of the Salutation Street Police Station back in December 1916, but newspapers and politicians were quick to raise the specter of the much-feared anarchist groups. Jake had his doubts. He hadn't seen the type of internal injuries he expected from a blast. And it bothered him that the nearby second story windows had not exploded.

When Edwin came back into the room, Jake tossed the pen he'd been clutching onto the desk. "What do you say we visit Mr. Patrick Ryan at his place of business, Edwin?" His assistant bowed in agreement. "You've got to learn to speak up, Edwin," Jake said. He rose and grabbed his coat. "I worry about you, sneaking around in the corners." He got his arms through his jacket and added an overcoat, following Edwin to the outer office. The young man turned away, and Jake felt an urge to aim a kick at him. No sense being overly sensitive in this rugged world.

Chapter Eighteen

The Jug of Punch pub was in a brick building planted on a corner, surrounded by three-story wooden tenements. Jake's specially modified Model T, Suffolk Sue, raised a few eyebrows when Jake and Edwin pulled up a block away. Inside the club, men leaned elbows on a long mahogany bar, balancing a foot on the brass railing at the bottom. They mostly wore the cloth caps of workers, some in overalls, and others in worn woolen suits or denim pants with thick boots on their feet. Wide mirrors behind the bar reflected clouds of smoke rising to the hammered tin of the ceiling as Jake shuffled through sawdust on the floor.

Edwin followed, hunched forward, a cloth cap on his head, looking for a dark spot. Out of the corner of his eye, Jake could see his assistant fade to the end of the bar. Sound echoed from the carved wood on the walls and the wood floor. Men turned slightly to stare at the newcomers. There were no chairs, only standing room for men with mugs of beer or glasses of whiskey. A sign plastered on one mirror advertised a political rally for a local city councilman. It was a rough crowd, nothing like the upper-class medical students Jake taught. But he had plenty of practice meeting men like this and preferred them to the sometimes-precious youths from Harvard.

"'Scuse me, 'scuse me," he called out, elbowing his way through. "Got a thirst to quench."

"In a hurry, are you?" a tall man in a cap, a rolled neck jersey, and denim pants challenged Jake. He looked like a sailor.

"The countdown's begun," Jake said. "Got to get it while it's still available." That drew a guffaw from men around him, and they opened a way to the bar. He knew they all were well aware that prohibition had finally passed a few days before, and, in a year, serving liquor would be banned. It wasn't a popular issue with these men. Why should it be? Saloons like this were where they found rest, entertainment, and fellowship after long hours at hard labor.

Jake ordered a pint for himself and another for Edwin down at the end of the bar.

"A shy one, is he?" the sailor asked.

"Shy in the city, but I heard he wasn't a bit shy at Belleau Woods. Ran screaming at the Boches like a madman," Jake said. It wasn't true, but he got the message across that Edwin was a veteran. A few of the men raised their glasses toward the ex-soldier, then left him alone. They knew others who'd returned from the war, and Jake had noticed that workingmen like these were more sensitive to the privacy of returned soldiers than the ladies and gentlemen in the polite society of Beacon Hill.

Patrick Ryan recognized Jake as he pulled the pints of beer. He wore a white apron over rolled-up shirtsleeves and a vest. After delivering Edwin's pint, he came back to Jake. "It's Dr. Magrath, isn't it?"

"Yes, Mr. Ryan. I wanted to ask you a few questions about Mrs. McKenna, if you don't mind."

"Call me Pat. I heard Billy McKenna arrested that soldier. Poor Maggie. Come on down to the snug, and we can talk."

Jake followed him to the opposite end of the bar, where there was a small closet with three stools. "It's where we let the women have a nip, don't you know," Pat told him. Jake had heard of the practice of having a hidden away space for women to drink in the forbidden pubs. He couldn't imagine Fanny subjecting herself to such a penance—having to hide away to sip a drink. On the other hand, he could sympathize with hardworking women who wanted the relief of a drink after a long day just as much as their spouses and brothers.

"Pat, I heard the police arrested Lt. Bradley, but both Mrs. Lee and Mrs. Ryan think they've got the wrong man. They say there was another soldier who was spending time with Mrs. McKenna."

Pat frowned. "I canna say. I heard she was seeing some soldier, but I never met him."

Jake wondered if Pat had been told the dead woman was bearing a child. He shook his head as he removed his fedora. It was stuffy in the little room. "That's not really what I'm here about. That's not my investigation. But I'm looking into the explosion of the molasses tank. Some people think it was due to an anarchist bomb."

Jake had meant it when he told Fanny he couldn't investigate Maggie's murder. But he was obliged to rule on whether the deaths from the molasses flood were due to accident, negligence, or criminal actions. If that led him to question the role of Maggie's Italian workmates, he had every reason to question Pat Ryan about them. At least that was how he rationalized it to himself.

"Aye," Pat looked out toward the crowded bar. "It's what they're all saying."

"You mentioned there were two colleagues of Mrs. McKenna who were Italians. And I thought Detective McKenna indicated they were anarchists."

Pat nodded his head. "That's right. Luigi Spinelli and Tony DeCarlo. They worked with her. She used to buy a bottle and drink with them. It wasn't right, but if she didn't get it from me, she'd have gone to someone else. I figured it'd keep her out of the North End if she came here to get it. Theresa worried her sister was too close to them dens of iniquity in Scollay Square. I told her drinkin' in her rooms was better than that anyhow." He seemed worried what Jake would think of him for selling liquor to the dead woman. "Say, are you thinking them Eyeties had something to do with the molasses tank? Did they bomb it? Maybe Maggie knew something, and they shut her up."

"I wouldn't jump to conclusions, but I'd like to have a talk with Mr. Spinelli and Mr. DeCarlo, so I was wondering if you knew how to get in touch with them."

"Those dirty Eyeties. If they had something to do with Maggie's death, we'll get them. I'll tell Billy, and we'll teach them something."

"Now, now, Mr. Ryan, please do nothing of the sort. I'm sorry I brought the subject up." Jake rose from his stool, bending to keep from hitting his head, but Pat grabbed him.

"No, that's all right. I know Billy is a wild man. I'll not say a word to him unless you tell me it's true. It's just that we all of us tried to warn her." As Jake pulled away, Pat clutched the wool of his coat more tightly. "As to where you can find them, I know from Billy that them anarchists get together at each other's houses. There's one of them lives on Salem Street, above a grocer, and the other's about halfway down on Fleet. They've got a rooftop where they get together. The Florence Hotel. It's a roomin' house for men there."

Jake stopped and looked down at the bartender still perched on a stool. "Thank you, Pat. That's what I need to know. But I will hold you to your promise not to say anything to Detective McKenna or anyone else about this." He ducked out the door and made his way to the other end of the bar, where Edwin appeared to be cornered by a short man in overalls and a cloth cap.

"Dr. Magrath, this is Gerry Doyle. He was in the same hospital as me in France," Edwin said.

The lively young man with a huge mustache turned to shake Jake's hand. "Ed here says you're the coroner, dead bodies and all. Sounds downright ghoulish, if you don't mind my saying." He had a narrow face and dark eyes that were alight with interest in Jake's profession.

"I'm medical examiner, as a matter of fact, and Edwin is a very fine assistant."

"You don't have to tell me," Dolan said, slapping Edwin on the back. "My man here is a hero, you know? Did he tell you about that?"

Jake could see that Edwin was suffering, shrinking back into the corner, turning toward the bar as he tried to get away from his overly rambunctious comrade. He wondered if the young man felt guilty about something.

"Well, it's great to meet you, Mr. Doyle, but I'm afraid I'll have to bring your reunion to a hasty conclusion. I'm very sorry, but I need to take Edwin away with me. We have more business tonight."

"Business? You got more dead bodies?" Doyle's mouth formed an "O."

"Nonsense, nothing of the sort. Come along, Edwin." Ignoring the loud young man, Jake pushed his way through the mostly genial crowd to the door and found Edwin right behind him.

"Thank you," Edwin said.

"No thanks needed. I meant it. We have business in the North End."

Chapter Nineteen

At Salem Street, they had no luck. Jake had parked on the outskirts of the North End. It was the oldest part of the city, where narrow streets were crowded with people and rubbish, as well as wheelbarrows and wagons left for the night along the sides of the brick streets. They learned that Tony DeCarlo lived in one of the brick buildings, but neighbors claimed he wasn't home. The inhabitants looked on them with deep suspicion and frequently answered in Italian. Jake heard scolding behind them when they turned from a little old man who had told them DeCarlo was out for the night. A woman in a black shawl appeared to be berating him in Italian.

Laundry flapped on ropes strung from window to window as they trekked through alleys and found their way to Fleet Street. Jake walked along unselfconsciously, although he could see that Edwin was wary. As medical examiner, Jake had been called to tenements in the area plenty of times. He knew where police raids had left broken jaws and bruised bodies. He had retrieved the dead ones. It was still unexpectedly warm for late January, and the sweet smell of molasses filled his throat even though Fleet Street was far above where the tank had burst.

At Hanover Street, they started down the hill toward the docks. Jake asked a passerby for the Florence Hotel, and the man pointed to a doorway halfway down Fleet Street. A couple of women pulled in laundry above them. Looking up, Jake could see dark figures and the glow of cigarettes on the roof of the hotel.

They entered a ground-floor café smelling of garlic and tomatoes. Women of the night hung on men near the bar and at some of the tables. Jake spotted a doorway at the back. He pushed the unlocked door open, then he and Edwin climbed four stories of a steep and narrow staircase to the roof. They stepped from the musty interior into the chill of winter.

Candles guttered around the edges on low brick walls that surrounded the roof. A group of men sat on cartons and packing boxes near a chimney. Most were smoking. A few held tin cups, and bottles of wine were passed from one hunched figure to another. A ripple of Italian followed by a burst of argument filled the air, then a couple of the men turned and yelled at Jake and Edwin.

Jake knew no Italian and was preparing to explain himself with hand gestures when Edwin spoke up behind him. Apparently, he knew the language. He was a godsend and he continually surprised Jake with his competencies.

After some patter, a man stepped forward. He was jaunty, a solid man of medium height with dark curly hair covering his forehead and ears. He had a magnificent mustache, which he smoothed with one hand as he reached out his other. "I am Luigi Spinelli," he said. The hand was hard with calluses when Jake shook it. "This is Tony DeCarlo. His English is not so good. I talk for us both. Why do you want to see us?"

As Jake explained who he was, the other men slipped away into the shadows, out of the flickering candlelight near the chimney.

"You police?" Luigi asked.

"No, nothing like that. I'm here about Mrs. McKenna. Maggie McKenna. I believe you know her. You work with her, don't you? I'm sorry to say she's passed away and her sister, Mrs. Ryan, asked me to find out what happened." Jake lied easily. It was a better story than one about how he suspected them of bombing the tank. If these men were anarchists, there was no need to rouse their suspicions.

Luigi glanced at his friend and translated. Tony was shorter than Luigi and plump. He looked distressed by the news. They had an exchange punctuated by hand gestures.

"You ask about Maggie? But she died in molasses. That's what they told us at the company. Her building was knocked down by the molasses, right?"

Jake studied the man. His face was half hidden in the flickering light.

"Terrible luck," Luigi said, nodding to Tony. "We were there the night before. Tony and me. We visited Maggie, had a couple drinks. Lucky the tank didn't burst then. We'd be dead, too. Huh, Tony?" He waved at his friend.

"You visited her the night before the molasses flood?"

"For sure. Maggie's a friend. Drinking buddy, you know? She left her husband. He beat her up all the time. Me and Tony helped her cheer up sometimes."

"I see. You were friends. When did you leave that night? Was Maggie all right when you left?"

"Sure. Of course, she's all right. What do you mean? She was happy. All cheered up. But somebody else was coming, so we had to leave."

"Who was coming?"

"She didn't say. Maggie had secrets. Not our business. Why you want to know?"

Jake decided he might get more from the two Italians if he told them the truth. "Maggie was dead before the molasses tank exploded the next day. She was shoved under the faucet in the bathtub and held down until she drowned."

Luigi's eyes opened wide, and so did his mouth. Tony badgered him with questions in Italian, grabbing the sleeve of his pea coat until Luigi answered in a few words. Jake sensed movement from the other men in the shadows at the edges of the roof.

"Somebody killed her? You're not thinking it was us? We were friends," Luigi said.

"Do you know of anyone who wanted to hurt her?"

"Crazy mad cop husband. She's afraid of him."

"Did you see him that night?"

"We never saw him, ever." Luigi stopped to listen to his friend. They argued with gestures that Luigi translated. "Tony says there was somebody out front when we left. I didn't see nobody." Jake recalled that the police detective had known about the Italian friends. He wondered if McKenna had been following his wife in secret.

"What did he look like, the person Tony saw when you left?"

After conferring, he said, "Not sure. Maybe wearing a uniform." McKenna wore plain clothes.

"What can you tell me about a soldier that Mrs. McKenna was seeing?"

Luigi had to discuss this question with Tony before answering. "Yeah, she had a soldier friend. Very good friend. You know what I mean? She wanted to run away with him, but he ain't got no money. Then she told us he can get money so they can run away."

"What's his name?"

"Only met him once. She calls him Eddie. When he's around, we don't see Maggie so much. Past few weeks, though, he's not around. Maybe she worried he got the money and ran away without her. She didn't tell us that. We guessed. She's a little sad after Eddie's gone."

"Could he be the one she was meeting that night?"

Luigi conferred with Tony. "Tony thinks he saw a man outside. Not me, though. And she was still worried when we drank a bottle that night. She said she's going to find out what's going on, so I don't think it's her soldier boy that was coming."

"Did she say anything that might help us find out who did this to her?"

More vigorous discussion in Italian. "She said she was getting money. Enough to get out of town, stop working for bad men. Go looking for Eddie."

"What bad men?"

"The tank company. United States Industrial Alcohol. Big capitalist oppressing workers company." He shook a finger in Jake's face. "You know, we got a friend told Mr. Wrentham that tank was a big problem. Makes noises all the time." With his hands, he drew a big tank in the air. "Huge tank, full of molasses, all dripping from the sides. You know what they do when he tells them? They tell him 'paint the tank brown' so nobody can see the molasses leak. All for the money. They exploit the workers, don't care about people." When he raised his hands in a dramatic gesture, Jake could hear a murmur of agreement from the shadows.

"Do you think Maggie knew something about the tank?" Jake asked.

"We all knew. Everybody knew." Luigi threw his arms wide. Then he dropped them and looked left and right before sidling up to within an inch of Jake's face. "Maggie was maybe a little too friendly with the boss man. You know what I mean?" He jiggled his eyebrows. "Too friendly. Maybe she got money to run away from him."

"You think she got money from Jeremy Wrentham?"

Luigi jumped back. "I'm not saying nothing. Tony, too. We're not saying nothing."

Jake wasn't sure what to think about the voluble Italian. One minute he was friendly, telling them everything he knew about the dead woman. The next minute he shut up. Unsure what to believe, Jake began to feel some apprehension. When he looked around, he realized Edwin had already disappeared through the door. Other men, nothing more than silhouettes, loomed nearby. They could easily overwhelm him. Nonetheless, he felt compelled to take an extra step toward Luigi.

"The company is saying that anarchists blew up the tank with a bomb. Do you know anything about that?"

Luigi stared at him, then translated what he had said for the others. Jake felt a surge of energy like lightning as bodies on the rooftop stiffened and moved toward him.

"Liars!" Luigi yelled. "They lie about everything."

Jake heard calls and grumbling in Italian. Concern for his safety prompted him to mumble a thank you and head for the door. The men behind him were quickly consumed in a debate and when he looked over his shoulder, he saw Luigi had grabbed Tony and was shaking him. Jake found Edwin at the head of the stairs, and they both hurried down.

When they escaped to the street, Jake said, "Well, that was instructive. Not sure how much of it I believe."

"And what about the 'other one'?"

"What?"

"Luigi and Tony argued in Italian. I couldn't hear it all, but Tony kept saying 'What about the other one?' What did he mean?"

"I have no idea. They did meet Maggie's soldier, however. They ought to be able to say if he and Lt. Bradley were one and the same."

"But would the police believe them?" Edwin asked.

Chapter Twenty

F anny received a terse reply to her letter the following day. Her father's friend, Senator Henry Cabot Lodge, had looked into the matter of Lt. Bradley and would receive her in his suite at the American House on Hanover Street promptly at ten that morning. She was surprised the senator worked on the Sabbath. She would skip her usual church service to get his help for Lt. Bradley. His note instructed her to bring her account books for the Wendell House, which the senator would review as a favor to her father.

Fanny was appalled. She wanted help for Lt. Bradley, but the home was her special project. She didn't need or want help running the place from her father and his friend. Wendell House had been established by a women's committee in Boston. The Massachusetts Branch for Women of the Special Aid Society for American Preparedness funded it. Fanny's mother and her Monday Morning Reading Class in Chicago provided money for the home's cafeteria.

The first wave of returning men had caused problems. Discharged soldiers thronged the streets and parks because their homes and jobs had disappeared. The Boston and Chicago women had worked to set up a sort of way station in Boston to connect returning men to their families before they moved home.

Fanny's mother saw the project as an opportunity for Fanny to do something that would make her feel useful. Since her divorce, Fanny had been as unhappy as she was in her marriage. What she thought would bring her freedom had barely lightened the constraints she felt were holding her back. The main problem was money. Her father had settled money on both of his children but, while her brother was free to manage and use his money, Fanny's settlement was controlled by her husband. When she divorced, her husband kept the marriage settlement while she received a reduced allowance from her father. Her husband paid the school fees for the children, and her father even gave money to her son John for extra expenses, but her own allowance left little room for extravagance.

Fanny's mother had pointed out her daughter's qualifications to the Boston committee. Fanny had experience running a household. She was the perfect person to manage Wendell House. Fanny would keep an account book to be reviewed periodically by the board that oversaw the home. Her mother had hoped the disgrace of divorce would be greatly lessened by distance and good works. Fanny had welcomed the offer as a way to start a new life that was more in her own control.

Yet here she was a mere three months into the project, and her father had asked Senator Lodge to review the household books. The senator was on the board of the house, but nevertheless, Fanny felt like a student called to the principal's office. She could have cried with frustration, but she knew she needed the help of a powerful man like the senator to get Lt. Bradley released. She was deeply disappointed by Jake's refusal to intervene. What else could she do? She couldn't let the poor young soldier rot in jail due to the incompetence or corruption of Detective McKenna.

Fanny wore her most elegant black brocade walking suit and carried the large flat account book, tied with string. She arrived a few minutes before ten o'clock. The American House was a five-story venerable hotel on Hanover Street that had been reopened under new management the previous year. Fanny had been told that Senator Lodge always took rooms in the centrally located hotel when he was in town since his family home in Nahant was inconveniently far to the north.

A bellboy took her up an elevator to the senator's suite on the top floor, where she was ushered into a drawing room by a young male secretary. Chairs and sofas were all turned toward a massive desk behind which stood Senator Lodge. He took the account book from her hands and gestured to a wing chair. Nearly seventy years old, Lodge was a trim man with thin curling hair laid flat against his head and turning white at his temples. He stood straight as a martinet, his white collar stiff under a short beard and generous mustache. Knowing that he was currently battling with the president about the treaty to end the war and the proposed League of Nations, Fanny was ashamed to take him away from such weighty matters to concern himself with her household accounts. He laid the book on the desk, splaying his hand over it.

"Mrs. Lee, I'm pleased to meet you. I told your father you must call upon me if you ran into any difficulties."

"Thank you so much, Senator. I would hate to take up your time, only a most serious injustice has happened, and I didn't know who else to turn to."

"Yes. I read your letter. This Lt. Bradley that you're concerned about—we looked into the matter. We also contacted your father, who assures us Lt. Bradley is a young man of means."

"Yes. Unfortunately, we only just learned his family all passed away during the influenza epidemic. My brother is working with lawyers to allow the lieutenant to access his inheritance."

"I'm sorry to hear about his loss. But the family estate will provide a bond to allow his release, according to your father." He was still standing and, when he snapped his fingers, his young secretary handed him an envelope. "Money is being wired, and in the meantime, a bond has been placed. This is a written order for the young man's release."

"Oh, Senator, I don't know how to thank you." Fanny moved to get up, but Lodge waved her back to her seat.

He sat down himself, carefully placing the envelope in front of him and pulling forward the account book, which he opened. "I spoke with your father. I'm happy to help, and he asked me to review your progress." He put on a pince-nez and scrutinized the entries. Fanny clenched her jaw shut to keep from questioning the senator's right to review her books. She answered to the full Wendell House board. While it was true that Senator Lodge was on the board, he was a single member, and her father had no authority over the soldiers' home at all.

"That is too good of you," Fanny said, instead of protesting. What was the use? As she watched him run a finger down the columns, and turn the pages, he reminded her of an opera singer who had played Mephistopheles in a version of Faust. There was something about the mustache...

"I see you are using a butcher in the West End. I highly recommend Savenors on Charles Street. The prices may be a little higher, but it's much closer to your home and safer. There's been an influx of non-natives in some areas of the city, which makes it prudent to support established institutions, like Savenors."

"Savenors, certainly. I'll speak to my cook." Fanny vaguely recalled that Lodge was known for wanting to restrict immigration. He had proposed literacy requirements in a recent bill, and he supported the exclusion of some categories of people, including anarchists. She wasn't sure how cook chose a butcher, but she felt it was well within her prerogative to insist on Savenors based on the senator's words. She was relieved. If that was the only objection he could find in her books, she'd be glad to follow his recommendation.

There was a knock at the door, and the secretary entered, followed by an older woman in a dark cloak and hat that Fanny recognized as a style from a dozen years before. She'd noticed the conservative, slightly old-fashioned cut of dresses on many of the women she saw in the shops that lined Charles Street. It seemed a peculiarity of Beacon Hill to be slightly out of fashion.

Lodge rose. "Yes, thank you. Mrs. Thornwell let me introduce Mrs. Lee. Please, have a seat." Lodge explained that he had invited the older widow to meet Fanny because she was also on the board of Wendell House. There hadn't been a formal meeting of the board since Fanny's arrival, so she had yet to meet the members. "Mrs. Lee is quite new to Boston and, as a favor to her father, who is a friend of a friend and a great supporter of the Republican Party, I thought perhaps you could take her under your wing. Show her around. Introduce her to some of the ladies' activities, sewing groups, and that sort of thing."

Fanny tried to protest that she was busy enough with work at her home for soldiers, but the senator insisted there were many ladylike pursuits that she really must come to know. "It's our Brahmin culture, Mrs. Lee. I promised your father I would make sure you're initiated, and there's no one I could rely on to do that more efficiently than Mrs. Thornwell here."

Fanny groaned inwardly but kept her face frozen in a smile. She feared the schedule of formal visits and parties that she had escaped when she left Chicago was going to be imposed on her again. Social life in Boston would creep out and entrap her like the ivy vines gripping the walls of all these brick townhouses.

Mrs. Thornwell had sharp little eyes that gleamed in her smooth and gentle-looking face. "Why, Mrs. Lee, I believe you are the lady who has produced an entire copy of the Chicago Symphony Orchestra in a miniature. Is it true? I met a lady from Chicago on my voyage to Europe last year. We became quite good friends on the ship home, and she told me all about the wonderful way you captured the entire orchestra right down to tiny musical scores on the music stands. And we're all grateful to your mother and her group for providing funds for the cafeteria at Wendell House."

Fanny was speechless. How could the woman know about the miniatures? Mrs. Thornwell smiled kindly and went on and on about it.

Fanny had hoped to leave that period of her life behind. It was after the divorce. Her parents were terribly disappointed in her, and she wanted to make it up to them. Once they accepted that she was determined to end the marriage, they did their best to support her. Her mother, in particular, never complained or reproved.

Fanny adored her mother but couldn't replicate her talents. Mrs. Glessner was an accomplished pianist who entertained professional musicians at her table. Mr. Glessner was on the board of the Symphony, and many of the players were friends. Her parents were patrons of the arts, purchasing works they displayed in their beautifully furnished home.

Fanny herself was never talented in the arts. The only success she had was when she created a miniature copy of the orchestra for her parents. She had fashioned tiny chairs and instruments by hand, sewed the clothes, and stuffed the little dolls. The orchestra music director, Frederick Stock, painstakingly wrote out the minuscule score parts that sat on the little metal music stands.

Compulsion drove her to manufacture every perfect little detail. It took months. When the result was revealed at a reception in her parents' home, people oohed and ahhed. Even the musicians took great delight in the details exposed. But when it was finished, Fanny felt bereft. What had she done after all? Spent innumerable hours to produce a tiny, pretty, but useless little diorama. What was it worth? When she saw the futility of it, she'd nearly gone mad. She realized she had to find a way to do something more useful with her life. But here she was in her new life, getting thrust right back into the world she'd hoped to escape.

"I'm sure the ladies of my sewing circle will be very anxious to meet Mrs. Lee and to hear about her work with miniatures," Mrs. Thornwell said.

"Very good." Lodge clapped his hands. "There you have it, Mrs. Lee. I promised your father to introduce you. What could be better?"

"Thank you so much," Fanny said, swallowing her revulsion. "I really don't have anything to say to your group, though, Mrs. Thornwell. I've given up making miniatures."

"Come, come. You can't turn down such an invitation," Lodge said. Mrs. Thornwell looked on calmly.

"I'm really very worried about Lt. Bradley, Senator. May I take your letter to get him released? Can you tell me where to take it?"

Lodge pursed his lips, and his eyes narrowed as if he were about to snap out an order, but Mrs. Thornwell stalled him by asking mildly who Lt. Bradley was, and Lodge replied with a succinct explanation.

"How wonderful of you to get the young man released, Senator," Mrs. Thornwell said. "He must be at the Charles Street Jail, is that it? I know what we can do. I have my driver waiting in my motor. Why don't I take Mrs. Lee home. We can discuss the next meeting of my sewing circle on Friday and get all the details."

Fanny didn't like to contradict the woman, but she had no intention of joining a sewing circle, even for a single meeting. She could see the senator's expression lighten up at the suggestion, though. His face looked like a sky after storm clouds had blown away.

Mrs. Thornwell continued. "We could stop at the jail on the way, and my man can just run in with the papers and get Lt. Bradley. I'm sure that will relieve Mrs. Lee's mind." She rose and stepped to the desk to put a hand on the envelope. Lodge stood, a bit uncertain, but the little Beacon Hill widow leaned toward him. "I know just what to do. We had to go and get my grandnephew released when he was slightly inebriated after his club races. You know how these young men are. And my niece was anxious to keep it from his father. So, we just took care of it." She took up the envelope and beckoned to Fanny.

"Thank you, Senator," Fanny said. Her eyes followed the envelope as Mrs. Thornwell drifted to the doorway.

Lodge coughed. "You're welcome. Here's your account book." He held on to the book for a moment and looked directly into Fanny's eyes. "I'll tell your father you've joined the sewing circle."

"Yes, of course." Fanny took her book and hurried after Mrs. Thornwell.

Chapter Twenty-One

"Call me Cornelia, dear." Mrs. Thornwell patted Fanny's arm in the back of her chauffer driven motor car. "May I see the release papers?"

Fanny had taken the precious papers from the widow as soon as they reached the car. Reluctantly, she handed them back.

"Yes, I see. This will do it." Cornelia explained what they would do once they reached the Charles Street Jail. "Men believe they are protecting us by taking care of things like this, but I've learned it's best to see to it myself. You'll find the process is faster if we ladies show up." There was a little smile on her face. "They don't know what to do with us, you see. So, they'll do the business as quickly as possible to be rid of us."

The motor car rolled to a stop. Trusting the woman instinctively, Fanny followed her into a granite building with high windows like a church. Inside, the clang of iron doors echoed up the four-story atrium. Fanny looked around at the black iron stairs and platforms clinging to the stone walls like spiders' webs. The women were quickly led into the warden's office, where a very big fellow wore an ill-fitting suit as if he were mimicking a man of business.

"Mrs. Thornwell, Mrs. Lee, these papers appear to be in order. We have certain procedures we must attend to..." he started to say, but when Cornelia sat down in a wooden armchair, he hurried to the doorway. "It's not necessary for you to stay, but I can see that is your intention."

Cornelia smiled angelically and patted the seat next to her for Fanny to sit down. The man obviously didn't want them to stay, but he seemed to recognize the older woman and to be resigned to the fact that the only way to get rid of her was to release the prisoner. Fanny was glad for Cornelia's help.

"I have some friends who are suffragists," Cornelia whispered. "He remembers them."

When the guards brought Lt. Bradley in, Fanny was relieved to see he looked tired but well. He was admonished not to leave the city, then the three of them were escorted out. Inside, there was plenty of light from the great windows, but the gray-painted walls were stained with water, and she felt a dankness begin to infect her soul. She had to keep herself from stampeding to the door. Outside, flakes of snow fell as they got into the motor car. A blanket of soft white covered everything, and the cold air was crisp as newly laundered sheets.

Lt. Bradley was grateful and reported that he'd been treated well enough but had been fearful of a long confinement. "With nothing to do, I couldn't help falling back into memories of my time over there," he said. Fanny remembered the nightmares of his fellow soldier and grimaced at the thought of the young man alone with his memories of the battlefield in that great gray building.

Fanny didn't have enough time to explain how his bond had been raised before they stopped in front of the brownstone on Hancock Street.

Cornelia put a hand on her arm. "Let me extend an invitation to our sewing circle. It meets tomorrow night. You must promise me you'll come. In fact, I'll pick you up here. The house is only a few steps away at 55 Mt. Vernon Street."

Fanny couldn't refuse after the help Cornelia had given, even if she had no desire to attend. Then she remembered Jake's request. "Would it be all right if I brought someone? She's new to the area and wants to meet people. Her name is Mrs. Wrentham, and she was recommended to me by a dear friend."

"By all means, bring her. Miss Nichols, our hostess, is always looking for new people. I'll see you then. Take care of your young man." She nodded to Lt. Bradley, who waited at the bottom of the stone stairs, talking to two workmen.

Fanny said goodbye to Cornelia and turned away in time to see one of the men gesturing with his hands. She thought she heard the name "Maggie." "What do they want?" she asked Bradley.

He silenced the man with a wave of his hand. "They came to give their condolences to Mrs. Ryan," he said. "I think they were friends of her sister. They were just leaving as we arrived."

Both men straightened up and bowed stiffly to Fanny. "We go now," one of them said. "We're very sorry about Maggie."

"Yes. We're very sorry, too," she said, taking Lt. Bradley's arm to mount the stairs. She had no objection to Theresa having visitors. She assumed the men must be Maggie's Italian friends. She could guess they would not be welcome at the funeral. Maggie's husband would have lashed out at them for sure.

Fanny took the lieutenant into the parlor and explained how Senator Lodge had assisted in getting the bond posted for his bail. When the grateful young soldier had gone away to bathe and rest, Fanny used the telephone to speak to Jake. She told him that Lt. Bradley had been released on bond and asked for Mrs. Wrentham's address and telephone number. She was glad to sense that he was taken aback by her boldness in seeking out the senator's help. He obviously hadn't expected her to invite Mrs. Wrentham so quickly, either. She liked the idea that she could surprise him.

"That's very good of you, Fanny. I'm sure Mrs. Wrentham will be grateful."

"Yes, and I'll see what she has to say about her husband's business." She wanted to remind him that he'd claimed she could help with the investigation by talking to Mrs. Wrentham.

There was silence. She looked at the heavy black handset and wondered if she'd been cut off. Then she heard a cough. "Yes. Very good. But listen here, Fanny. Be careful."

Chapter Twenty-Two

Jake was impressed. Fanny had used the influence of Senator Lodge to get her soldier released. And so quickly. She must have contacted her father. He had the impression that was the last thing she wanted to do, but she'd compromised. He wondered what concessions she'd made to get what she wanted.

And she was inviting Wrentham's wife to a Beacon Hill sewing circle. When he'd challenged her with that task, he hadn't really thought she'd do it. Good for her. He would have congratulated himself on his insight if he didn't have an uneasy feeling about all this. Something the Italian, Luigi, had said bothered him. He'd hinted that Maggie was having a relationship with the USIA manager. Jake was sure that Wrentham was being secretive, but he wasn't sure it had anything to do with the tank disaster. He'd only meant for Fanny to pump Wrentham's wife about her husband's business worries, but who knew what gossip or jealous imaginings the wife would confide to another female. He hoped Fanny wasn't about to stumble on an illicit relationship when she approached Mrs. Wrentham. Oh well, too late now. If Wrentham's secret had anything to do with the molasses flood, Jake needed to know.

Jake put it from his mind as he attended to a mountain of paperwork that had grown while he was doing autopsies on the victims of the tank explosion. By the time he finished, it was late, and he moved restlessly around his office, finally shrugging into his jacket. As he looked around, he worried. Maybe telling Fanny to get information from Mrs. Wrentham was a mistake. He found his hat under a pile of untidy papers. Dusting it off, he told himself there was no danger to Fanny at a meeting of Beacon Hill matrons unless someone put arsenic in their tea. It was silly to worry. Still, a woman had been murdered. Although he had no reason to believe the death was related to the tank explosion.

The telephone jangled.

Jake waited, expecting Edwin to answer it in the other room. When the shrill ring continued, he hurried out to the laboratory. Edwin must have already left. It was unlike him, but it was well after working hours.

"North Grove Street Morgue," Jake said.

The voice at the other end belonged to a policeman. "I'm calling to report a death. A body has been found in the North End. A man fell from a building on Fleet Street."

"This is Dr. Magrath. Fleet Street," Jake repeated. An odd coincidence. "I'll be right there."

He hung up and cursed. He could have used Edwin's help, but he realized he wasn't being fair. The medic stayed late most nights. It was only by chance that he was absent for this call out. The police couldn't move the body or reopen the street until Jake looked at the dead man and had him carted away. He put through a call to Massachusetts General Hospital, where he knew a couple of staff were available to pick up the body and bring it back to the morgue. It was a regular arrangement for backup in the evenings.

In the morgue's garage, Jake cranked up Suffolk Sue, then climbed into the high seat and honked before plunging onto Grove Street. It was chilly, but he relished the rush through the dark streets, clanging Sue's bells and roaring the engine. This time he drove right through Hanover Street and turned down Fleet. Sure enough, the police had cordoned off a space in front of the Florence Hotel, the same building where he had met the Italians the night before. Jake had a bad feeling about this.

After directing a light from Suffolk Sue on a bundle in the street, Jake climbed down. The police parted for him, several of them turning to examine Suffolk Sue. Beside the lump on the street, he recognized Detective McKenna pacing back and forth. Jake caught a whiff of whiskey.

"Doc, it's one of them wops got himself dropped from the roof up there, we think." The ungainly detective rocked back on his feet and pointed up to the rooftop, where several people were peeking over the low walls. "Hey, get those people out of there. *Now!*" he shouted at a couple of uniformed officers who immediately ran into the building.

Jake pulled back the dirty blanket that covered the corpse. It was Luigi Spinelli. The man lay sprawled on his back, eyes open in horror. Beneath his head, a pool of dark blood turned sticky in the cold. Jake knew the bones would be a mass of broken sticks from the fall. He'd seen that kind of impact before, most recently a young girl who jumped after finding herself pregnant. He couldn't help remembering. But Luigi? Jake didn't believe the man would end his life by jumping from a rooftop. Not willingly. And even if he had, Jake would expect to find the body face down. He'd never seen a suicide who had stood with his back to the edge before jumping. They always faced forward and landed on their front.

Looking up at the roof, he had a sudden vision of the voluble Luigi being pushed or kicked in the stomach and reaching out wildly to try to stop his fall. All Jake's instincts told him the man had been pushed.

He dropped the blanket over the body. The rest of the examination could wait for the lights and instruments at the morgue. He motioned to the ambulance drivers who had arrived. "You can take him away." He turned to McKenna. "I want to go up on the roof to see where he fell off." He stomped away. He found McKenna repulsive. Jake understood the man was in shock from the murder of his wife, but his shoddy investigative methods were exactly what Jake despaired of.

"A fight among the wops," McKenna said as he watched Jake go. "We'll never get a straight story from any of them. It's one of them did it, for sure...." His voice faded as Jake entered the hotel café. Puffing with annoyance, McKenna caught up when Jake started climbing the steep stairs in the back.

The detective cursed and didn't bother to follow Jake. On the roof, two patrolmen were holding two workmen who answered their questions in Italian. Exasperated, one of the policemen shook the man he held.

"Get an interpreter," Jake growled as he marched past to the edge of the roof above where Luigi had fallen. A few candles guttered in a sheltered spot by the chimney. The roof was mostly in shadows thrown from the gaslight fixtures in the street below. Jake couldn't tell if there'd been a struggle but, remembering Luigi, he couldn't believe the man wouldn't have put up a fight. Stepping to the chimney, he peered down and picked up an empty bottle. It was a colder night than when he'd visited. Still, in the cramped living conditions of the tenement, this might be the only place for a private conversation. Two boxes were pulled up where they would be sheltered from the wind. Jake wondered if Luigi had sat there drinking with someone else. Where was Tony DeCarlo? Was he the one who'd been up there with Luigi? Had they argued? A falling out among anarchists? He was pretty sure McKenna knew the two Italians had been drinking companions of his dead wife. He was on the squad that tracked anarchists. Jake shook his head and headed back down the stairs.

On his way down, he heard doors open and saw men peeking out from narrow rooms. He tried asking for Tony DeCarlo at open doors. The men stared blankly and retreated inside. He wished he had Edwin to interpret for him. On the street, he told McKenna to question the neighbors.

McKenna was not enthusiastic. "Not that they'll tell us a damn thing," he said. But he shouted instructions to his men. "They give you any guff, bring 'em down to the station, and we'll question them there. You done, Doc?"

"The autopsy will be tomorrow. It seems fairly obvious that he fell or was pushed from the roof," Jake told him.

"It'll be one of them Eyeties," McKenna told him. "They get drunk and fight each other like dogs."

"We'll see." Jake had no hope of teaching an old detective like McKenna to look for physical evidence instead of making assumptions. He only wished he had a way of training some of the younger men before they adopted the bad habits of their elders. It was a task that had defeated him so far.

Climbing into Suffolk Sue, Jake drove at a moderate pace back to the morgue to direct the storage of the body. He no longer felt the surge of excitement that had him clanging the car bells on the way out. Somehow, Luigi's brutal death only made the tangled mass of information about the tank explosion and the murder of Maggie even murkier. Would anyone ever find out what had really happened the night before the molasses flood?

Chapter Twenty-Three

Mrs. Jeremy Wrentham wore a flowery hat more appropriate for spring than the dead of winter. Fanny welcomed her into Wendell House promptly at four thirty Monday afternoon. After a brief tour, Fanny got into her own coat, and they were waiting at the door when Cornelia's motor car stopped out front.

"Good evening," the older widow greeted them. "I'm afraid you're about to be surprised by how short a trip it is to our destination." It was barely more than a block when they stopped again. "The Nichols are your neighbors at 55 Mt. Vernon."

Unlike most of the attached houses nearby, this one was a townhouse, with stone steps leading to a front door, which was on the side with a view down the hill toward Charles Street.

"Originally, they had a view all the way to the river," Cornelia told them. "Of course, that was 1804, so things have changed." Fanny and Mrs. Wrentham followed her into the hallway, where a maid took their coats and hats. There was a door into a kitchen on the left, and on the right, the office of Dr. Nichols. Like many of its neighbors, the townhouse had the rooms for entertaining on the second floor.

Cornelia introduced them to Mrs. Nichols, an older lady in a fine afternoon dress who sent them upstairs to the parlor, where she told them her daughter, Rose, was waiting. "With the other girls," she said.

Fanny and Mrs. Wrentham followed Cornelia up the circular staircase to a high-ceilinged room where a dozen or so women murmured in anticipation of the meeting. Fanny saw no evidence of sewing at all. She was relieved.

A tall woman in her late forties rose from a pink satin wing chair to greet them. Miss Rose Nichols had slightly waved brown hair cut in a bob. Her frame was gangly, and sharp brown eyes, like those of a raptor, raked her visitors. Satisfied, like an eagle who had found new prey, her gaze roamed around the room filled with a dozen other women.

After finding seats for the newcomers, she convened the meeting from her pink chair, explaining that the group had given up sewing a number of years before. There was a twitter from the others at that. First on the agenda was a discussion of plans for suffragists to greet President Wilson when his boat arrived in Boston the following week. Fanny was surprised to hear the women had every expectation of being arrested for their protests. The only question was which of the many volunteers would be the most newsworthy to fall into the clutches of the authorities.

"They'll be taken to the Charles Street Jail," Cornelia whispered to Fanny, as if they had a shared secret in having already visited the place.

Fanny suppressed a smile, noticing that Mrs. Wrentham was trying hard not to show her surprise at the topic of the meeting. She was giving the manager's wife a shock with this introduction to the matrons of Beacon Hill. Not quite what the woman had expected. Not quite what Fanny had expected, either.

Looking around, Fanny was curious about Rose Nichols. She decided her mother would approve of the taste of the Nichols family. A lovely Flemish tapestry hung on one wall, a French Empire settee below it. Italian portraits hung over a fireplace mantelpiece on which the gilded head of a Greek god was displayed.

"Saint-Gaudens is Rose's uncle," Cornelia whispered, pointing to the Greek god. Fanny realized she meant the sculptor Augustus Saint-Gaudens. She quietly shared the information with Mrs. Wrentham, hoping it would reassure her about this den of suffrage iniquity to which she had brought the woman from out of town. Mrs. Wrentham sighed.

Fanny was somewhat embarrassed to have herself introduced to the group as the creator of miniatures. She tried to demur, thinking as an activity it probably ranked with the sewing that had been abandoned, but the ladies appeared impressed and gratified by the skill, and several mentioned their own efforts in that area. As the group broke up to get tea from the dining room, Rose herself confided in Fanny that she both collected and created a wide variety of needlework.

"That's when she's not exercising her considerable practice of garden design," Cornelia told Fanny. "She's published books on the topic as well, and many magazine articles. But garden design is a profession for her, you see. And her younger sister has a carpentry business."

Fanny could see that Cornelia was enjoying her surprise. The older woman must have known that Fanny expected a group of narrow-minded society women engaged in critiquing fashion. Instead, she was meeting women with political and professional agendas far beyond what she had accomplished herself. It made her a little envious, but she thought Cornelia was purposely demonstrating the possibilities she had in her new city. For the first time since her move, Fanny felt less alone in her ambitions to do something meaningful with her life.

Realizing that she'd left Mrs. Wrentham to fend for herself for too long, Fanny turned to her and suggested they go to the dining room for refreshments. Rose and Cornelia waved them off as they started an earnest conversation with another woman, and Fanny threaded her way through women returning to the parlor with teacups and plates of petit fours.

"Oh, my, isn't this handsome?" Mrs. Wrentham said as they entered the dining room. Gold leaves on a red background covered the walls in what looked like leather wallpaper. Large pieces of dark mahogany furniture stood on an Oriental carpet. Solemn looking ancestors looked out stoically from the walls. Fanny thought the room was weighted down with too many ornaments in an old, stuffy style, but it appealed to Mrs. Wrentham. Food and tea were on the center table, and chairs had been grouped around the periphery.

Fanny led the way to the table, then when they were furnished with tea and goodies, they found a couple of seats in a corner. Fanny took advantage of the break to ask Mrs. Wrentham about herself and her family.

"Andrew's away at school now, and since we don't have any other children, Mr. Wrentham felt it was right to take advantage of this opportunity to manage the operation here. I must say it takes so much of his time I've been at my wit's end to entertain myself," Mrs. Wrentham told her.

"You must come into town often, then," Fanny said. "I'm sure you're glad you were here when the tank catastrophe happened. It was lucky your husband was at lunch with you. Weren't you relieved you chose that day to accompany him?"

"Oh, you don't know how thankful I was! He could have been killed! I tell him it's too much, the time he spends on all of this. But I didn't accompany him, I came to town by myself." She seemed proud of the fact. "It was another of those times that he had to spend the night in town. I hadn't seen him for several days, in fact, so I decided to come and make sure he spent some time with me. I was worried for his health. That's one thing about the tank explosion, there's still so much he has to do for the company, but I'm glad to say he's spending a lot more time at home. It was such a shock."

Fanny took a bite from a pretty petit four, then swallowed a sip of tea before casually asking, "Your husband stayed in Boston the night before the molasses flood?"

Mrs. Wrentham wiped her mouth with a napkin. "Yes, he often did. They had such a large shipment delivered, and he had to see to get it transported to the plant over in Cambridge." She watched for Fanny's reaction as if she were suspicious. "I always spoke to him on the telephone nights he was *forced* to stay in town. He hated being away from me." Fanny wondered if she was trying too hard to defend her husband's actions. She also wondered if Wrentham looked for opportunities to get away from his homesick, bored wife. Or perhaps there were problems with the tank. She reminded herself that Jake would warn her not to jump to conclusions. Nevertheless, she thought she had something to tell him after all.

"Was your husband concerned about that tank before it exploded?"

"No, no, nothing like that. He might have been concerned about those anarchists. He told me they're pretty sure it was a bomb. Can you imagine? They really should do something about those people. My husband could have been killed."

"What people, dear?" Cornelia had wandered over to them. She had a petit four in her hand, but she hadn't bothered with a plate or teacup.

"Those anarchists who blew up my husband's company's tank," Mrs. Wrentham said.

"Oh, the molasses flood. I thought there was some question about the structural integrity of the tank. Have they found out it was a bomb that caused it?"

Other women around them had gone quiet, listening in on the conversation.

"My husband's company hired leading experts to investigate, and they definitely think there was an anarchist bomb," Mrs. Wrentham said. Fanny thought she looked like a cat whose dander had risen at some unwelcome noise.

Chapter Twenty-Four

Tuesday, January 21, 1919

"So, Jeremy Wrentham was in Boston the night before the molasses flood," Jake said when Fanny sought him out at the morgue Tuesday morning with the news.

"Yes. His wife came into town by herself that day, and I think she insisted he have lunch with her. I had the impression she was none too sure of what he was up to all those nights he spent in town," she said.

If Wrentham's wife was suspicious of him, Jake thought Luigi Spinelli might have been right that there was something between the USIA manager and Maggie McKenna. Jake looked down at his desk, searching around under some forms. He was trying to keep his face expressionless, but Fanny was too sharp.

"What is it? Tell me. You know something. Did you already know he'd stayed in town that night?"

"No, it's not that. It's just that someone suggested Maggie might have been, well, friendly with her employer."

"Maggie? Do you mean they had a love affair? Theresa never said a word about that. Wouldn't she know? Who told you that?"

Jake's face screwed up in a grimace. He really didn't want to tell Fanny his suspicion, but she had found out information that he'd asked for. Surely, she wouldn't be that shocked to learn of a possible liaison between Maggie and Wrentham, but it was only a guess and he hated to think she would tell

Theresa.

"Jake!"

"All right. All right. But take it from whence it comes. It was one of the men who worked with Maggie and used to drink with her. He didn't give any details."

"Well, ask him."

"Not so easily done, I'm afraid. He's on a slab in my operating theater, waiting to be autopsied. I've kept him for my class today. That's right, it's a shock. He fell or was pushed from a rooftop in the North End Sunday night."

Fanny closed her open mouth. "Do you think Wrentham could have done it?"

"Now, stop that. I told you not to jump to conclusions. Detective McKenna thinks it could be fellow anarchists who got rid of him to keep his mouth shut."

"McKenna. He's the one who arrested Lt. Bradley. He doesn't know what he's doing."

"Fanny, he's an experienced police detective. While I have serious reservations about how men like him read a crime scene and whether they're open minded enough to collect all of the facts in a case like this, still, he has a point. If the tank explosion *was* caused by anarchists, and if they saw Luigi Spinelli with the Lieutenant or with a police detective, they might have thought he was talking to the authorities. They could have gotten rid of him." Jake remembered the men had seen Luigi talking to him on the rooftop Saturday night. How many of them knew English well enough to understand what was said? What if they assumed Luigi had been cooperating? Or even giving information unwittingly? Could they have concluded he was a threat based on his talk with Jake? And, if so, was Jake in some way responsible for his death?

"Was the tank explosion due to a bomb?" Fanny asked.

"I don't know." Silence. She was instinctively reading his mind, and he found it irritating. "I don't think so, but I can't say definitively that it wasn't a bomb."

"Hmm. What if Wrentham heard you were talking to this man? One of the other men who worked for him could have told him. Maybe he has his own spies. What if he found out you were told of his connection to Maggie? Or maybe the man knew something about how the company was responsible for the tank explosion? Mrs. Wrentham was very defensive when it was brought up. She insisted the company had 'experts' who would prove it was a bomb. Maybe that man knew it wasn't, and Wrentham killed him to keep him quiet. We've got to find out where Wrentham was that night."

"Fanny, stop it. You have absolutely no evidence that Wrentham was involved in the death of Luigi. You can't go around maligning the man on a whim."

"A whim! He purposely misled you into thinking he wasn't in town the night Maggie died. Doesn't that tell you something?"

"It tells me he was in town that night, nothing more." Jake remembered the suggestions he had heard that Maggie and her soldier were expecting to come into some money. Fanny didn't know about that, and he wasn't going to encourage her wild imaginings by telling her. He might wonder himself whether Maggie had been in a relationship with her boss and whether she'd tried to blackmail him, but he wasn't about to suggest that to Fanny. It was much too sordid, and he had no proof whatsoever. "Besides, your reasoning makes no sense. First you want to accuse Wrentham of killing Luigi because he knew something about the tank failure, then you want to say he killed Maggie."

"Maybe she knew something about the tank."

"Fanny, Maggie died *before* the molasses flood. It makes no sense to think Wrentham killed her because she knew something about a tank failure that hadn't happened."

"Are you sure?"

"Don't be ridiculous. You just don't like it that he might have been lying to his wife when he stayed in town so often. Surely, she was suspicious about that?"

Fanny sighed. "She defended him to me, but of course, she would. I just think someone should be looking into Wrentham's actions. If Detective

McKenna is determined to convict anarchists for the tank explosion and Lt. Bradley for his wife's death, justice will never be served. You say you're not the detective, you can't investigate Maggie's death, but the man who is the detective is biased and incompetent."

Edwin stood in the doorway.

Jake suspected Edwin had some news for him, but he concentrated on Fanny anyhow. "Look here, Fanny, I thank you for the information from Mrs. Wrentham. That is helpful. But now you must leave it alone. I'll be reporting to the authorities about the cause of death for the victims. Then they'll battle it out with the USIA if they must. You need to let the police find out what happened to Maggie McKenna and Luigi Spinelli. Your job is to run that home of yours." She looked as if he'd slammed a door in her face. Jake could feel frustration emanating from her like waves of heat from a fire. She was too fixed on the idea that Wrentham must have had something to do with Maggie's death based on the fact that he'd misled Jake about where he was the night of her death.

Jake wracked his brain for some innocuous task for her. "Listen, the one thing you could do is to talk to Mrs. Ryan and ask her if she remembers anything else, anything at all, about what she saw in that bathroom before the molasses flood. If there's a clue there, it could lead to the arrest of the right person for her sister's death." Of course, she'd have to convince the police, but they'd listen to Theresa Ryan if she remembered something. It was all he could think of to distract her. He doubted it would work. All that concentrated energy. He wished he could direct Fanny towards something worthwhile. "Normally, I'd have examined the place where she died to determine the circumstances."

"Yes. I see." She stood up. "I'll let you know."

Jake knew he'd let her down. Before she reached the door, Edwin entered, followed by Theresa Ryan. "What is it?" Jake asked.

"It's Billy McKenna. He's come back. I'm afraid he'll take Lt. Bradley away again."

"He can't do that," Fanny said. She turned back toward Jake.

"He was asking if Lt. Bradley was in all Thursday night," Theresa said.

She gulped a breath, still panting from running. "I sent someone to find his roommate, but I don't know if Billy will believe him."

"Of course, he was home. He'd only just been released from jail," Fanny said.

"He went out for a drink with some of the lads," Theresa said. "I'm sorry, Mrs. Lee, but I told some of them to take him with them. He'd a need for a drink after his experiences."

The girl looked so worried, Jake had to restrain himself from comforting her, and he could see that Edwin felt the same.

Fanny was not so sympathetic. "Oh, Theresa, I wish you wouldn't encourage them." When the housekeeper covered her face with her hands, Fanny took a step backwards. "I'm sorry, my dear. It's not your fault." She turned toward Jake. "Does he think Lt. Bradley had something to do with Luigi Spinelli's death? That's absurd. He'd never even met the man."

"I have no idea," Jake said.

Theresa lowered her hands to her mouth, a frightened look on her face.

"What is it?" Fanny asked.

"Luigi Spinelli? He came to see me. It was Sunday. He wanted to say how sorry he was for Maggie's death."

"Oh, good heavens, we met him as he was leaving. But Lt. Bradley didn't know him any more than I did," she told Jake, then turned back to Theresa. "Did Mr. Spinelli know something about your sister's death?"

"No. He didn't tell me anything about that." She looked drawn.

Jake was vexed that Fanny didn't seem to see the strain her young housekeeper was under. He watched Edwin restrain himself from touching the woman's arm in an attempt to comfort her. "Well, perhaps you'd better get along and see what the detective wants," he told Fanny.

"I'll do that." She flung herself through the laboratory, closely followed by her housekeeper.

Jake mused as he watched them hurry away. Could Luigi's visit to Wendell House be connected to his death? Had someone seen him and feared he would reveal secrets? Did Luigi kill Maggie? Had he left the grieving sister feeling guilty enough to throw himself from the roof of the Florence Hotel?

Or could McKenna be right after all? Did Luigi see Lt. Bradley with the dead woman, and had the young soldier found out and killed him?

Jake could think of no reason for Fanny's soldier to have thrown Luigi from a rooftop. If McKenna *was* accusing him of killing both Maggie and Luigi, the police would still have to prove Bradley had even known Maggie. The fact that he'd been overseas until December made it impossible that he was the father of Maggie's child. Jake was more worried by the fact that another soldier—his assistant Edwin—had been absent when the Italian was killed. It bothered him.

"Well, Edwin, what do you think of that? Could this Lt. Bradley have known Luigi Spinelli or is Detective McKenna blinded by rage and jealousy, as Mrs. Lee insists?"

Edwin stood tentatively in the doorway as if he couldn't decide whether to come in or leave. Jake had a sinking feeling. Was there something the young man needed to tell him? He waited. The medic had been such a godsend when he applied for the job some months previously. Jake had come to depend on his quiet, steady work.

Edwin seemed to consider before answering the question and, when he did, Jake sensed an underlying fury. "McKenna is a coward and a bully. He's afraid. He needs to blame someone else, don't you see? It was him who drove his wife out of her home, wasn't it?"

"You think he killed Maggie, not Wrentham?"

"If he found out she was carrying another man's child, what do you think he would do?"

Jake shook himself. "It's all speculation. That's no good. We've ruled the death a homicide. The police have to find the man who did it. That's no longer our concern. But I still haven't completed my report on the tank explosion. And if the death of Maggie McKenna is related, then it makes a difference to me. I'd discounted the suggestion of a bomb, but her Italian co-workers do seem to be anarchist sympathizers. What if she knew something about that? Or what if Wrentham is lying and she was blackmailing him about something to do with the company? Luigi said there'd been complaints about the tank."

"Or she was killed by a jealous husband," Edwin insisted.

Jake wondered at the man's certainty that McKenna was to blame. It almost seemed an obsession. He knew so little of his usually quiet assistant. What had made him hate the police detective so fiercely? McKenna had struck some chord deep in Edwin.

"Or a frightened lover. I'm afraid we have to consider that Wrentham may have been the father of Maggie's child. He certainly wouldn't have wanted that known. It wouldn't be the first time a married man killed a mistress to keep her quiet."

"The woman always gets the blame," Edwin said.

Chapter Twenty-Five

Fanny hurried back to Wendell House with Theresa. She had assumed Lt. Bradley was safe from the harassment of the police detective once he'd been released on bail. She thought the protection of a powerful man like Senator Henry Cabot Lodge was enough to prevent McKenna from pursuing the young soldier.

After a breathless hike up Beacon Hill, Fanny entered Wendell House at the Hancock Street entrance and found a uniformed police officer outside the parlor where McKenna was interrogating Lt. Bradley. She marched to the door and opened it. The young policeman stood by helplessly. He couldn't very well tackle a Beacon Hill matron.

Inside, McKenna was planted in a wing chair with Lt. Bradley leaning on his cane before him. The detective frowned at her. "What do you think you're doing? I'm in the middle of an interrogation."

"Detective McKenna, I demand you leave this house and stop harassing this young man. He is already out on bond. If you wish to speak with him, please have the courtesy to allow him to summon his lawyer." She looked down at the red-faced detective who struggled to rise from the chair. He had a pencil and notebook in his hands.

"For the love of God, woman," he said. "This is a murder investigation. Keep your bloody nose out of it."

"How dare you? I am manager of this house, and I demand you leave. Immediately."

McKenna was not as easily cowed as the policeman on the door. When he took a step toward her, seething in a way that made veins rise on his forehead,

Fanny began to lose confidence in her ability to control the situation with the unwritten rules of etiquette that usually protected her. This man had a deep well of black anger in him, and she could imagine it swelling up and bursting out to lash at anything in his way.

"Please, sir, Mrs. Lee is just trying to help me," Lt. Bradley said. He raised an arm between them, transferring his cane to the other hand. "Thank you, Mrs. Lee, but Detective McKenna was just asking about my whereabouts Sunday night. Stiller, here, was saying how I was out all night with him and some of the other men. It's not about Mrs. Ryan's sister, you see. It's something else."

Only then did Fanny look away from the hulk that was McKenna to see another young officer sitting on the sofa with his back to her. He rose when his name was mentioned. "It's all right, Mrs. Lee. We were just telling Detective McKenna which bars we visited."

"These men didn't even know Luigi Spinelli," Fanny said. She wanted McKenna to know she had already learned about the Italian workman's death.

"That's right," Lt. Bradley said. "We told him. Apparently, that man came to see Mrs. Ryan here at the home, but Lt. Stiller and I didn't meet him. We were just explaining that to the detective." He reached out to touch Fanny's arm, as if calming an anxious horse.

She took a deep breath.

"It's none of your business what I ask these men," McKenna said. His voice was harsh and gravelly. He had instinctively stood and pulled off his bowler hat in deference to Fanny but now he sat back down in his seat and placed it firmly on his head. There were pouches under his rheumy eyes. Had he pushed his wife into a tub and held her down until she stopped thrashing? It was an alarming picture conjured up by Fanny's imagination. "I'm not finished, so you can leave, or I'll have patrolman Lynch there drag you out." He sneered.

"Your behavior is unspeakably rude," Fanny told him. "And I will report it to the highest authorities if you don't leave this house immediately."

The two young army officers just gawked at her. McKenna rose again, his knees creaking as he did so. He walked right up to her and stuck his face in hers. She turned her head away at the smell of whiskey. "Don't threaten me, lady. If you're not out of here in ten seconds, I'll be taking these two down to the station, and they can sit in lockup overnight before we finish this conversation."

Fanny was stymied. If he delivered on his threat, they'd be sunk once again in the mire of officialdom, and she'd be hard-pressed to extract them. Besides, the detective seemed to be indicating that if he finished the interviews here, he wouldn't detain them. Realizing she had probably been wrong in her assumption that the man was here to arrest Lt. Bradley, she regretted her outburst. She wouldn't let him know it, though.

Without a word, she turned on her heel and marched out of the room and down to her office, where she pulled out ink and paper and began another long missive to Senator Lodge. McKenna didn't even know that Jeremy Wrentham had been in Boston the night of Maggie's death. The detective was an incompetent, and she was going to expose him.

Chapter Twenty-Six

Wednesday, January 22, 1919

The next morning Fanny was summoned to the American Hotel by Senator Lodge. She was gratified at his prompt response, but she entered his suite a little worried about the strong language she'd used in her letter. Overnight, she'd tossed and turned, remembering her phrases calling McKenna a bumbling incompetent. She'd probably gone too far by comparing him to comic portrayals of cops in motion pictures. She'd also accused Wrentham of being an unfaithful husband who used political "pull" to cover his vile actions. She knew Jake would say she had no proof, and her father would have been coldly angry at her accusations. By morning she wished she'd tempered her words a bit.

Still, she had gotten a prompt reaction, and she was glad of it when the young acolyte she'd met before led her into the room dominated by the senator's huge desk. She was surprised to see half a dozen people seated in chairs arranged to face the senator. There was one older man, and the rest were women. All talk stopped at her entrance.

The young man led her to a single chair placed in the middle. She felt a tingling of hairs on the back of her neck as she sat down. Telling herself not to be silly, she told herself they must be impressed by her pleas for help dealing with the incompetent police detective. She took a deep breath.

The door behind her opened, and everyone turned to see who it was. Cornelia Thornwell was ushered in and led to the one remaining empty chair. "Senator Lodge, I only just received your message. I was out of town visiting my daughter. It was lucky I decided to return early, or I might have missed your call for an emergency meeting. What, pray, is the emergency?"

Emergency meeting? Fanny realized these people must be the board of Wendell House. She was glad the senator had convened the group to help defend Lt. Bradley. It was more than she had hoped for.

Senator Lodge coughed. "Mrs. Thornwell, happy you could make it. I knew some of the board members were out of town, but we've received a very serious complaint against Mrs. Lee, and for the sake of Wendell House's reputation, we need to address it immediately."

"What?" Fanny was shaken. A complaint about her? But she was the one with complaints.

Fanny saw Cornelia's eyes narrow, and the older woman leaned forward. "What kind of complaint?"

Lodge stood and picked up a sheet of paper. Fanny recognized her letter. "Mrs. Lee has been accused of slandering a prominent member of the business community, and the proof is here, in her own hand." He grimaced at the paper as if it smelled bad. "Furthermore, she has maligned a member of the police force and refused to cooperate with a murder investigation."

Fanny felt the attention in the room concentrate on her. "No," she said. "I did no such thing."

Lodge's forehead creased. "You cannot deny your own words." He took the letter to the other male in the room. "Here, read it for yourself and pass it on to the others. I've never read such a disrespectful screed. It's hard to believe it came from a lady."

Lodge was a skillful politician. He must be to get elected as often as he had. He knew how to swing an audience his way.

"Senator Lodge, I'm sorry if you didn't approve of my choice of words, but I was just asking for your help."

Out of the corner of her eye, Fanny saw the male board member shake his head over the letter and pass it to the woman beside him.

"Lt. Bradley is one of our soldiers at the home. He has been repeatedly harassed by a police detective and accused of things he couldn't have done.

And that policeman has refused to question the manager of the USIA Company even though he lied about where he was the night of the murder of Maggie McKenna, who worked for his business."

Lodge's face was suffused with red. "How dare you? Who are you to question the work of an experienced detective? Who are you to accuse a respectable businessman of lying? No, Mrs. Lee, you have far exceeded your authority in this. You were hired to manage the housekeeping at the home and to provide food and lodging to the veterans. Nowhere in your charge is there any permission to question authorities or involve yourself in criminal investigations. Already the man in question has threatened to sue Wendell House for your actions. We cannot have this." He looked around at the seated board members. "I propose we dismiss Mrs. Lee from her position as Resident Manager of Wendell House immediately to protect the reputation of the home." He placed both hands on the desk and leaned forward, staring at the board members.

Fanny felt cold and heavy, as if she'd turned to stone.

There was a polite little cough. Fanny's letter had been passed around until it reached Cornelia Thornwell. "Mrs. Lee certainly expresses strong feelings about what she believes is harassment by this police detective."

"She accuses Detective McKenna of incompetence," Lodge said. "She has no competence herself to make such a statement."

"Yes, however, the issue of Mr. Wrentham's lying about where he was is something the police should investigate, surely?"

"These are issues for the professional investigator to pursue, not some housekeeper." Lodge snapped. Fanny realized with a jolt that the mere "housekeeper" he mentioned was herself, not Theresa Ryan.

"I have talked to Detective McKenna," Lodge said. "He's hot on the trail of Italian anarchists involved in both the bomb at the molasses tank and quite possibly the murder of his own wife. These are matters for the authorities. Not Mrs. Lee. Her attempts to blacken the name of the manager of USIA are a disgrace and an embarrassment."

"Perhaps we could caution Mrs. Lee to be more discreet in the future?" Cornelia offered. It made Fanny's skin crawl to hear her friend concede to

Lodge. Fanny gritted her teeth and took quick breaths waiting for a moment to break in and offer to resign in protest.

"A caution is not nearly enough," Lodge responded. "No, I demand dismissal, and I warn you that if the lady remains, I will be forced to resign from the board and to inform all of the donors who support Wendell House of my decision. I will also advise them to withdraw their support." He shut his mouth with a click of his teeth.

Fanny could see Cornelia frowning over the letter, calculating a response. She heard rustles of movement as the other board members settled uncomfortably in their chairs. That Lodge would go as far as he threatened shocked Fanny. Why should all the poor returning soldiers suffer just because Senator Lodge found her impertinent? Why had she ever imagined the powerful senator would listen to her and go against a wealthy man like Wrentham? If Lodge began a campaign against Wendell House, of course, he would succeed. He was a politician. He excelled at campaigns.

Cornelia caught Fanny's eye. Fanny folded her hands in her lap and lowered her head. She kept her lips firmly closed. Cornelia nodded slightly.

Cornelia glanced around at the others and sighed. "Of course, we very much want your support and continued work on the board, Senator. If you feel so strongly that Mrs. Lee should be replaced, I think we can do that. However, Wendell House is a large operation, and we'll require some time to fill the position." She looked up at Lodge, who was frowning. "Until the end of the month...if that's agreeable."

Lodge looked serious, his wiry eyebrows furrowed, but Fanny thought she sensed an air of relief under his pretended concern. He must have been prepared for a longer fight. "Of course, I'll leave it to you ladies to arrange for an adequate replacement. You know more about such things than I do." He waved a hand. "I'm very sorry to have to take such a step, Mrs. Lee, but it's best for all of us to cut this off before there are lawsuits. Thank you all for coming. If you don't mind, I'll have to leave for another meeting. My assistant will show you out."

He turned away, and Fanny felt a hand on her arm. "Come along, dear," Cornelia said. "There are some things I should tell you."

Chapter Twenty-Seven

"So, you wrote a letter, and they fired you?" Jake asked. It was Wednesday, one week after the molasses flood, when Fanny appeared at his office. Chastened, she was much calmer than when he had last seen her the day before, and he thought she looked downright demure in a walking suit of black wool trimmed in a shiny brocade.

She sighed. "Cornelia says it's because of the suffragists. I had no idea how much the senator despises suffragists." It was only *after* the hastily called meeting of the board that Cornelia Thornwell explained how Lodge had carried on a major strategic battle with the women's movement over the last several years. So far, he'd been victorious in preventing an amendment that would give women the vote. He was vigilant in stamping out any new attempts to raise the issue. As a result, Lodge was incensed when he learned that the gathering attended by Fanny at the Nichols home was a hotbed of suffragist conspiracy. Much as he despised his rival, President Wilson, he hated the uppity women demanding the vote even more. He was furious when he learned via a feminine grapevine that Mrs. Thornwell had led Fanny into the den of iniquity that was Rose Nichols's parlor. When he received Fanny's letter accusing the USIA manager, Wrentham, he assumed she was another of those bothersome suffragists who were his enemies. That explained his harsh reaction.

Jake pulled out the front page of the *Boston Globe* and turned it toward her. "This may be why."

"Oh, dear." The headline read "Militants Think Their Jail Treatment 'Lovely'" and the story described the fates of fifteen women who had been arrested for demonstrating against President Wilson's boat when it arrived in the harbor. The women cheerfully refused to pay their fines or even give their names to the police. They were jailed. "I'm afraid some of them were at the meeting at Rose Nichols's house, but Senator Lodge was the one who insisted I attend. I can see how their happy-go-lucky attitude could annoy him. But I had no part in the demonstration. He was angry that I wrote to him about Mr. Wrentham being in town the night of Maggie's death. I was dumbfounded by his reaction."

Jake stared at her with open mouth, then asked, "Whatever were you thinking, writing to Lodge about that?"

"I was *thinking* Detective McKenna was incompetent. Poor Maggie deserves to have her death investigated by someone who knows what they're doing."

"I take it Senator Lodge didn't agree that Wrentham should be investigated?" Jake could see that Fanny was completely deflated by her experience. She'd finally realized she couldn't expect men with power to bow to her demands. She'd been squashed like a bug, and he felt sorry for her.

"Oh, no. He was furious that I would 'assail the good name of an important member of the business community.' Especially when McKenna told him he was investigating anarchists. It seems Lodge is virulent in his opposition to Italian immigrants as well as female suffragists. That I would dare to impugn Wrentham when it was obviously an *anarchist* plot that blew up the tank and an *anarchist* assassin who killed Maggie McKenna was too much for him. Without giving me a word of reply, he called an emergency meeting of the Wendell House board to have me removed as resident manager. Cornelia tried to rally votes when she heard about the meeting, but it came as a surprise to her, and they pushed the thing through. I've been dismissed."

"I'm so sorry, Fanny. I know you were doing good things for those young men."

"But you're not surprised. You warned me. I was just too impetuous… again."

"What will you do? Are you out on the street?"

"I have till the end of the month. I can't go back to Chicago, not in disgrace like this." Jake could see she found the prospect of facing her relatives with such a failure too grim. "I think I'll go to The Rocks," she said, referring to her family estate in New Hampshire.

"It'll be awfully cold up there this time of year." Jake found himself wishing she would stay in the city. It surprised him. He'd never imagined he'd have such a gut-wrenching reaction to news that she would leave. He hadn't even seen her that much in the short time she'd been there. She looked much more relaxed now that she finally realized how very wrong she'd been in all her assumptions. He wanted her to stay. "Do you really want to go hide in the White Mountains at this time of year? There'll be nobody up there but a few natives."

"I expect I'll survive," she said. "I just wish I could do something to help find out what really happened to Maggie McKenna. I feel like I'm deserting Theresa and Lt. Bradley." She made a face. "I hope I haven't made it worse for Lt. Bradley. I'm afraid McKenna will go after him just to spite me now."

Jake didn't know what to say to that. It was certainly possible. She'd been terribly clumsy in her attempts to clear that young soldier by finding out what really happened to Maggie McKenna. He wished she had never become involved in that mess. He had a very uneasy feeling about the circumstances surrounding the woman's death. He wondered if Fanny would really want to know the truth if it was as sordid as he imagined. Yet he understood her need to do something to help. "Was Mrs. Ryan ever able to remember more about what she saw in the rooming house before the molasses flood?"

"I haven't asked her. What do you think she could remember?"

He dropped the pen he was holding. "It makes a difference to really look at the scene of a death. Sometimes a small detail will clear up a hundred questions. At the moment you first walk into the room, the action that preceded the death is imprinted on the place. You'd be surprised. A footprint, a mark, something out of place, it can tell the story of what really happened. In this case, someone followed Maggie into that bathroom and held her down in the water until she drowned. He might have left something behind." Jake glanced at his bookshelf and pointed. "Locard is a scientist who's been doing a lot of work in France. He says it's impossible for a criminal to *not* leave some trace evidence at the scene of any crime. Most police in this country haven't been trained well enough to find that trace. That's why it's so important to see the scene of a crime." He sat back, realizing he'd been riding his hobby horse. "Anyhow, if Maggie's killer left any trace in that bathroom, it was wiped away by the molasses flood. That's the only reason I thought getting Mrs. Ryan's memories of the room might help. It's too late now."

Fanny was staring at him intensely. It touched him to realize she'd listened to his rant. Few people sympathized.

"In the time remaining, I'll ask Theresa what she remembers. I might even have a way to help her remember." She gave a short laugh. "Lord knows I have few enough skills to contribute. But you've given me an idea. I'll let you know if she remembers anything."

"Any little thing, any detail, could be significant."

"I see. I'd better get back to Wendell House and decide how to tell my soldiers I'll be leaving. Gracefully, of course." She stood.

He stood to lead her out. He hated to think how soon she'd be gone again from his life. At the street door, he stopped. "Fanny, you must let me treat you to dinner. How about tomorrow night? At Marliave. It's just at the bottom of the hill on Bosworth Street. I'll come for you. Say, seven o'clock?"

She looked surprised, then near tears. Nodding, she turned quickly away.

By the end of the day, Jake felt as if he were being tortured by a mosquito. Something was whining in the back of his mind and would give him no peace. Finally, he dropped his pen and called out, "Edwin!"

When his assistant appeared at his door, he stood and grabbed his hat. "Let's go. I've got a little reconnoitering to do."

Chapter Twenty-Eight

I t was colder than the day of the molasses flood a week earlier. Jake and Edwin parked Suffolk Sue on a side street and walked carefully over to the harbor side of Commercial Street, where men were rebuilding structures demolished in the flood. Firemen had spent the week pumping saltwater over the area to dilute the remaining sludge of molasses, and a lot of it was gone. But there were still brown streaks embedded between bricks everywhere, and even in the frigid cold, he could taste the molasses in the back of his mouth.

What a mess. At least twenty adults and one child had died. All because a tank exploded, dumping over two million gallons of molasses onto the crowded streets. And the catastrophe had led to Fanny's dismissal, driving her out of his life just as suddenly as she had appeared in it again. If he could raise his hands and hold back that tide of roiling brown muck, he would. Too late. So many consequences from a rupture that took seconds to occur.

Jake spotted Jeremy Wrentham in a long overcoat with an alpaca collar directing some workmen. Jake hated that Fanny had been booted from her place in Boston by the concern for this self-righteous little prig who lied about where he was the night of Maggie's death. Jake knew Fanny was right to question McKenna's investigation. Someone as prominent as Senator Lodge would lead that policeman by the nose. Wrentham would easily overwhelm McKenna and keep him from considering the USIA manager as a suspect. Even in the death of his own wife, a man like McKenna would be intimidated by the likes of Lodge and Wrentham.

When Wrentham recognized the medical examiner and his assistant, he led them into a temporary metal structure. Several oil lamps hung from the low ceiling, and tables acting as desks had blueprints spread over them. A small oil heater sat at one end of the long building.

Wrentham pulled off his gloves and rubbed his hands over the heater. "This is all temporary. We need it for the engineers who're doing the reports," he told them. "It's not terribly convenient, so they only use it when they have to. What can I do for you, Dr. Magrath?"

There was no one else in the place, so Jake plunged into his inquiries. "No doubt you've heard that one of your workers, Luigi Spinelli, died last week."

"Yes. They say he jumped off a roof in the North End. The police think he was involved with the anarchists who planted the bomb. Either he felt guilty enough to take his own life, or his fellow conspirators turned on him and threw him off. I hope this proves to you, doctor, that the tank explosion was caused by a bomb."

"That's one theory," Jake said. It would suit Wrentham and his company to blame anarchists for the flood. "I understand Luigi was friendly with Maggie McKenna."

Wrentham stopped rubbing his hands and looked up. "That's right. Perhaps he had something to do with her death as well. Maybe she knew about the plans to bomb the tank, and they killed her to keep her quiet."

"I spoke to Luigi the other night. He said there were complaints about leaks in the tank."

"Nonsense, the workers are always looking for something to complain about. The tank was sound."

"So you say. He also mentioned that Maggie had received money from you and expected to get more. What was that about?"

Wrentham jolted upright, then moved to put the table between himself and Jake. "That's a lie. Mrs. McKenna received her salary, nothing more."

"Did you know Maggie was pregnant when she died? Did that have anything to do with the money she expected from you?"

"What? No. What are you saying?" He looked back and forth between Jake and Edwin.

"Someone must have fathered the child, and Maggie hadn't lived with her husband since before the conception," Jake said.

Wrentham stared at him. His eyes widened as if mesmerized. "You can't think I had anything to do with her condition! She was married."

"Married to a very jealous man who is also a policeman. I imagine if he found out she had a lover, he would seek revenge."

"I had nothing to do with Maggie McKenna. Not like that. There was a soldier she was seeing. Everyone knew she was in love with him. Her husband drove the man away, and she was trying to get money to go after him. She wanted to leave town."

After this outburst, Wrentham looked down and fumbled with the layers of blueprints in front of him. He bristled.

"How did you know she needed money to follow her lover?" Jake asked.

Wrentham hesitated as if weighing the risks of answering. "Well, she came to me. She asked for money—an advance on her salary." He dropped the papers and shuffled a few feet away.

Jake stepped around the table to force Wrentham to face him. "She didn't ask for an advance, did she? She demanded money, or she'd tell your wife and her own husband about the baby. Isn't that what happened?"

"No, you've got it all wrong." Wrentham was sweating now. He took off the fedora and brushed back his slick hair. He stared at Jake wildly as if looking for some weakness or sympathy. He found none. All Jake would take from him was the truth, and Jake was in a position to make trouble for Wrentham if he didn't get the answers he wanted.

"Listen, this is what happened." Wrentham swallowed as if he had trouble speaking. "Maggie saw me at a place where I shouldn't be. It was a brothel, if you must know. She threatened to tell my wife. That's all." He leaned his hands on the table and hung his head. "I gave her a hundred dollars in December. I thought that would be it. But then she came to me and demanded more. She promised it would be the last time. She planned to leave town to follow her lover. He must have fathered her child, not me."

While Jake considered this revelation, Wrentham tried to excuse himself. "Look. You're a man. You know how it is. Sometimes you just need something. But I wanted to spare my wife. You can understand that, can't you?"

Jake saw Edwin roll his eyes. "You did see Maggie the night before the flood, didn't you? You were at her rooms."

"I brought her the money she asked for," he said in exasperation. "Maggie said she was leaving town the next day. She said Luigi and Tony were coming, so I gave her the money and warned her not to come back to work. Then I left before they got there. I saw Luigi and Tony coming down the street, and I hid. They must have killed her. Either they wanted the money, or they let something slip about the bomb, and they killed her to keep her quiet. I can testify they were there that night. They're anarchists."

Jake glanced at Edwin. He couldn't prove or disprove Wrentham's story. One point struck him. "What brothel?" he asked.

"What?"

"Where did Maggie see you?"

"Mrs. Lake's on North Street." He was red in the face. "Is that all? I need to consult with the engineers on when they'll complete their report."

Jake thought it was curious that the brothel Wrentham named was the same one he and Edwin had visited to investigate the death of the unidentified soldier in the morgue. He grunted a farewell to the USIA manager and followed Edwin out the door into the cold.

Fanny was right in her suspicions about Wrentham, or almost right. He had not only been in town the night of Maggie's death, but he had been to her rooms. Jake suspected the man would deny everything he had said if confronted by authorities. There was no way to prove Maggie had blackmailed him without his own testimony. Why had he admitted as much as he had to Jake? It seemed that Wrentham was more afraid of the accusation that he had fathered Maggie's child than that he had visited a brothel. Perhaps he feared revenge from Maggie's jealous husband or his own wife more than the embarrassment of the admission he'd made. Jake had no hope that McKenna would be willing to pursue the USIA manager as a suspect. Fanny was right to be frustrated.

He wasn't sure whether telling Fanny what he had learned would be helpful or only make her mad. It wouldn't get her job back for her, even if she ran to the police with the man's admission that he'd seen Maggie the night of her murder. Jake thought a relaxed dinner at Marliave would go a lot further towards smoothing Fanny's ruffled feathers. He'd think about whether or not to share Wrentham's admissions with her. He thought not.

Chapter Twenty-Nine

Thursday, January 23, 1919

Thursday afternoon, Matt Bradley heard women's voices coming from Mrs. Lee's small office. Should he interrupt? He wanted to tell Mrs. Lee how much he regretted his part in her disgrace. When he heard she'd been dismissed as resident manager, he knew her efforts to protect him had gotten her fired. It was a very long time since anyone had sacrificed anything for him. Except for one magnificent instance on the battlefield. But he'd never expected to find that kind of loyalty in civilians. So he was very touched by Mrs. Lee's actions. He didn't know how to thank her.

Taking a breath, he straightened up and knocked.

"Yes, come in," Mrs. Lee called out.

When he opened the door, he found Mrs. Lee sitting at her desk with Mrs. Ryan beside her. They were looking at an empty wooden crate. He thought how much he liked the way Mrs. Ryan perched at the edge of the desk, as if she were a little bird that might fly away any moment. Her given name was Theresa. He'd heard her mother-in-law address her that way at the relief station. Matt wondered how long a young widow had to wait before she could think of another man. She must miss the strong arms of her fireman husband. He had been a bear of a man. Matt thought he should be mourning his own fiancée since he'd just found out she was dead. Somehow the memory of that loss didn't stir him.

He noticed the top and one side of the box had been removed and wondered what the women were up to. Mrs. Lee greeted him when she saw him approach. "Lt. Bradley, you've heard the news. I'll be leaving at the end of the month. Don't worry. I've warned Mrs. Thornwell about Detective McKenna's irrational vendetta against you, and she's promised to keep an eye on him. She's also engaged a prominent attorney for you. She's on the board for the home, so you should be all right."

Mrs. Thornwell was the ancient lady who'd been with Mrs. Lee when she rescued him from the jail. It was a relief to know she'd continue to support him. "I'm so sorry, Mrs. Lee. I feel terrible that you've lost your position because you tried to help me."

"Nonsense. It's not your fault. If it hadn't been you, I'd have run afoul of them for someone else. You mustn't worry about it at all." She peered at him. "Here, take a look at what Mrs. Ryan and I are up to. It's a miniature."

He stepped around the desk. Inside the crate, they'd arranged some small boxes, papered the walls, and added little fixtures fashioned from hairpins and ceramic cups. Mrs. Lee held a little stuffed doll in her hands. The legs were bent upward. He felt the hairs on the back of his neck rise. "It's a bathroom," he said.

"Yes. Very good. I'm glad you can recognize it. There's more to do, of course. But I'm working with Mrs. Ryan to help her remember what she saw when she found her sister. It was all washed away by the molasses flood, but there might have been something there that would point to who did this."

"A clue?"

"Yes. Something like that. We're going through what happened and adding details as Mrs. Ryan remembers them. Try again, my dear," she said to the housekeeper.

Matt wanted to object. How painful it must be for the poor young widow to remember what happened that night. He wondered at how kind and sympathetic Mrs. Lee could be to her soldiers, yet how cold and analytical she was about this death. While he knew her efforts were meant to clear his own name, her blunt determination to find the truth gave him pause.

"I went to the bedroom first," Mrs. Ryan said.

"That's right. We haven't set up that room yet, but we can do that next," Mrs. Lee said.

"There were a couple of chairs, and the bed was mussed, as if some people had sat there drinking. I thought they were drinking because I saw the bottle on the floor of the bathroom."

Matt realized they were talking about the morning Theresa Ryan had found her sister right before the wave of molasses swept the building away. He was repulsed by the idea of reliving that awful experience. What were they thinking?

"That's right. We'll have to find a tiny bottle. You tripped over it, didn't you?" Mrs. Lee asked.

"I don't think so. I tripped over something, I felt it on my ankle. A stick or something, maybe a mop or broom. Then I stumbled into the bottle and it rolled away. I remember the sound, before the noise of the molasses tank exploding."

"Hmm. Do you remember any labels on the bottle? Was there liquid left in it?"

"I don't recall but, when I stumbled, I grabbed the side of the tub. That's when I saw her." The young widow trembled at the memory.

As if to distract her, Mrs. Lee consulted a paper diagram and placed the little doll on her back on the floor. Matt realized that was where Mrs. Ryan...Theresa had found her sister in the bathtub. "Wait a minute," he said. "I'll be right back."

He tromped up the stairs, cursing his damaged leg, went into a bathroom, and hobbled back down, holding a ceramic piece like a trophy. "Here you go. I knew when I saw your miniature that this would be perfect. It's Stillman's soap dish. He keeps his lavender-scented bar in it." Matt rolled his eyes, and the two women exchanged a glance. Stillman was fussier than most of the men. "Hey, at least he smells better than Rodgers. We're not sure that one's used soap since he got back." Matt shrugged.

"That's very good," Mrs. Ryan said. She looked at him with astonishment. "It looks like the tub, just the right shape."

"I remembered it," he said with pride. "The soap dish. I thought it might do the trick."

Mrs. Lee placed the little doll in it, with the legs splayed in the air and the head deep in the tub. Mrs. Ryan put a hand to her eyes. Mrs. Lee reached for the woman's other arm. "It's just meant to help you remember," she said. "I hope it doesn't cause you too much pain."

"No, it's all right. I'm just trying to picture it to see if there's something else...."

"What about the bedroom?" Matt asked. He had an idea. "If someone like Wrentham left something, wouldn't it be there? Shouldn't we put together that room?"

Mrs. Lee sat back and looked at him. "It would be helpful. It takes time. More than you might think. I've made these types of miniatures before, and they can capture all your attention and eat up all of your time." She sighed. "It can become an obsession."

"Well, it's worth it if we find something that links someone to the death of Mrs. Ryan's sister, isn't it?" Matt asked.

Mrs. Lee smiled. "Yes, of course. If you want to help, you could gather some materials for the second room, and we could try putting it together tomorrow. I'm going to dinner with a friend tonight, so it will have to wait."

"What do you need?"

"Another crate, perhaps. Then pieces to make a bed, a couple of chairs."

"A bureau and a mirror," Mrs. Ryan added. Matt thought she looked sad. His mind raced, thinking of where he could salvage materials and how he could sit down with the nice widow and find out what else she remembered. He could do that.

Mrs. Lee rose. "Good. You find some materials, and tomorrow we'll start again. Theresa, don't try too hard to remember. Don't force it. Let your mind drift back for a while and if you think of any details, write them down here." She gave a pencil and notebook to the young woman. "And we'll work on it again tomorrow." Mrs. Lee turned to Matt. "Thank you for your help, Lt. Bradley. You go along and see what you can find. I have to prepare to go out, and Mrs. Ryan will need to oversee dinner in the big house."

As Matt followed her out, he glanced back at Mrs. Ryan. The young woman's hair was softly lit from behind by the setting sun, and as she stood looking down at the little diorama, he thought she was a very handsome young woman. It was such a shame that she had to experience such tragedy.

Chapter Thirty

Jake had spent all Thursday in the morgue. He finished some paperwork and planned to leave early to dress for dinner. Edwin had been too quiet all day. He was in the laboratory cleaning instruments at the soapstone sink. Jake hesitated, then pulled up a stool and picked up a towel to dry some of the equipment as Edwin finished rinsing it.

"So, do you believe Wrentham's story?" Jake asked.

Edwin shrugged.

"Come on, man. You've got to have an opinion." He wasn't going to let the young man fester. He had touched on some deep antipathy before, and Jake wanted to explore it. His assistant had shared very little about his own history, and Jake found he wanted to know more.

Edwin handed him a glass beaker and stared at the cold tiles on the wall for a moment. "I don't believe Mr. Wrentham was the father of Maggie McKenna's child. I can believe he went to whores. But Maggie wasn't a whore."

Jake raised an eyebrow. For someone who didn't know the dead woman, he seemed very certain. Why was he so defensive of a woman he'd never met?

"I could go to the brothel and find out if he was known there," Edwin said.

Uh oh. Jake didn't think it was a good idea to give a young man like Edwin an excuse to go to a brothel. Imagine what Fanny would think. "Ah, no. Don't do that. Leave that to the police. I'll make sure McKenna knows about Wrentham's claim that he was at a brothel."

Edwin slammed a pile of Petri dishes into the soapy water, splashing

136

himself and Jake. Afraid of provoking another tirade against the detective, Jake thought of a task for Edwin. If he was busy making himself useful, he wouldn't have time to brood. "What you might do is to see if you can find Tony DeCarlo. Somebody knows where he is, but they don't trust the police. And perhaps he saw something or knows something about what happened to Luigi. The fact that you can speak Italian might make all the difference. I'm taking Mrs. Lee to dinner tonight, but if you're not engaged, perhaps you could go to the North End. See what you can find out and report back tomorrow morning."

The tension in the young man's back muscles eased as he thought about that for a moment. Jake was relieved when he agreed to the plan. He hoped it would keep the medic out of trouble.

"By the way, how does a nice Irishman like you learn Italian?" Jake polished the dishes with his cloth.

Edwin hesitated, but then Jake sensed that he was willing to drop some of his defenses to let him a bit closer. "I grew up on the west side of Chicago. There were lots of Italians there."

Jake suppressed his surprise so as not to put him off. Chicago. Edwin knew Fanny came from Chicago. He wondered why Edwin had never mentioned this before. "I see. So, you learned it on the streets?"

"No, actually. At Hull House...the settlement house."

"Hull House. Of course. Everyone's heard of it. Did you know Miss Addams? She's quite famous, although she's been criticized lately for her pacifist views about the war."

Edwin handed him another rinsed beaker. "My mother worked there. She enrolled me in classes."

"Italian language classes? Lucky for you. Very broad-minded of your parents to encourage it, too." Jake knew there was a bitter enmity that grew up between immigrant groups, and the dislike between the Irish and the Italians was fierce in Boston. He could only assume the prejudice was just as strong in Chicago.

Edwin snorted. "My father tried to stop me. He hated the 'Eyeties' as he called them. He forbade it, so I did it anyhow."

Edwin must have had a poor relationship with his father. "That was brave of you," Jake said. "Going against your father like that."

"He was a drunk and a bully." Edwin pulled the plug to drain the water. "My ma was the one who encouraged me to take classes at Hull House. She wanted something better than manual labor for me and my sisters. The drunk only wanted money on the table for more whiskey."

Jake was quiet for a moment thinking of that. This explained why Edwin hated McKenna on sight. He reminded Edwin of his abusive father. Still...

"Edwin, I had no idea you have family in Chicago. Mrs. Lee's home is a place where they help soldiers reconnect with their families. She's been dismissed, but the work will go on. She'd be able to help you if you want to go back, even if only to visit." Selfishly, Jake didn't want him to relocate.

"There's nothing for me there."

"But surely you want to tell your family you're all right." Jake wondered if the burn injuries made the boy ashamed to go home.

"There's no family left." The sink was empty now, the remaining water slurped down the drain, and Edwin turned toward him, wiping his hands on a towel. "I got drafted. After I was gone, my mother died. Then one sister died of the flu, and the other ran away with a man."

Jake didn't ask about the father. He also didn't ask about how Edwin's mother had died. He had to wonder if a wife who worked at Hull House and encouraged her son to educate himself could survive the anger of a drunken husband like McKenna. No wonder Edwin was convinced the police detective had killed his wife. It was a repeat of a sad story.

He didn't try to convince his assistant he could be wrong. He just gave him a wad of cash and sent him off to use his hard-earned Italian in the North End. Then Jake headed home to prepare for dinner with Fanny.

Chapter Thirty-One

Jake dressed with care, as if it would help him convince Fanny that Boston was the place for her. He took a cab to the Hancock Street entrance of Wendell House. It was cold but still. There was no wind. A fresh snowfall dusted the ground, but the brick walks of Beacon Hill had been shoveled. It was a good evening for a walk, and he wanted to show Fanny how close she was to civilization. She'd like Marliave. He was sure of it.

Fanny said she was happy for the walk. She wore a coat with fur cuffs and collar, a matching fur hat, and sturdy boots. Her frock and coat were short enough not to drag in the wet. It gave him satisfaction to feel her gloved hand clutch his arm as they walked down Joy Street.

Lights twinkled on the Boston Common and along Beacon and Park Streets. The air was sharply clean, freezing his nose, while the city sounds were hushed by the heavy layer of new snow. They didn't talk. It was cold enough to sting if you opened your mouth. They just listened to the quiet and took care not to slip on patches of ice.

By the time they climbed the stairs to the restaurant, Jake was ready to appreciate the warmth and smells of garlic and tomatoes that filled the well-lit room. A girl took their coats, and the maître d' led them to a corner table covered with white linen and lit by a candle. The room was more than half filled and hummed with conversation. There was a cheery fireplace burning wood on the far wall. Jake grinned. He used the menu in his hand to point out two actors and several artists to Fanny. He wanted her to know not all of Boston was as stuffy as Beacon Hill. A local newspaperman came over to chat, and he could see Fanny enjoyed the man's description of Jake at the scene of an accident, racing in on Suffolk Sue, horns blaring and lights shining.

When they had glasses of Chianti in their hands and had ordered the veal scaloppine, a city councilman came over to speak to them. Jake was delighted to find Fanny held her own in banter with the arrogant windbag. Sipping wine redolent of warm Italian nights, Jake realized Fanny had been brought up in a very social family and had no problem making small talk with self-important people. He couldn't help thinking it was a valuable trait in a city like Boston. He sighed as the man was called back to his own table by his wife.

"Pay no attention to that fellow," he mumbled to her. "He's full of himself."

Fanny laughed. "I know the type. He was quite complimentary about you, though."

"That's not who I brought you to meet. I wanted to show you another side of the city. This place is completely egalitarian. You've got artists and writers and actors as well as society folks and academics. That's the dean of women from Radcliffe sitting over there, and there's an MIT professor in the corner. It's a great place to meet interesting people."

"Boston's Bohemia? It's very nice. I like the wine, and this bread is so fresh."

"Wait till you taste the veal. It's great." He slid his chair closer and hunched over his butter plate, tearing warm bread with his hands. "You said you don't want to go back to Chicago, but there's no reason to bury yourself in the mountains. Stay here. You've barely gotten to know the city."

She sipped her wine. "I'll miss the musical concerts. This is orchestra season in Chicago."

"You've got to hear the Boston Symphony. Our hall is known as one of the best in the world." He knew Fanny's family were patrons of the Chicago orchestra. She was brought up communing with musicians. "And there's the Handel and Haydn Society. You could join. I'm a member. I'll introduce you. We do several performances every year. It's great fun."

She laughed. "Sorry. Afraid I can't carry a tune. Totally tone-deaf. I do want to hear the Boston Symphony, though. I've got tickets for next weekend."

"Great. They're doing Beethoven's Seventh and some new stuff. Stravinsky. I'm not sure what to think of him."

"Very vigorous," she said.

"Hah! You've got it." They spent a pleasant half-hour discussing music. When they stopped to let the white-aproned waiter deliver plates of veal and bowls of pasta, Jake sat back and thought what a long time it had been since he'd had such a lively discussion about the music he loved. He was frankly amazed at Fanny's knowledge. But she had her own opinions on music as well, preferring chamber music to the sonorous orchestral bombast from the end of the last century. He couldn't agree with her distaste for Wagner, but he thought he could wean her away from such heresy if he could take her to some really good performances.

She exclaimed over the meal, relishing the velvety taste of the veal. Jake concentrated on his own food, rolling the flavors around in his mouth, then taking a sip of the luscious red wine. As he breathed in the smells of garlic and tomato, he felt a pang of regret. That's what came of getting older. You could savor a special experience, but you knew in your bones it wouldn't last.

"Why won't you return to Chicago?" Jake asked as he patted the last drips of sauce from his mustache. "Don't get me wrong. I want you to stay here. But don't you miss your family?"

Fanny ate her last bite of pasta, then answered. "I've been such a disappointment to them. And now I've done it again."

"Surely not."

"It's true." She reached across a hand to cover one of his. "Jake, I remember all those years ago how you encouraged me to go to Radcliffe. I remember that so well, and I'm grateful to you still." She withdrew her hand and gave a little laugh as the busboy cleared the plates and the waiter emptied the wine bottle into their glasses. "Thank you," she told him.

When the waiter had moved away, Jake stirred in his chair. "It's too bad if you feel you missed out, but there's still time. You're a comparatively young woman."

"Young? Hardly. Not continuing my studies was entirely my own choice. My parents thought I was too young to marry. Did you know that? They wanted me to wait. But I was headstrong. I wanted to marry and show them I could be as famous a hostess as my mother. More so, even."

She sipped her wine, and Jake fiddled with the saltshaker. "I'm sorry that didn't work out as you hoped."

"I've no one to blame but myself. But, really, who am I to complain? At first, Blewett and I were happy, and I adore my children. I may not be the best mother in the world, but I tried to give them everything they needed."

"Oh, nonsense."

"It was fine when they were young and needed me, even though my parents bought us the house next door to my brother George and his wife. But between them and the rest of the family a block away, I struggled not to have my every move monitored and criticized. Not that my parents didn't mean well. Of course, they did. But when it came time to send the children off to schools, I couldn't very well demand to keep them with me. That would be selfish. But they were the only thing that made my life worthwhile."

There was an uncomfortable pause, but Jake let it rest there. He'd never married and had no children himself, so didn't feel qualified to comment. He wanted to know what really caused the break with her family.

"It turns out I'm not much of a hostess," she said, taking another swallow of wine. "What a mess I made of that. Do you know what my problem is, Jake? I'm too blunt. I'd say the first thing that came into my head and manage to offend everybody. My mother and sister-in-law sat me down one time to explain it to me, and I was livid. What they told me was that I needed to lie politely. I couldn't do it. I couldn't toady up to a mean old woman just because her husband ran one of the railroads. And I couldn't spurn the social newcomers with their vulgar tastes and impertinent remarks. I laughed. Or worse, I agreed with them.

"As a social butterfly, I was a complete failure." She sighed. "It was only when I started inviting some of the homesick young soldiers and sailors from a nearby naval base to family dinners that I finally felt I could do something right. They didn't mind my bluntness."

"So, that's how you came to Wendell House?"

"Yes. My mother's reading class was in touch with the committee here. They raised funds for the house. My mother suggested I would be good at the job. But now I've ruined that. You can see why I don't want to go back."

"Stay here."

She ignored his suggestion. "I'm thinking of starting a business in New Hampshire. My oldest girl, Frances, isn't happy at her school. I'm thinking she could come with me and open a shop. There's an old schoolhouse near The Rocks that we could use. She and I love riding around, finding antiques. After seeing Miss Nichols's home, I realized there are people who want to buy antiques. We could search out rare finds and sell them up there."

"You've already been thinking about this?"

"Yes. Last summer, when we were up at The Rocks, we imagined what it would be like. So, now, I may as well make it happen. Frances will be excited."

"And it's an excuse not to go back to Chicago. But what about Lt. Bradley and Maggie McKenna's death? I thought you wanted to find out what really happened." Jake felt he was clutching at straws to find a reason for her to stay in Boston.

"That's the one piece of unfinished business. But I've got an idea about that."

Chapter Thirty-Two

Edwin turned up his collar and wrapped a wool scarf around his face, then put on a cloth cap. It was bitter out. As he walked down Charles Street toward the North End, he jiggled coins in his pocket. He needed to do something. Mrs. Lee was right about McKenna. He was a bully and a thug. Just because he had a badge, he didn't have the right to push people around.

Edwin had smelled whiskey on the detective's breath the first time he saw him—when McKenna came to the morgue to view his wife's corpse. He didn't believe the drunken tears McKenna shed as he sat beside his dead wife. Edwin knew only too well how repentant a drunk could seem.

The fierce cold made him hunch over, hiding within his wrappings so he could only see a slice of the snow whitened streets between his scarf and hat. It cut him off from the outside world, forcing him back into his memories. He thought of his return from overseas. A year before, when he finally reached the familiar tenement in Chicago, he found his father passed out on an unmade bed. A neighbor had to tell him that his mother and one of his sisters had died. Ushering the soldier into a tiny set of rooms, the old man next door told him about his sister Mary's death in the flu epidemic, and Edwin wept and asked if his mother had died from nursing her.

The old tailor hesitated. Edwin took him by the shoulders. "Tell me. What happened?"

"It was before the flu. It was one night...."

Edwin shook him. "It was him, wasn't it? It was my father."

"I'm sorry. There was a fight, you know, they argued. But they argued all the time. Your sisters ran away when it got too bad. There were sounds of breaking glass. Some of us neighbors were worried, then all of a sudden, it got quiet. We knocked and knocked. Somebody got a policeman. Finally, he opened up." Edwin let go of the man, his eyes blinking as he fought back tears. "I'm sorry, boy. There was nothing we could do. It was too late. Your father was mad with grief. He was terribly sorry."

Edwin shook his head wildly, trying to rid himself of tears. He felt a tide of anger rising from his stomach up through his stiffening shoulders to his head, where a hammer pounded an anvil.

The old man looked worried. He shrugged. "They said she fell. Your sister, Mary, got ill right after the funeral. Your father was good then. He wasn't drinking. But she passed, and then Joanna left without telling him. She just ran away. We heard later she married a soldier. She's in Iowa. You wait a minute; I'll get you the address." He patted Edwin's shoulder and pointed to a chair, then trundled away and returned with a slip of paper. He made Edwin stay with him that night, then put him on a train to Iowa the next day.

Edwin found Joanna in Iowa. She was happy enough working on a big family farm with her husband. She wept when she told him how his father had finally beaten his mother to death and how Mary had fallen ill and died. They offered him a job on the farm, but he had other plans.

Back in Chicago, he returned one last time to the tenement. Avoiding the old neighbor, he waited in the dark for his father to return from the bars. He saw revulsion in his father's face when he looked at Edwin's burn scars. The drunk railed at him, complaining about how in Edwin's absence, he'd had to endure the deaths of Mary and Edwin's mother, as if that were the son's fault. Edwin listened in silence as the man got nastier and nastier. When the old man finally raised a hand to his son, Edwin struck him and threw him against the walls until he was a shivering mass huddled in a corner, whining and weeping. Shaking his head as if to wake himself up, Edwin stomped out of the door and down the stairs. He left Chicago that night on the first train he could book. He would never go back.

Edwin pushed up his hat as if to escape the enclosure of his memories. It

145

was no good thinking back. Looking around, he saw he was just entering the North End. The narrow streets cut off the wind. Shouts and grumbles in a ripple of Italian distracted him from the past. He was pulled back into the freezing present as he hopped over snowbanks and slipped around slower people walking on Salem Street.

When he turned down Fleet from Hanover, he slid on ice under the top dusting of snow. Grabbing the brick corner of a building, he righted himself. He saw lights in the windows of the Florence Hotel café and hurried toward it. Stepping out of the cold, he peered around the busy dining room. He saw a small table in a corner. The red and white plaid tablecloth reminded him of towels in his mother's kitchen. An empty wine bottle in a straw casing held a yellow candle that dripped wax down one side. Sitting down, he brushed away crumbs from the last customer.

He didn't see Tony DeCarlo in the clump of men around the bar drinking red wine from small glasses. A woman plopped down opposite Edwin as he tried to melt into the corner shadows.

"Hi, mister." She smiled through a layer of scarlet lipstick. Spots of rouge stood out on her white pancake makeup. Edwin thought she must be in her forties, a skinny woman in a low-cut dress with fraying ribbons tied in bows on her arms. "Looking for something warm?" she asked. "This is the place for it, you'll see. Why don't you take off that scarf and hat? You'll get hot in here." She reached out a playful hand, but Edwin swatted it away. "Aww. That's not nice." She pouted. "You owe me a drink for that." She squirmed around to wave at an aproned waiter.

It was hot. The scarf felt scratchy on Edwin's face, and a drop of sweat rolled from his forehead into his eye. But he was frozen by the stares of people around him who were curious about a newcomer. He only nodded when the woman ordered a carafe of wine. He could see she thought she had the upper hand now, so she continued to tease him until the wine showed up. Edwin paid the waiter while the woman poured herself a glass and drank it greedily, her eyes on what she could see of his face. Slightly pinker in the cheeks and emboldened by the wine, she poured herself another glass and one for him. She slid it toward him.

"Don't be shy, honey. Have a sip." She smiled slyly.

Edwin gritted his teeth. He wanted to be rid of her, but he hated how he was forced to do it. He took off his cap, slapping it on to the table, then he unwound the scratchy scarf.

She choked on her wine, putting a hand with red nails in front of her mouth as her eyes got wide. "Oh, Lordy. That's awful. Oh, oh, oh." She got up from the chair and backed up. In the end, she turned and pushed her way through the crowd near the bar. Some of the men laughed at her, then looked back at Edwin. The sight of his face made them quiet.

Edwin tossed the scarf on top of the hat and swallowed a large gulp of wine, then poured himself another. Backs turned toward him as people who had been watching from other tables looked away. Of course, they'd know he'd come by his scars from the war. But they wouldn't want to look at him. He reminded them of times they wanted to forget. He was used to it.

He gulped another mouth full. The wine was slightly sour. He beckoned to the waiter. When the man came to take his order, he kept his gaze on the red checkered tablecloth. "Sir?"

Edwin took a handful of half-dollar coins from his pocket and stacked them on the table. The waiter watched the coins. "I'm looking for Tony DeCarlo," Edwin said, picking up the coins and letting them fall back one at a time on the table in a neat pile.

The waiter pursed his lips.

Edwin repeated the request in Italian, adding that he wasn't police and just wanted to talk to the man. He picked off one of the coins and held it out.

The waiter grabbed it and hurried away. In a few minutes, Edwin saw Tony DeCarlo making his way through the crowd at the bar. His eyes darted around, as if he expected a trap. Edwin sat quietly, clicking his pile of half dollars.

Tony was mesmerized by the coins when he stopped across the table from Edwin. With the tank gone, he'd be out of work and desperate for money. Edwin was counting on that.

"Sit down, have some wine," Edwin told him in Italian. "Don't worry. I just want to talk." He held out a coin.

Taking the coin, Tony dropped into the chair and poured himself a glass of wine. "What you want?"

Edwin replied in Italian so the man couldn't pretend he didn't understand. "What do you know about what happened to Luigi Spinelli?"

Tony looked away. Then he drank down the glass of wine. He replied in Italian. "I remember you. You're not police. You're with the doctor, yes?"

"That's right."

"I wasn't there when Luigi fell from the roof. The cops say he killed himself."

"Did he?"

Tony glanced around and shrugged. "How do I know?"

Edwin took a roll of bills from his pocket. It was the money Dr. Magrath had given him. He peeled off two one-dollar bills and put them on the table. Tony stared at them. "Luigi thought he was smart. Thought he could get money from a man."

"What man?"

"You think I know? I just told him he's crazy. Look what happened to Maggie."

"You think whoever killed Maggie threw Luigi off the roof?"

"How do I know? I told him we need to stay away, but he made me go see Maggie's sister."

Theresa Ryan. Edwin thought of the thin woman who was housekeeper to Mrs. Lee. He felt sorry for the poor woman who'd lost her husband and sister on the same day, but he remembered that she'd hoped Maggie might reconcile with her husband. Edwin couldn't understand why she thought the man would change his cruel ways. "What did he want to tell Mrs. Ryan?"

"Not to tell. To ask. He wanted to see how much she knows."

"About what?"

Tony moved restlessly, looking around the room as if he expected someone to jump out and pounce on him. "Luigi thought Maggie was getting money from someone. He thought he could get money, too."

"Who from?"

"I don't know. Luigi said Maggie was waiting for somebody to bring money that night, then she was leaving town. But Luigi said lots of things. Most of them not true. He said Mr. Wrentham gave her money, but somebody else was bringing more."

"Who?"

"I don't know."

"Who was the 'other one' you were talking about when Dr. Magrath came to see you on the roof? I heard you say to Luigi, 'what about the other one.'"

Tony reached out for the dollar bills, but Edwin held them down with his hand. "The other soldier," Tony said. "I saw a soldier outside when we left Maggie. She told us to go like she's waiting for somebody."

"A soldier. Was it the man she was seeing? Her lover?" Edwin asked.

"No, not him. At least, I don't think so. Maggie made it a big secret about her lover. She wanted to run away with him but was afraid her husband will find out and kill him. She didn't introduce him to us, but we saw him sometimes with her. I don't think that's who was outside her place that night. There was something different about that soldier."

"What?"

"I don't remember. Honest."

Edwin let go of the bills, and Tony took them, carefully folding them up several times until they were a small rectangle that he stuffed into a pocket in his pants.

"Did you see Luigi the night he died?"

"I said hi to him in the street, but he ignored me. I figure if you're gonna be like that, I don't care. Then somebody said he fell from the roof. I was pretty scared. Maybe they'll kill me. So, I hid."

Edwin sat back, fingering the roll of bills in his hand. "There's nothing else you can tell me?"

Tony licked his lips. "No. I don't know nothing. I just know Maggie was gonna leave and find her soldier. He was supposed to get money so they could leave town, but he didn't. She was worried. Maybe he got scared of the husband and ran away. I don't know. But she was gonna go after him. She said she was gonna get the money he didn't get and bring it to him so they could live together." He shook his head. "Poor Maggie. Poor Luigi. It's not gonna be poor Tony, though. I don't know nothing." He slipped off the chair and vanished into the crowd before Edwin could stop him.

Tired and hungry, Edwin decided to go to one of the pubs he liked near his rooming house for a meal. He wound the scarf around his face and put on his hat, handing a tip to the waiter on his way out. As he slid down Fleet Street, he looked up and saw a figure turn a corner below him. It was Detective McKenna.

Chapter Thirty-Three

Matt Bradley put down his hammer and looked at his work with pride. He was in a basement room of Wendell House that evening. The furnace clanked away, staving off the freezing temperatures. He'd gone down to the Haymarket area and found some broken crates and sticks that he brought back and used to fashion a crude bedroom for Mrs. Lee's miniature. He'd removed the top and one side of a crate, and he'd cut and shaved some smaller pieces of wood that he nailed together to make a rough-looking little bed and a couple of chairs. He'd emptied a cardboard box of nails and stood it on end to make a dresser. He figured Mrs. Lee could paint on fake drawers and make bedding for the bed from scraps of material. But he was satisfied that he'd procured what they needed to create an additional room. He was proud of his work, and he hoped it would allow him to get closer to the pretty widow.

He thought of the story as he'd heard them describe it that afternoon. Theresa had gone to the bedroom first, then gone to the bathroom. She'd stumbled on something and seen a bottle on the floor. They'd need some little glasses and something for a bottle of liquor. Apparently, Maggie McKenna had entertained men in her bedroom. Matt didn't think Theresa Ryan would have been guilty of such an indiscretion, but her dead sister must have been a much bolder type.

Matt wasn't confident the little crime scene would help to find the murderer of Theresa's sister. But he could only hope they could come up with a theory that would lead the police away from himself. He was grateful for Mrs. Lee's help in getting him out of jail, but he worried about how Detective McKenna seemed determined to blame him for his wife's death. Matt hadn't been in Boston long enough to be the dead woman's lover, but the detective wouldn't listen to that argument. He just wanted the investigation to be over so he could go on with his life. Surely with all he'd been through on the battlefields of France, he was owed that.

He would never return to Chicago now. He'd already decided that. He hoped that Mrs. Lee could still get her brother to help him claim his family fortune even though she'd been dismissed from her position. He trusted she would do it. He couldn't go back to Chicago, and it made it so much easier to have people of the Glessners' status to help him. He blocked the thoughts of his parents and fiancée from his mind. He'd have to start new somewhere else. Perhaps he could convince Theresa Ryan to go west with him. Or, perhaps, he'd have to just settle down here in Boston. Soon he'd have to decide. But not yet.

Looking at the crate, he tried to imagine how this would help Dr. Magrath to find Maggie's killer. He decided he needed to cut out a place for a window behind the bed, and he gathered some tools to do that.

As he worked, Matt thought about Dr. Magrath and his attendant, Edwin. Matt couldn't help envying Edwin his relationship with the medical examiner. It was obvious the older man considered himself a mentor to the younger man.

Matt was grateful to Mrs. Lee for her confidence in him, but he wasn't sure her support would be as helpful as Dr. Magrath's. Nonetheless, he wanted to show Mrs. Lee that he was grateful for her support, in the past and in the future. Perhaps she'd stay in Boston despite her dismissal. He hoped she would. Without her, who would take his side?

What a strange twist of fate that Theresa Ryan had found her sister's body, and then the whole building was swept away by the molasses flood. No one could have anticipated that. He wondered if it hadn't been for that, would they even have suspected Maggie McKenna was killed? Perhaps if other roomers had found her, they would have assumed she slipped and fell and died by accident. He wondered if Dr. Magrath had even considered that possibility.

As he carved out a rectangle for the window and then sanded the edges, Matt tried to think of a different explanation for Maggie's death. From what Matt had seen of Detective McKenna, he could easily believe the man had brutalized his wife. But if he were responsible for her death, it was unlikely the truth would ever come out. He'd be protected by his position in the police.

Apparently, they knew that she'd been seeing a soldier for some months. If it wasn't the jealous husband, perhaps she was killed by the lover. Surely that would be obvious. But where was this mysterious soldier? It was understandable that she kept his identity secret. She was afraid of her husband. There were indications that the couple was gathering money to leave town together. Blackmailing people, perhaps. What if the lover decided it would be better to take the money and run? Maybe Maggie thought he would run and threatened him, and he struck her down. That could be true. But how could the police find him? Matt really wanted them to find the killer, so Detective McKenna would have to give up his vendetta against him.

What could Theresa Ryan have seen in those rooms that would identify the killer? Medicine, perhaps?

He stopped working on the little bedroom and sat back, closing his eyes. He tried to remember what Theresa had said that morning. Concentrating, he swiveled in the chair, knocking down his cane with the movement. His eyes flew open. He looked down at the silver-headed stick. He knew Mrs. Lee had meant well by giving him the gift, but he hated what it represented, his lameness. As he bent to pick it up, he remembered something Theresa had said and wondered if that could help them to identify the killer.

Chapter Thirty-Four

Edwin looked up at the black door and the lantern hanging from an iron hook. He'd come to this part of town with other ex-soldiers before. But only to drink. When they mounted the stairs of a brothel like this, Edwin would fade into the shadows, unwilling to approach any woman, even a prostitute, with his ruined face. But, tonight, he was drawn to the black door. What brought Detective McKenna to this place? He recognized this house as the one where he and Dr. Magrath had found the dead soldier that no one had claimed. It was the same one visited by USIA manager, Jeremy Wrentham.

He remembered this was a "parlor house" run by a widow named Lake. Drinking and gambling took place in the downstairs rooms, which were decorated to look like a respectable middle-class home. But, for an extra price, there were private rooms available on the upper floors. At dusk, the women of the house would display themselves in the upper windows and call down invitations to passing men. It was too late, too dark, and much too cold for that now.

Edwin hesitated, sure he would be turned away when they saw his burn scars, but he fingered the roll of bills from Dr. Magrath in his pocket. The money gave him confidence. He suppressed the memory of Dr. Magrath, forbidding him to enter a brothel. Edwin put his head down and climbed the steps to push the door open.

A fat man in a bowler hat, no jacket, and black suspenders jumped up from an armchair to look over the new client. He held out a hand. "Four bits."

Edwin heard a bell tinkle as he fished out the coins. A young girl of about fourteen came up behind him, clutched his coat by the shoulders, and helped him to remove it. At the same time, a woman all in black with jet earrings and bracelets swept through a curtained doorway.

Reluctantly, Edwin released his coat and handed his cap to the girl. When he unwound the scarf, the woman took a breath, and stepped backwards. "Well, now," she said. "I'm not sure we can help you, mister. I don't want my girls upset." She pursed her lips.

There was a harsh jangle as the door was flung open, and two men rushed in. They slammed the door shut behind them, then leaned against it. "Cold enough to freeze your tits," one man said, grinning. "Oh, hey, O'Connell. What're you doing here? Good to see you." It was Gerry Doyle. Edwin had met him at the Irish bar.

Edwin wasn't sure what to say. He was painfully conscious that he hadn't convinced the woman in black to admit him.

The newcomer turned to her. "Mrs. Lake, how're you this fine evening?" Gerry said. "I was just going to introduce my friend Donny here. Private Donald Mack. But I see you've also just met my friend Private Edwin O'Connell currently assistant to the Suffolk County medical examiner." He pounded Edwin on the back, then turned to Mrs. Lake. "But the most important thing is Noreen. I promised Donny, here, I'd introduce him to Miss Noreen." He swayed a bit on his legs. Edwin could see the men had been drinking. Gerry prayered his hands to plead with the woman. "Please, Mrs. Lake, tell me we can see Miss Noreen."

She smiled at him. "She's been waiting for you in the parlor." They could hear a tinny piano in another room. "I know Mr. Mack from previous visits. But you say Mr. O'Connell here is a friend of yours?" She sounded doubtful.

Gerry turned to Edwin and blinked at the burn scars. "Oh, yes. He's a hero, Mrs. Lake. We were in the hospital together. He got injured fighting the Boches. You wouldn't turn away a hero now, would you?" He winked at Edwin.

Edwin could see that Gerry was adept at manipulating a situation no matter how drunk he was. It was a skill Edwin had noted in the man when they shared a hospital ward.

Mrs. Lake stood firmly in the doorway, still unconvinced. "I don't want my girls upset."

"No, of course," Gerry said. "But Noreen won't mind when I tell her he was wounded with me. He'll just come in and have a drink with us." He spotted the roll of bills in Edwin's hand. "In fact, he'll buy us all a round, won't you, O'Connell?"

Edwin nodded.

Mrs. Lake stepped back. "All right. Mary will take you in." She nodded to the young girl who'd taken their coats. "I'll send along Noreen and Tina for you and Mr. Mack. Mary can stay with you, Mr. O'Connell, but there'll be no upstairs for Mary. You understand? She's too young."

"Oh, sure, sure." Gerry waved Mary in and followed. He pulled Edwin after him.

Inside, there were a number of rooms with gilt and velvet chairs and sofas, an upright piano against a wall, and several alcoves with gambling tables. The air was thick with smoke from cigars and cigarettes.

Mary led them to a corner nook, and soon two young women in low-cut gowns with bare shoulders were putting their arms around Gerry and Donny. When Mary saw that, she stood in front of Edwin as if she wanted to imitate the older girls by sitting on his lap. But Edwin took her by the shoulders and sat her down beside him on the sofa. He saw Mrs. Lake looking on from the doorway, and she nodded approval.

Noreen and the other girl stole curious glances at Edwin's face but didn't seem to be put off by the scars. When they had drinks on a low table in front of them, Edwin saw an opportunity to get information. He mentioned that he'd seen a police detective go through the door.

"You must mean Bill McKenna," Noreen said. "He lives here. He's got a suite on the third floor." When Gerry expressed surprise, she said, "I suppose it gives Mrs. Lake some protection. It's not likely we'll get raided with a policeman on the premises, is it?" She lowered her voice. "of course, his bosses at the police don't know. He keeps his old address, but he's here most nights." She looked around to be sure no one was listening. "I heard his wife ran away from him, and he's been staying here ever since. I can see why she ran. He likes it rough. We stay away from him, don't we, Tina? Poor Sherry has to put up with him. He's one of her regulars. But he's a brute."

Edwin gritted his teeth. What nerve the man had. He beat up on his wife, then he beat up on a prostitute, and they let him get away with it. The women even let him move into the brothel with them. He knew some cops took advantage of their power. It was true in Chicago, too. And he'd seen something like it in the army. Some men were bullies. He could tell Magrath about the crooked cop, but Edwin had grown up in a city where you learned that it didn't pay to get on the wrong side of someone with power like McKenna. It was better to wait and let them hang themselves when they eventually slipped up. They always did in the long run. He asked if McKenna had been at the brothel the night before the molasses flood.

Noreen wasn't sure. "I suppose so. He's here most nights, although sometimes he goes out again. I couldn't say. I was here that night with Gerry. You were here, weren't you, sweetie?"

"Do you think you could ask Sherry if McKenna was in that night?" Edwin asked.

"I don't know."

Edwin fanned out a few bills.

"Well, I can ask her. But not tonight. She's busy. But I'll ask her tomorrow."

Edwin decided Noreen was going to be a helpful informant. "Do you know a Mr. Jeremy Wrentham? He's the manager of the company that owned the molasses tank that exploded."

"Oh, yes. He uses another name, though, Mr. Blank." Noreen laughed. Gerry kissed her.

"Does he like it rough?"

Noreen glanced at Tina, and they both giggled. "Not likely. He's a little lamb, that one. Judy sees him, and she bosses him around like you wouldn't believe." Noreen snickered.

Edwin wasn't surprised. Wrentham had seemed a sniveling sort of man. Edwin was sure the USIA manager had never been in the trenches, but he thought he was the type of man who wouldn't last long if he had been. He was the kind of man who would be seen crawling around, diving into holes at every sound, and soon falling to pieces.

Edwin asked if McKenna's wife, Maggie, was known to the women. He wondered how she had found out about Wrentham to blackmail him.

"Oh, no. Heavens, wouldn't that be a thing? No, the detective's wife would never show her face here. What are you thinking?" Noreen said.

Edwin realized Maggie must have learned from someone else about the cheating Wrentham. He wondered if her husband could have told her. Or perhaps Luigi or Tony. Noreen said that Mrs. Lake entertained Italians as long as they had money, but Noreen didn't think she knew Luigi or Tony when he described them.

"What about the soldier who died here?" Edwin asked. When he had come to the house with Dr. Magrath, Edwin hadn't seen Mrs. Lake or any of the girls. Police had interviewed them, and they'd stayed away from the staircase while the medical examiner looked it over.

"Oh, that poor boy," Noreen said, and the other two girls looked away. "Mrs. Lake said not to gossip about that, especially not to the clients." Her head shot up and she checked the doorway to be sure the madam wasn't watching. "But he wasn't a regular at all. He just rented a room to meet somebody."

"Could it have been Wrentham, or McKenna?" Edwin asked.

"I don't know. Like I said, Mrs. Lake doesn't like us talking about it."

Edwin paid for two rounds of drinks but, as the other couples became more amorous, he became more uncomfortable until he announced he would leave. Little Mary looked jealous as the other women took Gerry and Donny up a rickety staircase, but Mrs. Lake gave him a civil goodnight at the door.

The sharp breeze outside woke Edwin from the haze the beers had thrown over him. He trudged back to the morgue. He wanted to get one more look at the unidentified soldier who'd died at Mrs. Lake's. Somehow, he felt close to the man and wondered if he could shed some light on what went on at the brothel and why Maggie McKenna had been killed.

When he closed the door of the morgue behind him, he thought he saw a figure in the alley. For a moment, he thought Dr. Magrath might be there, but he shook off the feeling. It was the guilt he felt for disobeying his boss and going to the brothel. He didn't want to disappoint the man who he knew was trying to mentor him, but he felt more obliged to find out who had killed Maggie McKenna. Someone should bring her justice by punishing her killer.

Chapter Thirty-Five

When Theresa finished her evening chores at Wendell House, she looked out the window. Tall feather strokes of snow blew on frigid brick walks that had been hastily swept. She was glad she didn't have to trudge through the streets to get home.

Mrs. Lee had insisted she take a room in the house. Theresa still felt some guilt for accepting the offer. She'd left her mother-in-law and Patrick in the rooms they all shared in the South Boston triple-decker. After Tom's death, it became a burden to move through those few rooms seeing him everywhere.

The dining table was where they would settle every night after Patrick went off to the pub. Tom would tell them about the fire station, and Mrs. Ryan would fill him in on neighborhood gossip. In the parlor, Theresa could barely pull her eyes away from the big old, cushioned chair where Tom would sit on Sundays while his mother treated her cronies to tea. Neither of the women could bear to sit in that chair, or even look at it. And the feather bed where they had lain together warm and close was a hole of dark despair for her now. She couldn't stop hearing their voices planning how they'd find a bigger place and fill it with babies of their own. It broke her heart that she had no child of Tom's to hold onto. It was cruel to try to sleep alone in that room filled with the scent of him and echoes of his deep voice. She faced a dilemma when her mother-in-law wouldn't hear of Theresa trading Pat for the smaller room. But Theresa knew the old woman prayed her remaining son would bring home a wife. How could he do that with his brother's widow still living in the biggest room?

She didn't know if Mrs. Lee had sensed her pain when she first offered the room at Wendell House, but when she noticed Theresa's puffy eyes and weary slump, Mrs. Lee insisted Theresa must have a room at the house for the winter months. Even Mrs. Ryan agreed to the plan. Theresa would return to the family on Sundays and her day off. And by her first Sunday visit, she realized her mother-in-law was also relieved by the change. She'd never admit it, but Theresa saw how the shadow of grief and memories weighed down the old woman when she saw her widowed daughter-in-law. Looking at each other, all they had lost of Tom stared back at them. So, Theresa was glad she didn't have to go out in the cold that night. She could retire to the cozy room that represented the start of her new life without Tom.

But first, she did her rounds of Wendell House to be sure all was in place for the morning. Dinner in the large dining room where the enlisted men ate was done. She pushed in a few chairs and straightened some throw rugs. In the lounge, a few men played cards or read newspapers. She would tidy up there in the morning before they were down. Some of the men were returning from the cold at the front door on Mt. Vernon, and she reminded them to wipe up after their wet boots and to use the hooks for their coats.

"Yes, ma'am, Mrs. Ryan," they said.

She didn't bother with a coat for herself when she slipped out the back door and across the courtyard to the smaller building on Hancock Street. All of the officers were out or already retired to their rooms. She banked the fire in the parlor, so it could die out. After her inspection there, she returned to the basement kitchen in the big building and chased away the last of the dishwashers who had to go out in the cold to travel to their homes. The cook, who was wrapping a shawl over her head before ascending to her room on the top floor, wished her a goodnight.

As Theresa turned back for a final look at the room, she tripped and nearly fell, grabbing the edge of the black iron stove.

"Oh, that Henry," cook said. "I told him not to leave that stuff around. Are you all right then, Mrs. Ryan?"

Theresa disentangled herself from a mop that had been left leaning in the doorway. "I'm fine," she said. "It's my own clumsiness. Go on up, and good night to you." As she watched the cook trudge up the backstairs, the sensation of the mop handle touching her ankle stuck in her mind.

Theresa stood for a moment, thinking. Then she slipped out the back door again and across the courtyard to the other building. Inside, she could hear someone on the stairs, but there were no other sounds. The parlor was still empty. She tiptoed to Mrs. Lee's office and opened the door. The miniature bathroom was perched on the corner of the desk. She stared at it and caught her breath just as a sharp blow fell on her neck, and she saw a burst of light.

Chapter Thirty-Six

Fanny had listened while Jake described the merits of Boston as a place to live. She was flattered that he was worried she would leave. She didn't deserve such consideration. It wasn't as if she'd lived here for years. She'd only been in the city a few months. Would he really notice her absence once she was gone? After all those years when they'd hardly seen each other at all?

And yet, as Jake beckoned the waiter and ordered after-dinner brandies, Fanny realized she would miss his company. Why hadn't she spent more time with him while she was here? When they met and talked, like tonight, the years apart just fell away, and they spoke to each other as if he was still an undergraduate and she was still being tutored at home. Those days and nights up in New Hampshire with Jake and her brother, they had spoken of anything and everything and emptied their hearts with ease. She hadn't talked to anyone like that for years, but it came naturally with Jake. How was it possible?

The waiter brought round glasses and poured in a rich amber liquid. When he left, Jake raised his glass. Fanny raised her own.

"To old friends," she said.

He pursed his lips. "And new adventures," he added.

The small sip trickled down her throat like a little ball of fire.

"New adventures here in Boston," he said, wiggling his wiry eyebrows.

He was nothing if not persistent. Fanny knew it was impossible. Her father would never let her spend the amount of money it would take to keep a home in Boston. The house in Chicago was still her family home. The children needed a place to come when they were off from school, and her parents would never let her give up the house they had built her so close to their own. Her father would point out they had The Rocks up in New Hampshire if she needed a change of scene. Fanny even had her own place up there, the Camp, a separate building she'd managed to acquire for just her own little family. Her father would contribute money to support The Rocks and the house on Prairie Avenue, but he would never let her start another household in Boston. She couldn't explain all of that to Jake Magrath without criticizing her relatives. He was still a close friend of her brother's, and she feared he'd take sides with the family no matter how much he tried to convince her to stay in Boston.

She took a large breath. "Enough about me. What about you? It seems you're very happy with your life these days. All these activities, rowing, singing with the Handel and Haydn Society. Do you still chase after fires?" Fanny remembered her brother George's tales of how he and Jake would chase fire engines, riding bicycles across town to watch the men put out the fires in burning buildings.

"Good Lord, it's a long time since we did that. Happy? I suppose I am, if happiness means you're busy trying to move things along to a better place. I couldn't say I'm satisfied, though." He shook his head. "No, I'm not ever satisfied. There's too much to do. It confounds me how so many deaths go unexplained, how much evidence is mishandled, how many times an autopsy is not even attempted for sudden or violent deaths. It's a Sisyphean task to get the authorities to understand what a travesty of justice it is to leave a death unresolved."

"That happens?"

"Daily. Well, weekly, at least. I tell my medical students all the time, the medical profession has got to take responsibility for alerting the legal authorities when there's a suspicious death. The police lack the training to investigate when there's any question. They abdicate responsibility, and it's a disgrace for a civilized society to operate in that way."

He picked up his glass and chugged a mouthful of the brandy.

Fanny was surprised. She wouldn't have guessed that he was laboring under so much frustration. To her, it seemed he was fully in control of the world around him, a recognized expert, in charge of all the deaths in Suffolk County, a teacher of Harvard medical school students. That he should feel so helpless in the face of the world shocked her.

"I'm sorry. I shouldn't complain to you. But you can't believe it's smooth sailing out there in a world where so many can be killed and maimed by an explosion like the molasses tank. And will we find the cause of it? Or will we just blame the nearest group we have a grudge against?"

"They're saying it was an anarchist bomb. Is that what you mean?"

He rolled his eyes. "An anarchist bomb that never blew out the windows above ground level, sure."

"But if it wasn't that, what was it? Someone mentioned a possible defect in the tank itself." Fanny remembered hearing someone say that at Rose Nichols's house.

"Fanny, you've seen yourself what happens if you dare to impugn the reputation of an important businessman."

"Mr. Wrentham."

"Right. Look what happened when you accused him of involvement in the death of Maggie McKenna in your letter to Senator Lodge. They dismissed you. Imagine the reaction if he's accused of responsibility for twenty-one deaths."

"*Was* there something wrong with the tank?"

"There must have been. And it was negligence that allowed it to deteriorate to the point that over two million gallons of molasses flooded the streets. One of the workmen had complained about creaking noises and leaks. Wrentham just had them paint over it. But whether he or anyone will be brought to task for it...."

Fanny had never heard Jake so despairing. She wished there was something she could do to encourage him.

"Look at the death of Maggie McKenna. If your housekeeper hadn't been there, they would have assumed she was killed by the flood. And we haven't gotten any further on finding out who killed her, either."

"I've got something to show you about that," Fanny said. "It's not finished, but Theresa—Mrs. Ryan—and I have made a copy of the room. To help her remember details, like you asked."

"A copy?"

"A miniature. Of the bathroom where Mrs. Ryan found her. I do want to help prove who killed Maggie before I leave. I believe it's Mr. Wrentham. But I know you said we need facts, so we put together what she remembers. We plan to make a miniature of the bedroom, too."

"Has it helped her to remember anything?" Jake looked at her with a frown of concentration.

"I don't know that she's remembered anything that proves Mr. Wrentham was there yet, but—"

"This is good. Very good." Jake pounded a fist on the table. "I'd like to see this miniature."

"It's not finished yet."

"Still." He looked at her with hope, and Fanny worried she'd suggested her experiment was more than it really was.

"Well, it's in my office. You could come back now and see what we've done so far."

"Yes, yes, yes." Jake waved at the waiter for the bill. As he settled it, Fanny got their coats and boots from the cloakroom.

Before she could think, they were walking arm in arm up Park Street toward the golden dome of the State House. It was even colder. They ducked their heads against the wind as they climbed the hill on Joy Street. At the top, they saw a commotion to their right, at the corner of Hancock.

Rushing over, they saw a white truck with a bold red cross. "An ambulance," Jake said.

Fanny ran to the stretcher bearers who were carefully maneuvering down the stairs of the Hancock Street brownstone. They ignored her questions, but Matt Bradley and some of her other soldiers in shirt sleeves followed.

"It's Mrs. Ryan," Matt told her. "She's been badly hurt."

"Theresa," Fanny tried to follow, but the stretcher bearers loaded the bundled stretcher into the back of the ambulance and rang their bell as they started up. They shouted to Jake that they were headed for Massachusetts

General Hospital when he asked.

Fanny shivered as the ambulance pulled away and another dirty black motorcar slammed its brakes in front of them. Detective McKenna leapt out. "What's going on here?" he asked.

"Mrs. Ryan was attacked," Matt said.

When McKenna saw it was Matt Bradley, he grabbed him by the shirtfront.

"Stop," Fanny yelled.

The front door banged open again, and two uniformed officers dragged a man down the stairs. "It's not that one, Detective," one of the officers said. "This is the one who did it."

Edwin's bloody, scarred face hung down as the policemen held him up by his arms.

Chapter Thirty-Seven

"Edwin," Jake muttered when he recognized the man in the arms of the police.

Fanny was saved from attacking McKenna when he let go of Matt. "What're you saying?" McKenna barked at the uniformed officer.

"It's this guy beat up the woman."

Fanny stepped back as McKenna chucked Edwin under the chin. The young man's eyes were rolled back in his head, and his hands and legs dangled. He was bleeding from nose, arms, and stomach. She couldn't believe the quiet, damaged morgue assistant could have attacked Theresa.

"Why would he do it?" Fanny asked. She was facing Matt Bradley and three other young officers.

"It's true," Lt. Stillman said. "We were in bed when we heard noises. We came down and found him sneaking out. We grabbed him, and Matt called the police."

She thought they must have done more than grab him, when she saw his bleeding, unconscious figure. Could it be that whoever attacked Theresa had also beaten him? But they said he was sneaking out.

Detective McKenna slapped Edwin's face, right, left, right.

"Stop," Fanny yelled. Jake put out an arm to hold her back. He was white faced.

McKenna glared at her, then turned back to the policemen as a paddy wagon pulled up, bells ringing. "Take him in." He pushed the men toward the vehicle. "You." He pointed at the young soldiers. "Follow me."

McKenna pounded up the steps. Matt looked hesitantly at Fanny, and Jake then motioned to Stillman and the two other men to follow. They carried baseball bats stained with blood. Fanny felt sick at the thought that they had used the bats on Edwin. Jake helped her up the steps.

It was dark in the hallway with a dim light from the dying fire in the parlor. Light glowed straight ahead, coming from Fanny's office in the back. It threw the hulking figures of the men in silhouette as she followed them.

They stopped and made way for her at the office door. She caught her breath. The miniature room was smashed. Pieces had flown around the room. The ceramic soap dish was split apart, and there was a pool of blood congealed over the desk and a spray of dark drops painted on the opposite wall and ceiling. A bloodied bat lay on the floor. Someone kicked it under the desk.

Matt stepped forward. "We were upstairs in bed. We heard something, so we grabbed the bats." He took one from one of the others and held it up. "We found Mrs. Ryan on the desk. It was awful. It looked like he'd beaten her to death with that plank." Matt pointed at a block of wood on the desk. It was a slat from one of the packing boxes they had used for the miniature rooms. "He tried to escape. We stopped him."

Fanny could feel the leftover tide of rage flowing from the young men in waves like heat from a fire. She took a step further into the room, shuddering at the sight and smell of blood. Jake stepped up and put an arm around her. She sank against him, stifling an impulse to sob. Instead, she shivered while he looked around sharply. "Mrs. Ryan was lying on the desk?"

"Yes, sir. We thought she was dead," Stillman said.

"He's an animal, a bloody animal," McKenna growled.

"She's not dead, though, is she?" Fanny asked. She felt like she was scrambling up a hill, trying to outrun a blackness that threatened to engulf her. She wouldn't faint.

"No. They took her to the hospital, so she's not dead," Jake told her. "Come away, now." He squeezed her close to him and nudged her out the door and down the hallway into the cold parlor. Matt and Stillman followed while the others talked to McKenna.

Jake sat her in an armchair and pushed her head down between her knees.

"Here, you need the blood flowing to your head. Keep it down like that till you're steady." He held her hand, feeling for a pulse.

Matt knelt beside her. "Can we get you anything?"

"Some brandy," Jake said.

Stillman went to the drinks trolley and poured a small glass. After a minute, Jake sat her up and had her sip it.

"I must go to Theresa," Fanny said. "We must tell her family."

"That's all right. I'll get McKenna to send someone to Patrick's pub to tell him," Jake said.

Fanny tried to get up. "I must see how she is." Pressure from Jake's hand on her shoulder kept her from rising.

"In a little while. Pour me a glass of that, will you?" he asked Stillman.

The slender officer poured three more glasses and doled them out to Jake, Matt, and himself.

"I'll go," Matt said after a swallow. "I'll find out how she is for you."

Fanny saw fear in his eyes. He was still kneeling by her, staring into her face. A vein jumped in his neck. "No. I need you and the other men to stay here. To see to the house," she said.

"She's right," Jake said. "I'll take Mrs. Lee to the hospital but get one of the others to find us a cab." He sat down heavily on a sofa. "Go," he commanded.

Matt and Stillman scurried away while Fanny and Jake caught their breath. The silence was heavy. There was nothing worth the breath to speak. In a few minutes, they returned. They had a cab waiting.

Jake helped her up. "Keep an eye on McKenna," he told Matt. "But whatever you do, don't start a fight. I'll bring her back as soon as possible."

The young officer tried to protest but was ignored.

At the hospital, Jake found out that Theresa had lost a lot of blood and was suffering from multiple broken bones. They had set what they could and given her morphine for pain, but she remained unconscious. A nurse allowed Fanny a peek at Theresa, swathed in bandages. There was nothing Fanny could do but wait.

Jake admitted the doctors had little hope Theresa would survive her injuries, which brought Fanny to tears.

When Patrick and his mother arrived, Fanny agreed to let Jake take her home.

In the cab, she looked across at Jake and realized how drawn he looked, as if he might faint. He was abnormally quiet. She knew what bothered him. "Edwin. Why would he do this?" she whispered.

Jake's eyes were red. "I should have known there was something wrong. I knew he was out when Luigi was killed. I didn't want to believe it."

"You think he killed that man? Do you think he killed Maggie, too?"

"I think he was her soldier."

Chapter Thirty-Eight

Friday, January 24, 1919

Fanny spent a restless night. She couldn't stop her mind from revolving round and round. Edwin was Maggie's soldier? Had she rejected him, and he killed her? Had the Italian seen something? Had Theresa remembered something? Why would Edwin kill these people, even if he was Maggie's soldier?

Jake had told her how much Edwin hated McKenna. Had Maggie decided to return to her husband? Perhaps Theresa convinced her sister to go back. Had Edwin killed her in a fit of passion? Fanny cringed from the dark swirl of emotions. Edwin? Theresa? The young people she knew? It wasn't possible. Edwin had strong emotions roiling beneath his quiet exterior, but Fanny was sure he admired Theresa Ryan. There was a sympathy there. Each time she entered the room, the young soldier looked up like a shopkeeper who'd heard the bell tinkle when the door opened. There had been a connection there, she was sure of it.

She roused herself in the morning to do the tasks that should have fallen to her housekeeper. As she straightened the parlor in the big house and consulted with a shocked cook, Fanny's mind buzzed with thoughts about Theresa. Did she live through the night, and would she ever recover? Fanny wondered if there was anything from Theresa's room she could bring her. Even if she survived, how could she return to work after such severe injuries, and how could she live without her pay if she couldn't work?

This last thought gave Fanny something to grab on to. She would write a check for Theresa's salary and deliver it. She choked back tears as she crossed the courtyard to the brownstone. She couldn't promise Theresa her job would be waiting for her. Fanny herself had been dismissed and would be forced to move out by the end of the month.

In her office, she could smell the taint of blood. She felt sick. Splinters of the miniature crunched under her feet. A bat lay under the desk, but she shrank from moving it. She got the checkbook from a drawer and took it with pen and ink to the parlor. She was glad the young officers weren't up yet.

When she had written the check and prepared to leave, she heard footsteps on the stairs. Matt Bradley blinked in the morning sun pouring through the front door she'd just opened.

"I'm going to the hospital to visit Mrs. Ryan," she told him.

He jumped down the last few steps. "Let me go with you. Please, Mrs. Lee."

He looked white as he brushed past her to grab up his overcoat from the rack.

"I'm not sure they'll let us see her."

"I'm coming," he insisted.

Outside, she was grateful for his arm on the snow dusted brick walks. They descended the steep hill and hurried to the hospital.

Theresa Ryan lay in semidarkness, her mother-in-law asleep in a chair beside her. Her head was hidden in bandages and both arms encased in plaster. She was so motionless; she could have been dead.

"Mrs. Lee?" Patrick Ryan, Theresa's brother-in-law, came up behind them as they looked through the doorway.

"How is she?" Fanny whispered. They shuffled away from the room while Matt lurked in the doorway, straining to see in the dim light but reluctant to cross the threshold.

"She's no better. Who did this?" Patrick asked.

Fanny still couldn't believe it. "They claim it was Edwin O'Connell. He works for Dr. Magrath. They think he was Maggie's lover, and that Theresa must have seen him or seen something to incriminate him, so he attacked her."

Fanny nearly swallowed her words, it was so hard to pronounce them. She had a sudden memory of Maggie's undignified corpse, legs spread, lying in the morgue. How could Edwin have assisted in her autopsy if he loved her? It was unthinkable.

Patrick frowned. She could sense anger rising in him. What good would it do? Fanny reached out a hand to his arm. "Mr. Ryan, I'm so sorry. We all care for Theresa very much. I would do anything to help if I could. But at the very least, I wanted to give you this check for Theresa's wages. And if there's anything she needs, for her care, please let me help." She slipped the envelope with the check from her bag.

Patrick frowned. "We don't need your charity."

"Not at all. These are Mrs. Ryan's wages. They're owed her." If Fanny had increased the amount by a few weeks, she hoped it would make up for the fact that she couldn't guarantee Theresa's job in the future. She hated not being able to promise that Theresa could return as housekeeper. Looking through the doorway, she knew that by the time the broken girl recovered, she herself would not even be in Boston. "Please." She forced the envelope into his hands.

He sighed. "I only hope we'll not need it to bury her."

"Oh, please, not," Fanny murmured. Patrick brushed past Matt Bradley and went to his mother, who was just waking.

"Lt. Bradley, come. We can do nothing here."

The young soldier followed her reluctantly.

At the street door, Fanny decided she had another visit to pay. She attempted to send Matt back to Wendell House, but he resisted. "Where are you going?" he asked.

"To the morgue."

Chapter Thirty-Nine

The door to the morgue on North Grove Street was unlocked. When no one answered the bell, Fanny and Matt entered. It was past ten o'clock on a Friday morning, but no one was about. On the door to the operating theater, a handwritten sign announced that the day's class was cancelled.

Feeling uneasy, Fanny continued through the laboratory. A body on a table was covered except for the face. She thought it was the unidentified young soldier that Jake had showed her. She felt a pang of sorrow for the poor unknown man with no family to bury him. At least Theresa and Maggie had people who cared about their fate. Matt skirted the body as if afraid of contagion. She didn't know why she herself felt no such scruple. It was as if she were already inured to death and coldly scientific in her interest. The morgue was Jake's place of work to her, and she still envied him that work, despite all the terrible things that had happened.

Jake's office was in darkness, but she could see him slumped over his desk, an empty bottle in front of him. When she stepped into the room, she sniffed. The air reeked of whiskey. "Oh, Jake." Taking a breath, she moved forward and pulled at his shoulder. "Jake, wake up. What's the matter with you?"

Stirring, he grumbled, and she stepped back. Matt hesitated in the doorway. "Looks like the doctor really had a snoot full," he said.

"Hmm. Jake, come on."

Jake raised a heavy head, shaking like a dog. He coughed and wheezed, sitting back to glare at Fanny through half closed eyes. "What do you want?"

"I want you to wake up, Jake. What is this? Are you drunk?"

He peered at her through narrowed eyes. "What?"

"Are you drunk?" she asked, disgusted.

He growled at her and grabbed the empty bottle. "What if I am?" A look of surprise spread over his face, and he lurched up. Fanny retreated to the other side of the desk as Jake grabbed a metal waste basket. Turning his back to them, he retched into it. Fanny collapsed into a chair she felt behind her legs and tried to hold her breath against the stench.

Finished, Jake pulled a handkerchief from his pocket, wiped his mouth, and sat back down facing Fanny. She shut her eyes to block out his red nosed, wrinkled face.

He coughed into the handkerchief. "Sorry to offend your sensibilities, but what do you expect? How stupid could I be? Here I was training that young man, helping him, feeling sorry for him, a valiant soldier wounded in battle, and all the time, he's a killer and a coward.

"These soldiers coming back," Jake said, pointing at Matt, who still stood in the doorway. "We're so busy taking care of them, you and I." He frowned at Fanny. "You, you're here taking care of these poor little boys in your home. But what are they really like, huh?" He leaned forward to glare at Fanny. She leaned back to get away from his breath. "What did we do to them when we sent them over there? How warped are they when they come back? How could he kill a woman like that, and attack another one? Did we make them all murderers?"

"You mean Edwin?" Fanny asked. She felt bad for poor Matt standing there, as Jake's accusations could apply to him as well. "I know it's hard for you to believe he could attack Theresa. I can't understand it either."

"Everything I thought about him is wrong. More fool me." Jake said.

He looked so old to Fanny. His face sagged, and his bleary eyes were unfocused. She felt panic, as if he was sliding down a hole away from her. "Jake. Do you really believe he was Maggie's soldier? Why wouldn't he say so?"

"Because he killed her," Matt said.

Jake stared at him, then back at Fanny. "Unlike your man, here." He motioned at Matt. "Edwin was in town all those months ago when Maggie found her soldier."

"Did you have any idea he was seeing her?"

"No, but she was a married woman. He's not going to tell me about that. And she probably hid him from everyone because of the scars. What woman would want to be seen with a man who was so damaged?" Fanny flinched at the thought that Edwin's disfigured face deserved his boss's comment. The burn scars were a fact that could never be ignored, no matter how sympathetic a woman could be. Jake sat back and wiped his eyes. "He must have seen his mother in her. His mother was beaten by his father."

"As Maggie was beaten by her husband," Fanny said.

"Yes. But, like his mother, Maggie must have decided to return to her husband. Edwin couldn't bear that. He couldn't let her go back to that."

"So, he killed her?"

"Perhaps he merely tried to stop her, to reason with her, but his passion got the best of him. And then it was too late."

Fanny remembered how Edwin had helped her find Maggie's body and bring it back to the morgue. If he had really killed her, how could he be so calm? He couldn't, surely. "Why are you so sure?"

Jake groaned. Matt shifted from foot to foot behind her. Jake looked as if he were peering over the brink of some dark abyss. "He was with me when I talked to the Italian workmen. Luigi, the man who died, knew more than he said. Edwin was there in the shadows when Luigi said he saw a soldier outside of Maggie's place that night. I know he was holding back something else. He must have recognized Edwin. When Luigi was pushed off the roof in the North End, Edwin wasn't here."

"And because he wasn't here at the morgue, you think he killed Luigi Spinelli?" Fanny could see how it wounded Jake to think Edwin had killed the man after hearing Jake question him. Jake blamed himself for Luigi's death. Edwin had been something special to Jake. Jake mentored the damaged young man as if he were a son. . She sensed how bitterly disappointed he was in Edwin.

Jake pounded a fist on the desk, making the empty bottle rattle. "I should have known something was wrong when he was absent. I never even asked him where he was. I was afraid, and now Mrs. Ryan has paid for my cowardice."

Now Jake felt guilty for the attack on Theresa as well. But Fanny's mind rejected the image of Edwin smashing Theresa and the miniature. "I can't believe he'd hurt Theresa like that."

"But he was there. We saw him." Matt stepped into the room. "We found him in the room, and Mrs. Ryan was covered in blood."

Fanny reached out to him. "I know, Matt. But it was dark. Are you sure he was the only one there? Are you sure there wasn't someone else?"

Matt froze, his eyes wide. Jake and Matt both stared at her as if she were mad.

"It's only that when I saw how hurt she was, so much damage…." Fanny gulped back a sob and bit her lip before she could go on. "It must have taken some time to do that. I wondered how long after it happened that you men came downstairs."

Matt staggered back a step. "I heard a noise. It took me a minute to wake the others. We grabbed the bats, ran down. O'Connell was standing over her. He had a board in his hand. We hit him before he could strike us. It had to be him."

"Fanny, why are you making excuses for him?" Jake said, his voice like gravel.

"I'm not. I just want to be sure. Why would he attack Theresa?"

"She must have known something, seen something," Matt said. "Or maybe he just wanted to destroy the miniature room, and she found him at it."

"He was here last night," Jake said. "He must have been. He should have prepared a body for the class, but he pulled out an old body instead, one already cut open and closed again. I don't know why he did that. He should have gotten a new body. There're two outside in the garage."

"He brought out the soldier who was killed at the brothel?" Fanny asked.

"Yes. He's still unidentified."

Matt looked confused and upset.

"It's a man who was dead long before Maggie McKenna," Jake said. "It has nothing to do with her death. But Edwin shouldn't have brought him out.

That body will be taken away for burial in a pauper's grave Monday. Edwin must have been agitated, not knowing what he was doing. He must have been building up to go after Theresa Ryan."

"Perhaps he went to look for Dr. Magrath at Wendell House and found the miniature," Matt said. "Then he was afraid it showed something about Maggie's death that would implicate him. Maybe Mrs. Ryan remembered something and accused him.

"Or perhaps he found her after she'd been attacked," Fanny said. She was stubbornly insistent on the possibility of Edwin's innocence. She didn't know why. "Did anyone even ask him?" She leaned across the desk toward Jake. "Go see him, Jake. Ask him what happened."

"Mrs. Lee!" Matt was horrified.

"Stop, Fanny," Jake said. He stood up slowly, as if he were eighty. He reminded Fanny of a fragile elderly aunt who moved as if her limbs were made of blown glass. "He's broken my heart. I'm so disappointed. I never want to see him again."

Fanny was stunned. His grief was so thick, it hung in the air between them. She longed to reassure him, but how could she? She had no reason to doubt Edwin O'Connell's guilt. Her mind just wanted to reject it.

As they stood frozen, they heard a door bang in the entryway and footsteps.

Jeremy Wrentham pushed past Matt in the doorway. His face was red from cold and anger. He thrust a leather-gloved handful of paper at Jake's face. "What's the meaning of this?"

Chapter Forty

He could have knocked the felt fedora from Wrentham's head or strangled him with the white silk scarf gently fluffed up at his neck. Jake's head throbbed as if a hatchet were stuck in his forehead, and the last thing he needed was this fellow prancing around before him. Jake was only too aware that he must look like a hobo in comparison, and he hated that Fanny was there to see him like that.

He grabbed the papers from the kid-glove covered hand. Jake smirked, even though it didn't help his head. "It's my report on the deaths from the molasses flood. You can't read?"

"I know that," Wrentham said. His nose wrinkled at the sour smell in the room. "Disgusting," He pointed at the report. "How dare you suggest negligence on the part of USIA? That tank was sabotaged by anarchists. It's outrageous for your report to ignore all evidence of an anarchist bomb."

Jake tilted a bit on his feet and had to grab the desk for support. *Damn*, he thought. *This is no time to stumble with this jackass making a fuss, and Fanny and her young soldier as witnesses.* He planted his feet firmly, dropping the papers on the desk. "That report is for the inquest. Chief Justice Bolster will decide if your company should face charges for negligence. The tank was structurally defective, and there's no evidence of a bomb. My report merely supports those conclusions. None of the injuries on the bodies showed any evidence of a bomb, either." Jake wanted to groan. His head was splitting, and he saw halos around objects. He wanted to close his eyes and sink down, down, down. But he didn't want to give this blustering incompetent the satisfaction of seeing him so weak, so he just gritted his teeth and frowned.

180

Wrentham rose on his toes and trembled with righteous indignation. "That tank was dynamited by anarchists. We have experts who can swear to it."

"If you're so sure of your innocence, why're you questioning my report?" Jake raised a hand and pushed his index finger into Wrentham's chest. "Because you're afraid of liability for the deaths and injuries, that's why. You should be held criminally responsible for manslaughter due to negligence. That tank wasn't constructed to hold as much as you put into it, and it's your responsibility." He punctuated his next line by pushing his finger into Wrentham again. "I hope those people who suffered from your incompetence sue you for every penny you and USIA have got."

Wrentham slapped Jake's hand away.

Jake's head was pounding so much now he thought it would burst. "Now, get out of my morgue."

"Not until you amend that report to say those injuries are consistent with an anarchist bomb." Wrentham looked around as if he thought he would get support from witnesses. Then he recognized Fanny and nearly erupted in a fit. It was almost enough to make Jake laugh, but he didn't dare chance the pain from such an action.

Wrentham pointed at Fanny. "You're in league with her! Let me warn you, madam, if you repeat any of the slander you've dared to utter in the past, you'll lose more than your position. The USIA lawyers are prepared to bring action against you if you so much as open your mouth."

"That's right, you little coward, attack a woman," Jake said. "You and the USIA lawyers are afraid of Mrs. Lee and other people like her who don't believe your lies. You just want to blame anarchists, so you won't be liable for the pain and suffering your negligence caused."

"This is outrageous. Boston is the chief vipers' pit for anarchists in this country. Everyone knows it, and Senator Lodge is determined to rid us of these assassins. Your refusal to support the fight against such dangerous criminals should be more than enough to remove you from office."

"When hell freezes over." Jake had really had enough of this man. He was a well-dressed clown. He might have Senator Lodge's ear, but Jake knew Lodge was a crafty old codger who just hated all immigrants and plotted to ship them all back to Europe. Except the ones who waited on him in his dining room or polished his boots, of course. But the USIA manager continued to argue, practically yelling about experts the company had hired to prove the tank was blown up by an anarchist bomb.

Jake spotted a wooden paddle leaning against his file cabinet. He'd brought it in for repair and never got around to fixing it. The paddle reminded him of something. He swooped past Wrentham's side and grabbed the oar. Wrentham staggered back a couple of steps. "As a matter of fact, I'll be seeing Lodge at the boat club Sunday night. I'll be sure to tell the old man you've been taking his name in vain. Now, get out of my morgue." He took a step forward, brandishing the oar, and Wrentham was forced to retreat.

"Don't think this is the last you'll hear about that report," Wrentham said. He turned and, with a huff, raced from the room.

Jake wondered if the man was expecting him to chase after him and slap him on the rear with the paddle. He didn't have the energy, and suddenly he remembered a duty he had to perform. Deflated, he brought the paddle to the floor with a clunk. "Fanny, Lt. Bradley, I'll have to ask you to leave as well." Jake's stomach was roiling. He needed to rid himself of observers, no matter how well-intentioned they might be. "I have to go home. He's reminded me I have the Union Boat House awards dinner Sunday night, and I'm master of ceremonies. I need to write a speech." He twirled the paddle in his hands. He didn't feel up to speeches, but he couldn't miss this annual appearance, and, besides, it was as good an excuse as any to drive them out of his office. Jake could have broken down in sobs as the pain in his head, and the twisting of his insides continued, but he called on his manly pride to remain standing.

"Jake, are you sure you're all right?" Fanny asked.

Even Fanny's sympathetic worry appeared grotesque to him in his present condition. He wanted her to leave, so he could puke in his basket again.

"Mrs. Lee, why don't I get a cab to take the doctor home?" Bradley suggested.

Jake could have hugged him if he weren't so near to puking again. He nodded carefully.

Bradley escorted Fanny out, and Jake sunk down gratefully with his head in his hands. He was not looking forward to the evening festivities at the boat house on the Charles River Sunday night. The thought of all that food and drink and cigar smoke turned his stomach, and he reached for his wastebasket again.

Chapter Forty-One

Saturday, January 25, 1919

Saturday morning, Fanny started to clean up her office. The men had found her a new box, but she didn't have the heart to work on a new version of the bathroom where Maggie had died. As she swept aside some of the broken bits of the miniature, she wondered if it was cursed. Was Theresa's attack the result of their attempt to conjure up the room where her sister had died? Was there something evil about reproducing the crime? She shook herself. She wasn't a superstitious woman. Like Jake, she wanted facts. But what had been so telling in the tiny room that it had been smashed and Theresa Ryan attacked? What could the room prove about the murder? Nothing. It had proved nothing.

Matt brought her his partially built bedroom, but he, too, had lost all enthusiasm for the project. When she asked him to find a replacement for Stillman's broken soap dish, promising to pay for it, he took the broken pieces, dumped them into a waste basket, and wiped his hands with a handkerchief. Then he escaped her presence without another word.

She knew he was shocked by her defense of Edwin O'Connell the previous day. He didn't understand. She wasn't accusing Matt and his roommates of making a mistake. She just wasn't convinced that in the darkness and confusion, they'd been able to see what really happened. She'd examined her own feelings, and she was sure she felt no particular empathy for the scarred ex-soldier. Jake was very fond of the young man, and so he was terribly disappointed. But she didn't know Edwin that well at all. Fanny was fired up by the need to know the truth of what had happened to Theresa and her sister, Maggie. Partial explanations wouldn't satisfy her anymore.

There was a knock on the door, and Cornelia Thornwell entered. She'd heard of the attack on Fanny's housekeeper, and she offered sympathy, but that was not the main reason for her visit.

"I wanted to extend a personal invitation from Rose Nichols for her Sunday Salon tomorrow. You really must come."

"Thank you for thinking of me, but I'm not sure I could sit still for a social gathering, what with all that's going on." Fanny couldn't imagine drinking tea with the matrons of Beacon Hill after her dismissal.

"Oh, no, my dear, it's not a social event at all." Cornelia perched on the wooden armchair opposite Fanny, and her eyes glittered with amusement. "Just like the so-called sewing circle, Rose's Sunday Salon is intended to provoke serious discussions. She only does it once a month. She serves tea, much to the disgust of her mother, who's appalled by the lack of hospitality. Mrs. Nichols is of an older generation with different expectations. She thinks Rose is being rude. But everyone knows to eat before they come." She grinned. "The most important thing is that Rose invites people who don't agree on a particular topic, then she starts a debate. There are some very spicy disagreements to be tasted in that parlor. Guess who she's invited tomorrow?"

Fanny was at a loss.

"Your Mr. Wrentham."

Fanny's mouth dropped open. After the man's performance at the morgue, she was dumbfounded. She feared Miss Nichols would give him a forum for more pernicious statements. He had tried to threaten Jake to get him to change his report. Of course, Rose wouldn't know that, but Cornelia was well aware that he was the one who'd gotten Fanny dismissed from her position. All the more reason for Fanny to decline. "I never want to be in the same room with that man again."

Cornelia waved her blue-veined hand. "No. You don't understand. You won't want to miss this. In addition to Mr. Wrentham, Rose has invited the alderman for the North End, the police commissioner, and the district attorney who'll prosecute USIA for negligence. They're already amassing evidence for a grand jury to convene after the inquest on Friday. Wrentham has no idea they'll attend, and they are all delighted to rehearse their arguments before the trial. There's an engineer from MIT who's doing a study of the tank construction, too. You don't want to miss this, Fanny."

It sounded like Rose and Cornelia were stacking the deck against the USIA manager, and Fanny *would* relish watching his comeuppance. "I see. As long as I'm not the one who has to talk to him."

"Not at all. Just sit back and listen to professionals take him apart. I tell you, my dear, this man will rue the day he got you dismissed, and don't think our board won't hear all about it when he's demolished in court next week. You must come to the salon. I need you there. You won't have to say a word. Just being there will get under his skin."

"All right, I'll come." She could see that Cornelia wanted her present as an irritant. Fanny felt she owed her that much for her help getting Matt out of jail.

"Four o'clock. By the way, I heard they arrested the man who attacked your housekeeper."

"Edwin O'Connell. He works for Dr. Magrath, the medical examiner." Fanny shook her head. She still couldn't believe in the young man's guilt.

"You don't appear satisfied. Is something wrong?" Cornelia sat back down, unwilling to leave without the whole story. "And what's all this?" She waved her hands over the miniature rooms.

Fanny realized it must seem odd to find her playing with dollhouses in the midst of tragedy. "Mrs. Ryan and I were building a miniature of the room where her sister was killed."

"Ah, the Mrs. McKenna whose death you believe Mr. Wrentham was involved in. Lt. Bradley was accused of her murder when he was in jail, wasn't he?"

"That's right. Now, the theory is that Edwin attacked Theresa Ryan and destroyed the miniature because it could have exposed him as Maggie McKenna's killer."

"But you don't believe that?"

"I don't know. The police say he was Maggie's lover, but I don't see how he could have been." She looked across at Cornelia. "Last night, the police took him away. But no one asked *him* what happened. Everyone believes he beat Theresa and killed Maggie, but no one, not even Jake—Dr. Magrath—who knew him, asked him *why* he beat Theresa."

"They arrested him?"

"They dragged him away."

Cornelia gathered her bag and gloves and stood up. "What are we waiting for? My motor is at the door. Let's go ask him."

Chapter Forty-Two

The warden of Charles Street Jail rolled his eyes when he saw Cornelia and Fanny led into his office. He threw up his hands when he heard their request. He didn't even argue. He just sent someone to bring Edwin. Snatching his coat and hat from a rack, he announced he was finished with his half day of Saturday work and stomped from the room.

Two guards brought Edwin in handcuffs. At Fanny's request, he was seated on a wooden armchair opposite the women who sat on a padded couch. Fanny heard Cornelia's intake of breath when she saw the burn scars as well as other bruises on the man. Fanny introduced Edwin and explained that he'd been burned in a battle in France.

One of his eyes was swollen shut, and his lip was split. He sat stiffly on the hard chair but remained silent.

"Edwin, can you tell Mrs. Thornwell and me what happened last night? Did you attack Mrs. Ryan? I can't understand why you would do such a thing?"

Edwin hung his head as if a stone were attached to his neck.

Fanny sat forward. "Please, Edwin, tell us what happened."

He raised his head slowly. "What does Dr. Magrath think?" he asked, and she saw tears pooling in his eyes.

"Dr. Magrath is disappointed in you. He was shocked—we all were—to find Mrs. Ryan beaten and you accused of having done it. He's devastated. He's very fond of you, Edwin."

Edwin shut his eyes. "Is she dead?" His eyes remained closed.

"No, but she's badly hurt. She's unconscious in the Massachusetts General casualty ward. We don't know if she'll live."

He slumped forward.

"Edwin…"

"You won't believe me." He opened his eyes and stared out from his ravaged face. Fanny felt that he was in a dark, cold place that she couldn't reach.

"How do you know she won't believe you if you don't tell your story, young man?" Cornelia asked. She sat erect as if she wore an iron rod down her back. Fanny recognized the training of her mother's generation in Cornelia's physical and moral rectitude. That some of the girls had actually worn iron contraptions to train their posture popped into Fanny's mind.

Edwin stared at Cornelia as if she were an animal of some unknown species. He scanned her up and down with alarm. But he had nothing to say to her.

Fanny was frustrated. Why wouldn't Edwin try to defend himself? She wanted to get up and put her hands on his shoulders and shake him. "Edwin, I'll tell you what Dr. Magrath thinks. He thinks you were Maggie McKenna's lover and the father of her unborn child. Everyone said she had a former soldier who promised to take her away. Dr. Magrath is worried that you are that man and that she decided to return to the husband who beat her, like your father beat your mother. He thinks you became angry, lost your temper, and killed her by mistake to keep her from going back to her husband."

Edwin watched her but remained silent.

"He thinks that Luigi Spinelli saw you outside Maggie's apartment, and you threw him off a roof to keep him from blackmailing you." She could see him begin to shake his head. At least he was listening. "Then, when Theresa Ryan remembered something, she saw at her sister's rooms that implicated you, you attacked her and smashed the miniature to hide your guilt. That's what Dr. Magrath and the police think happened."

"No, no, no," he muttered, shaking his head back and forth.

"What are you saying? Are you saying that's not true? What happened, Edwin? Why were you there if you didn't beat Theresa?"

"No. I found her." At last, he replied. "I never knew her sister. I was trying to help." He gulped, stumbling on his words. "I was at the morgue. I think he's her soldier, the dead man from the brothel. I pulled him out to see if I could prove it. The telephone rang. The voice said Dr. Magrath wanted me to come to your house on Hancock Street. I knew he was with you, so when I got the message, I went." He covered his face with his fettered hands.

"No, Edwin. Dr. Magrath didn't send for you." Fanny wasn't sure if she believed him. She looked at Cornelia, who raised her eyebrows in silent surprise. "What happened when you got there?"

He pulled his hands down and clasped a knee. "The door was slightly open. There was a light from the room at the end of the corridor…only a fire in the side parlor besides that. I called out. When there was no answer, I went to the door of the office. Something seemed wrong. I pushed the door open. Inside, Mrs. Ryan was covered with blood. I tried to help her. Then I heard footsteps on the stairs, so I picked up a broken piece of wood. They burst in with bats. I defended myself. I tried to tell them who I was, but they wouldn't listen. They kicked me and beat me with the bats."

Fanny sat back. "Was anyone at the morgue with you? Did anyone else hear the telephone? Why were you there so late?"

He shrank into the chair.

"Edwin, why were you there?"

"I thought…I talked to someone that night who knew about Maggie's soldier. The one who was killed at the brothel. I wanted to tell Dr. Magrath. McKenna lives at the brothel where that soldier was killed. If he was Maggie's lover, McKenna could have seen him there and killed him.

"He thinks I was Maggie's lover. Me? How could you think that? With my face? I'm a monster. Does Dr. Magrath really believe I'd do that?" He looked up at her, his swollen eye round and hard as a ball, the eyelid blue and green with bruising. "I would never hurt Mrs. Ryan. Don't you know that? Never."

Chapter Forty-Three

Fanny didn't know what to think. She got the name of Edwin's friend, Gerry Doyle, who he claimed could identify Maggie's lover. But Edwin didn't know where the man lived or worked. Fanny couldn't ask Jake or Detective McKenna to help find the man. They wouldn't believe Edwin.

Reluctantly, Edwin finally admitted he'd met the man at Mrs. Lake's brothel on North Street. It wasn't a place Fanny could even contemplate visiting. She'd be disgraced. A woman of her breeding didn't acknowledge the existence of such places.

On the ride back to Hancock Street, Cornelia said she was unable to decide whether the damaged young man was telling the truth or desperately making up lies to escape punishment. When she dropped Fanny off, she reminded her that she had promised to attend Rose Nichols's Sunday Salon.

Inside, Fanny retreated to her office. After hearing Edwin's story, she didn't feel like completing the miniature. She pushed it aside. What good was reproducing it if Theresa wasn't able to use it to search her memory for some detail that would identify her sister's killer? She didn't even have the energy to clean up the broken crate. Pieces had been swept into a corner.

Fanny thought of going to Jake to tell him what Edwin had told her. But, after his display of anger and despair, Fanny was certain he didn't want to hear anything Edwin had to say. Detective McKenna would be a worse choice, especially since the policeman still believed Edwin had been his wife's lover. She knew better than to expect rational thinking from a man in such a stew of emotion.

If only she could locate Edwin's mysterious friend. Jake could go to the brothel to find out more about Gerry Doyle, but Fanny couldn't. Going there would be a scandal that could ruin her reputation. Of course, Jeremy Wrentham and Senator Lodge had already ruined her reputation in this town. Nonetheless, going to a brothel was unthinkable.

She found Matt Bradley and brought him back to her office. As she described her visit to the Charles Street Jail, she saw his ears redden. "You can't be serious, Mrs. Lee. O'Connell battered Mrs. Ryan to a pulp. He very nearly killed her. She may yet die. You can't mean that you believe his story."

"I just want to get to the truth," Fanny told him. Any suggestion that Edwin wasn't the attacker touched a tender spot in the young soldier. "If he's lying, we should be able to prove that. But we must try." She attempted to convince Matt to go in search of Edwin's friend for her.

"No. Not after what he's done. The man is clearly warped. Can't you see that? I know other men who've come back scarred from the war. Not just outwardly, like O'Connell, but inside. They're lost in a dark place. They turn on the world because of the horrors they've seen, and they imitate the worst of it." Fanny could see the whites of his eyes as he said this. He gripped the arms of the chair. "You can't know what it was like over there."

Fanny looked at him with concern. She feared he would explode. As she moved back in her chair, her foot touched the wooden bat under the desk, and she felt a jolt of energy down her spine.

Matt noticed her distress and took a large breath to calm himself. "I know O'Connell's burn scars make you sympathize with him, but it's not just his face that's ruined. He's ruined inside. Look at what he did to Theresa Ryan. After killing her sister. He has to be stopped. This search for some supposed friend is a wild goose chase. A brothel? The fact that he's gone there and wants to send you there to find his 'friend' should tell you what kind of man he is. No, Mrs. Lee. I'm sorry, but I won't help you." He stood up, straightened his uniform jacket, and marched from the room.

Fanny relaxed. He was fond of Theresa and was grieving for her. Fanny should have known his reaction would be as bad as Jake's. She wished she could be as certain of Edwin's guilt as they were. Perhaps she was subconsciously sympathizing with Edwin because of his wounds, as Matt believed.

There was a soft knock on the door. "Come in."

Lt. Stillman entered, carefully closed the door behind him, and stood across the desk from her. His eyes scanned the room, lingering on the empty miniature room and stopping on Fanny's face. "I couldn't help overhearing part of your discussion with Matt. His voice carries. I was wondering if I could be of assistance."

Fanny was surprised.

"I heard you say you want to search for some person, but the only place that might offer useful information is a house of ill repute, as we say, on North Street. I probably shouldn't admit I've heard of the place but, since it's important to you, I could go there and make inquiries for you." He sat down opposite her.

"Matt is, let us say, very fond of Mrs. Ryan," he said. "I could see he was furious with her attacker last night. He released some of that fury on the O'Connell fellow, but I think Matt is still aching to take out his anger on someone. I myself have made a point to stay out of his way."

"So, are you offering to accompany me to the brothel?" Fanny asked. He looked shocked at her use of the term, but a brothel was a brothel in her parlance, and she saw no reason to call it something else.

Stillman coughed. "Yes, well, we could do that, or, alternately, you could tell me what information is needed, and I could go in your place."

Fanny frowned. She was tired of having to sort through secondhand accounts. Sending Stillman in her place might be the more appropriate solution, but she wasn't having it. "No, I'd like to follow through on this personally."

"Yes, I see. Matt must have sensed that." He cleared his throat. "Matt is a very good person, but he's a man and a soldier. It's quite possible he might fear some embarrassment if anyone recognized him in your presence. He'd feel bad about that, you know."

"Are you suggesting Matt has visited this brothel?" Fanny asked. It hadn't occurred to her that fear of recognition would be a problem for him, but she was not so naïve as to be shocked. She should have realized that he could have visited the brothel in the past.

"No, not at all. It's just a possibility. It's much more likely he's never been there."

"It's not a problem for you, though?"

"No. I won't be known at that place but, even if I were, I would bear the disgrace to help you. I'm not trying to make a good impression on poor Mrs. Ryan, like Matt, you see. I do hope…we all hope that she survives her ordeal."

Poor Theresa. Fanny was sure if she did recover, her place at Wendell House would be filled by someone else, and Fanny herself would be gone. So much for worries about the niceties of reputation either on Matt's part or her own. "I will take you up on your offer, Lt. Stillman. When can we go?"

Chapter Forty-Four

They took a cab to the corner of North and Clark Streets in the North End. It was late afternoon on a Saturday, and Stillman had suggested it would be wise to approach the "lady of the house" before the start of business in the evening. Fanny just hoped they would get the information they needed. She wasn't sure what she would do if they were forced to wait and watch for the arrival of Gerry Doyle at the brothel. What would the other young soldiers think if they saw her in this street?

They walked up North Street until Stillman questioned a man delivering a basket of fish. As the men put their heads together several feet away, Fanny felt the fisherman's eyes staring at her. She was as out of place as a peacock in a farmyard on this street. She shook some snow from the hem of her coat as she waited.

Stillman returned and took her elbow. "It's two doors down." He led her to a four-story brick townhouse between two workingmen's bars that were just opening their shutters. Stillman hopped up the steps and opened a door that gleamed with heavy coats of black paint. Fanny had never entered a brothel before. She caught a stench of old cigar smoke as she stepped over the threshold. Her parents would be appalled. She heard a bell jangle overhead as Stillman closed the door.

It was dim in the hallway. No one sat at the desk opposite the door, but a heavy-set bald man in shirtsleeves and suspenders came through a curtained doorway. "We're not open yet. Come back at eight." He pulled a white napkin from where it was stuffed in his collar and wiped grease from his mouth.

Stillman confidently flipped through a notebook on the table, and then smiled directly into the bald man's face. "Oh, yes, but we're not here for that. This is Mrs. Lee, and she'd be grateful for a few minutes of your proprietor's time." He fiddled with a matchbook from a silver tray on the desk. "It's Mrs. Lake, isn't it?"

The bald man's forehead creased in an effort to take in Stillman and the lady behind him—Fanny. It was all too much for him. He turned his back and retreated through the curtained doorway.

"I do hope he understands English," Stillman said. "He sounded like he spoke English, didn't he? You never know. Sometimes they memorize a few phrases, and that's it. Well, we'll see."

Stillman was babbling out of nervousness. Fanny felt even more uncomfortable and regretted her decision to come. She was about to insist they retreat when a woman about Fanny's age, all in black, stepped through the curtains. "Can I help you?"

Before Stillman could babble, Fanny stepped forward, introduced herself and tried to explain her errand. She needed to contact a Mr. Gerald Doyle, but she had no address for the man and knew only that he was last seen by her informant at Mrs. Lake's house.

Mrs. Lake frowned. She had unnaturally black hair without any trace of the gray that threaded Fanny's dark hair. She also had a wide mouth that was red with rouge. "We have a lot of people who visit. They all value their privacy."

"I see," Fanny said. "But it's important that we contact Mr. Doyle because a friend needs his help very badly."

"Exactly who is this friend of Gerry Doyle's?"

"Edwin O'Connell. He and Mr. Doyle are veterans of the war. I believe they met while recuperating in a hospital."

"He's the boy with the burn scars on his face?"

She nodded.

"He was here with Gerry."

"Yes, that's right. Can you help us to get in touch with Mr. Doyle? I'm sure he'd want to help his friend."

Mrs. Lake thought about that for a minute. She seemed to remember Edwin. His face would be hard to forget. Maybe his injuries would provoke enough sympathy for the woman to help her.

Mrs. Lake opened the curtains with one hand and called out. "Mary, find Noreen and bring her to me right now."

They waited in silence. Fanny was grateful that Mrs. Lake didn't offer them further entry into the house. They understood each other. It would be to their mutual advantage for the visit to be as brief as possible.

There were footsteps on the stairs. A young woman in a flowered robe slumped down to them, looking like she had been roused from sleep. "You wanted me?"

Mrs. Lake succinctly explained what was needed.

Noreen said, "Gerry Doyle? I think he's at the soldier's home on Lewis Street, off Commercial. There's a lot of the men take a room there. Brightstone Manor, I think they call it. Fancy name for a boarding house. Is this about his friend with the scars on his face? Poor guy. I really felt for him." She moved a finger around in her mouth as if trying to remove something stuck in her teeth. "That reminds me. Gerry asked me to find out from Sherry whether Detective McKenna was here the night before the molasses flood. He's one of her regulars." She saw Mrs. Lake glowering at her and shrugged. "Well, that friend of Gerry's—the one with the scars, asked. Sherry said McKenna wasn't here that night." She turned away from the brothel owner and looked up at Fanny. "I heard that guy O'Connell got arrested for beating up a woman."

Mrs. Lake's mouth opened, and she frowned, then sent Noreen back upstairs. "We don't want any trouble here," she told Fanny. "Good day to you."

"Thank you," Fanny said to her retreating back, then she followed Stillman out the door. When they reached the street, she noticed a man turn quickly to walk toward Clark Street. She thought she recognized the bowler hat and remembered that Edwin had said Detective McKenna lived at the brothel. Had he turned away to avoid her?

Chapter Forty-Five

It was a short walk to the corner of Commercial and Lewis Streets. The façade of Brightstone Manor was made of crumbling gray stone. Some of the windowpanes in the four-story building were broken and replaced with sheets of wood. Fanny thought it was a disgrace compared to Wendell House. She felt sorry for the returning soldiers who had to make do with such accommodations.

Inside, Stillman convinced the clerk behind the desk to send someone for Gerry Doyle. He and Fanny were directed to a cold parlor with shabby furniture. A few men read papers or napped in corners. Near a cold fireplace, Stillman and Fanny found an uncomfortable sofa to sit on.

Gerry Doyle looked as if he'd just woken up. His hair was mussed, and the shirt under his open jacket was creased. Like many of the veterans, he was still wearing the sturdy uniform that had been issued to him in the service. He was a short man with a flourishing moustache that looked too big for his face.

Before Stillman could speak, Fanny jumped in to explain Edwin's situation and his theory that the soldier who was killed at Mrs. Lake's brothel might have been Maggie McKenna's lover.

"You mean Eddie Reynolds?" Gerry Doyle asked. When Fanny didn't answer, he went on. "The thing is, we didn't talk about it in front of the girls the other night because Maggie's husband lives at that brothel, and they might let something slip. But Eddie had been seeing Maggie McKenna for months. In fact, he was raising money to take her back to California with him. He's got family in San Francisco. You're not saying he's dead, are you?

198

Eddie? I haven't seen him around, but I thought he must have left town after Maggie died. Come to think of it. I hadn't seen him since before the molasses flood." He stopped talking and appeared to be stunned, looking off into the distance.

So, Edwin was right. Here, at last, was Maggie's soldier. Fanny let out a sigh. "Mr. Doyle, can you tell me who Eddie Reynolds was? How did you know him?"

He looked at her, dazed. "Eddie and me were in the same company in France. We were at Meuse-Argonne together last fall. I got shot up pretty bad, and I was in hospital with O'Connell. Eddie was lucky. He made it back without a scratch. We kept in touch, so when he landed here, we got together. I got him a room here at the Manor. He was working stable jobs where he could get them, with horses, you know. That's how he met Maggie. He worked at the stable over on the pier next to where that tank exploded. I heard they had to shoot a lot of the horses." He stopped for a moment. Fanny remembered the shots she had heard the day of the flood. Gerry Doyle was obviously picturing the bizarre event as well. He shook his head and continued. "I never heard him talk about the molasses flood, come to think of it. I would have expected to see him at one of the bars, telling stories about it, but I never did. Anyhow, I knew he was gone from here." He gestured to the room. "At first, I figured he'd moved in with Maggie. Then, when I heard she died in the flood, I figured he gave up and left for the West Coast." He stopped to think, and his brow furrowed.

"But, listen, that can't be him was killed at Mrs. Lake's. He never went there. He knew Maggie's husband moved in there, so he avoided it. It can't be him."

Fanny pictured the unclaimed body in Jake's morgue. She hadn't believed Edwin's story about that body being Maggie's lover, but now she wondered. If Gerry Doyle could identify Eddie Reynolds, that would prove Edwin O'Connell wasn't Maggie's lover. Maybe it would be enough to exonerate him, or at least disprove his motive for attacking Theresa.

"Mr. Doyle, can you come to the morgue on North Grove Street tomorrow to identify the soldier who was killed at the brothel?"

He cringed at the word. Men didn't know what to think of a lady like Fanny actually mentioning a brothel, but Fanny had no time for such delicacy. "Please, Mr. Doyle, you do want to know if it's your friend, don't you?"

"I can't believe it's Eddie. I'm telling you he'd never go to Mrs. Lake's. But, of course, I can come and look at the body."

Fanny hesitated. Remembering her promise to attend Rose Nichols's salon the next day, she asked Gerry to meet her at the morgue at seven in the evening. The salon should be done by then, and she hoped to get Jake to meet them before his awards dinner. She wasn't at all sure she could convince him, but she had to try. If Edwin could be cleared, she knew it would be a great relief to Jake no matter how stubborn he was in his belief that his assistant had attacked Theresa Ryan.

Chapter Forty-Six

Sunday, January 26, 1919

O n Sunday, Fanny attended church and then supervised dinner at Wendell House. She had no intention of hiring a replacement for Theresa. Whoever they chose to appoint as the resident manager could do as they wished, but Fanny was determined to keep the housekeeper position open for Theresa as long as she could. She would take on the housekeeping chores herself until she left at the end of the month.

Ever since the attack Thursday night, Theresa had not spoken, and Fanny feared she might never recover. Matt visited at least twice a day and reported on the dwindling hopes for the young woman. Against all odds, he was sure she would return to them. Fanny felt sorry for him. He'd lost so many comrades in the war, and then his family in Chicago. She thought he had a romantic interest in Theresa. To lose her, too, after all the other losses, must be terribly painful.

By four o'clock, Fanny was able to take the short walk to Rose Nichols's house on Mt. Vernon Street. She was greeted by a maid and sent upstairs.

Tea was served in the dining room, then carried into the parlor for the discussion. A dozen people balanced bone china cups and saucers. More than half the guests were men this time. Cornelia had told her how important it was to Bostonians to be invited to the Sunday Salon of Miss Rose Nichols. Already Fanny could sense this meeting would be very different from the strictly female sewing circle.

She found Cornelia in a corner and turned her back carefully when Mr. Wrentham entered. She saw him attach himself to Rose's elbow, joining her conversation with Senator Lodge. Wrentham and the senator had caused Fanny so much trouble that she hated having to endure their presence. She was tempted to get up and leave. But Cornelia smiled across at them serenely. Fanny gritted her teeth and hoped her friend was proved right. Cornelia was convinced Wrentham would get his comeuppance at this meeting.

Everyone was invited to sit down in the chairs arranged in a circle. Rose sat enthroned in her pink satin wing chair, looking around impatiently while her guests found seats. Once again, she reminded Fanny of a hawk, perched on a branch, ready to sweep down on unwary prey.

Wrentham made sure he got a seat beside Rose, beating out a plump older woman who looked mildly offended. All of his attention was on Rose, however, and he ignored the other woman. Fanny noticed a few raised eyebrows at the man's blatant rudeness.

Rose called them to order by welcoming them and going around the room, introducing each person. Police Superintendent Crowley and a North End alderman were present. When Rose introduced District Attorney Pelletier, Cornelia whispered to Fanny that he was the prosecutor for the grand jury to be convened about the molasses flood. Next, an MIT professor was introduced, and Fanny felt a nudge in her ribs from her friend. She thought Cornelia was anticipating a good fight, like someone in a crowd at a football stadium before the game began.

Other civic leaders were introduced, including a judge who Rose said was not involved in the actions to be discussed. The women in the room represented various influential clubs and philanthropies. When Rose's introductions got to Fanny and Cornelia, Wrentham and Senator Lodge both looked away. Cornelia smiled.

Rose announced the issue for discussion as if she were throwing out a ball for someone to bat. "This week, there will be an inquest into the cause of the molasses flood that devastated the city. What caused the tank—which contained over two million gallons of molasses—to burst, destroying property and killing or maiming so many bystanders? And what can be done to prevent such a disaster from happening again?"

Wrentham jumped to his feet. "Anarchists. This city is plagued by many dangerous anarchists who plan to wreak havoc and spread terror. It's time the local authorities cracked down on those foreign criminals."

"It's not necessary to stand, Mr. Wrentham," Rose told him. "We are quite able to hear you from your seat." Fanny suppressed a smile. Wrentham was certainly doing his best to make a bad impression on the Beacon Hill matrons. Of course, the men wouldn't be as offended by brash behavior.

Wrentham's face reddened, but he remained standing. He put a hand in his jacket to pull out a paper. "I want all of you to hear this." He flourished the document over his head. "These words were found on placards stuck to buildings along Commercial Street in January." He brought the paper to his face as if to read from it. His tone became more and more agitated as he quoted from the placards. "First they condemn what they call the 'senile fossils ruling the United States' for passing the deportation law to get rid of anarchists. Then they say, 'Deportation will not stop the storm from reaching these shores. The storm is within and very soon will leap and crush and annihilate you in blood and fire. You have shown no pity to us! We will do likewise. We will *dynamite* you.'"

Wrentham's dramatic reading was greeted by a stir among the people in the room. Fanny shifted uncomfortably in her seat. She thought the man was a charlatan, but she worried others would be won over to his side. Wasn't that always the way?

Satisfied, Wrentham waved the paper again. "It's signed 'The American Anarchists.' What could be more clear? Dynamite. That's what caused the tank explosion."

He sat down, looking like a cat who'd licked the bowl clean, and nodded to Senator Lodge. That stiff-backed politician agreed without leaving his seat. "We need to deport all of these undesirables immediately."

Fanny felt a burn in her stomach that threatened to rise through her throat to her face. Wrentham, who had betrayed his wife and lied about his visit to the dead Maggie, was once more deflecting guilt from himself onto others. He'd turned her words against her to get her dismissed, and now he was turning the words of the anarchists against them to accuse them of bombing the tank. He and the senator had the power to crush anyone who dared to question them.

"Superintendent Crowley," Rose said, calling on the policeman for a response.

Crowley was a fit-looking man with short-cut graying hair. He grasped his knees as he looked across at Wrentham and the senator. "It's true we found those placards, but we alerted Mr. Wrentham and other businessmen in the area. We're sure this is the work of followers of Mr. Galleani, who is under a deportation order. We recommended to Mr. Wrentham that he rehire the private security guards who'd watched the tank until recently."

"And did you do that, Mr. Wrentham?" Rose asked.

Wrentham's face flushed. This time he remained seated. "We hired guards during the war to prevent sabotage. The alcohol distilled from the molasses is used for munitions. Or it was, during the war. Since the war's end, demand has been greatly reduced, and the cost of private security is prohibitive based on current revenues. Besides, the police were aware of the threat. We had hoped that was sufficient."

The police superintendent rolled his eyes. Fanny felt a faint stirring of hope. At least not all the men in the room would give Wrentham a pass.

Rose took back the conversation. "Mr. Wrentham has claimed that the flood was due to a dynamite explosion. But it is my understanding that local officials blame the tank itself and charge that structural failure caused the flood. District Attorney Pelletier, can you speak to those arguments?"

Fanny was amazed at Rose's sangfroid. The Beacon Hill spinster was unmoved by the dramatic claims of the USIA manager. She obviously had a plan of attack, and the question to the police commissioner had been only a first sortie. Fanny glanced at her friend Cornelia and saw that she was not at all surprised by Rose's tactics. Fanny sat back, eager to watch what was coming next.

The district attorney was a heavy man wearing rimless glasses. "That is correct. The evidence we've gathered shows that the huge tank collapsed by reason of faulty construction and not because of an explosion."

Wrentham jumped to his feet. "Untrue! The tank was designed to specifications that are safe and approved by the local building department."

Pelletier rebutted. "Isn't it true that you arranged for the building department to classify the tank as a receptacle rather than a building and thereby avoided inspection? And, furthermore, you failed to fill the tank with water as a final test before the first load of molasses was piped into it back in 1915. And, when leaks were reported, you had the tank painted brown to conceal the flaws. Isn't that correct?"

Wrentham shook with rage. He hadn't anticipated these attacks. Fanny imagined his wife probably led him to expect a group of ladies he could impress, rather than a room full of very professional adversaries. She crossed her arms and hugged herself, hoping the attacks would continue to hit home.

"We have experts who are willing to testify that the tank was completely safe and that it was a dynamite explosion that caused the flood. And Mr. Pelletier himself warned of anarchist attacks less than a year ago." Wrentham sat down again.

Pelletier responded. "I advised businesses to be vigilant in guarding their assets. I suggest that your unwillingness to hire guards is another instance of your unwillingness to spend adequately for safety. In this case, it was not lack of guards that caused the failure, it was a lack of care in the design and construction of the tank. That is a crime, manslaughter through negligence."

Before Wrentham could get up to harangue them again, Rose called on another man. Fanny wanted to applaud her agility in the fight. "Professor, do you have anything to contribute concerning the safety of the tank? I understand you're doing a study?"

A balding man in a gray tweed suit nodded. "I've been retained by the Boston Elevated, who leased the land for the tank to USIA. They asked me to examine the specifications. Our report is not yet complete, but we are finding that the steel plates were of insufficient thickness for the amount of molasses that the tank was holding at the time of its collapse, and also, there were too few rivets to fasten the tank. In my opinion, the failure is entirely due to structural weakness."

"That's not true," Wrentham barked. "You know this city is a hotbed of anarchist activity. USIA has received threats. A bomb was found in our New Jersey factory. Senator Lodge, you know how dangerous these people are. You agree with me, don't you? By blaming the company, they're letting the anarchists get away with this destruction."

Fanny was infuriated that Wrentham always turned to the senator for reinforcements. She was disgusted. The suffragists were right. Women needed the vote to rid society of this male conspiracy to defend businessmen, no matter how questionable or even guilty their actions proved to be.

To Fanny's surprise, the distinguished senator kept his seat. He gave his flourishing mustache a light brush with his fingers before speaking. "It is essential that we rid ourselves of the anarchist and the communist. As I have said before, they seek to solve social problems, not by patient endeavor, but by brutal destruction. That's why I supported the Deportation Act in Congress."

"You see," Wrentham said, pointing at the senator.

Rose stared at the USIA manager as he sat back in his chair, satisfied by his rebuttal. "I don't believe any of us here support the anarchist movement," she said drily. "But we must condemn them for acts they have actually committed. It won't do to ascribe every act of destruction to them because they are guilty of some."

"But there's no reason, madam, to give them the benefit of the doubt," Senator Lodge said. "Rather, we should ascribe to them acts they have clearly threatened to do, thereby eliminating the threat of future attacks."

Wrentham clapped his hands in support. No one joined him. Fanny was fascinated. She'd heard Jake's claim that none of the dead had been injured by an explosion of the type Wrentham insisted had taken place. But she hadn't known there was so much evidence of faulty construction on the part of the company. Maggie could have known about the problems and confided in her sister. Fanny still believed Wrentham should be a suspect in Maggie's death.

As the discussion became more heated, Fanny said her goodbyes and hurried off. She was unexpectedly cheered by the discussion and hated to leave, but she was anxious not to miss her meeting at seven. Unable to reach

Jake by telephone earlier in the day, she'd sent a note requesting that he meet her and Gerry Doyle at the mortuary.

Chapter Forty-Seven

When Fanny reached the Hancock Street house, she was disappointed to find a note from Jake.

> *Fanny,*
>
> *I'm not able to meet you. As you know, I must speak at the awards dinner at the Union Boat Club tonight. In any case, the body of the unidentified soldier has been released for cremation and burial in Potters Field. You may visit tomorrow during working hours and, in the event it has not already been picked up for disposal, someone will assist you.*
>
> *Jake*

Fanny was shocked by the way he brushed off her request. She hadn't given him details in her note because she didn't want to get his hopes up that Edwin might be innocent. She wanted it to be a surprise when Doyle identified the dead man as Maggie's lover. She was not only disappointed, she was angry. She knew Jake was disappointed by her decision to leave the city, but this request had nothing to do with personal matters. If he was angry with her, he shouldn't refuse a request that could mean the difference between guilt or innocence for Edwin. But it was her own fault. She hadn't told him how important it was to identify the corpse. And now, if the body was destroyed, it would be impossible to identify him as Maggie's lover. She blamed herself for not making it clear that her request was urgent.

She worried that Doyle would be waiting for her at the mortuary and might leave if she didn't show up, but she needed to find Jake and convince him to help. Seeing Matt pass by the open door of her office, she called out to him and asked him to do her a favor. She explained that she needed to reach Dr. Magrath, but there was someone waiting for her, so she couldn't go herself.

"You want me to fetch Dr. Magrath from the Union Boat Club?"

"Yes, it's on the river. It wouldn't be far for him to come back to the mortuary, and it's very urgent. I need to have him let me in with a man who can identify a soldier's body that I hope is still there." She hesitated to explain that the information could clear Edwin of the accusation that he was Maggie's lover. She knew Matt was convinced Edwin was guilty. "I'll keep the witness as long as I can, but you *must* convince Dr. Magrath to come."

"Witness?"

Oh, dear, the lieutenant is demanding an explanation. "Matt, I know you feel strongly that Edwin O'Connell is responsible for the attacks on Mrs. Ryan and her sister. But that is based on the assumption that Edwin was Maggie McKenna's lover. I've found a man who knew Maggie's lover, and it wasn't Edwin. He says he was in the same company in the army and could identify the man. I think it's the unidentified body in the mortuary. But that body is scheduled for cremation and burial. I must get Mr. Doyle to identify the corpse before it's incinerated. Please. You want the truth as much as I do. I know you do."

Matt stood still, as if stunned. She could see he was struggling to understand the implications of what she'd said, but she believed he was fair enough to give up his prejudice against Edwin and help. "He was in the same company?" he asked.

"Yes. He can identify the man and, if it's who we think it is, he's the man who was seeing Maggie. Please, find Dr. Magrath and bring him to the mortuary."

Matt sighed. He looked down at the cane she'd given him and said, "Yes, of course, I'll do it for you."

She was grateful Matt felt obliged to help, even if he doubted Edwin's innocence, and still hated him because he believed he'd hurt Theresa. At least he could see beyond his beliefs enough to help.

Matt was gone before Fanny had rebuttoned her coat and slipped back into her boots for the walk down the hill to North Grove Street. At the door of the mortuary, she found Gerry Doyle waiting. "I'm so sorry for being late," she told him. "I was arranging for Matt Bradley to go get Dr. Magrath to let us in. I hope we're not too late and the body hasn't already been taken away."

Doyle seemed struck by the news that she'd sent Matt to the boat club. "*Lieutenant* Bradley?"

"Yes. Do you know him? He's from Chicago."

He frowned. "Lt. Matthew Bradley from the 305th?"

"Yes." Why did he sound so skeptical?

"There must be some mistake, Mrs. Lee. Eddie and me were in the 305th. We knew Lt. Bradley. But he's dead, ma'am. Horrible incident. Buried alive. But he saved another man, a private. When they got dug out, Lt. Bradley still had his dead arms around the private, and he was stiff as a board."

Chapter Forty-Eight

The noise in the boat club was overwhelming. Jake's head still felt heavy from his drinking bout on Friday. He knew he was getting older when it took more than a day to recover from a binge that would have been cured by a pick-me-up the next morning in his youth.

As he looked around the second-floor room full of men in formal evening clothes, he was disgusted with himself. This is what his life came down to. Days of dead bodies followed by nights of steak and champagne with self-congratulatory, cigar-smoking blowhards—himself included.

He was in a funk. He'd sent Fanny a rude note, but she deserved it. He couldn't bear to hear her defend the young man he had so misunderstood. He was furious with himself for the trust he'd put in Edwin O'Connell. At his age, Jake should know better. He'd been used all along, and Fanny, with her female sensibilities, continued to be fooled.

That was the worst thing. He'd made a fool of himself over Edwin and over Fanny. He cringed at the memory of how he'd tried to convince her to stay in Boston. It was undignified. At least all these rowing enthusiasts surrounding him had no idea of his weakness. They knew him as a former champion who doled out advice and hearty jokes to the younger men coming up. He knew he was even envied by men of his own generation for his carefree bachelor existence. This was his world, and he thrived in it, he told himself.

He was chewing the last of his prime rib while he rifled through the pages of his speech when one of the waiters tapped him on the shoulder to say someone was asking for him at the door. He frowned. His staff knew he was unavailable tonight, no matter the circumstances. He'd left contact information for a doctor at Massachusetts General Hospital who was covering for him.

Looking around, he saw that the dinner would not be done and cleared away for another half hour, so he tore off his napkin and threw it down on his chair as he left. Downstairs at the door, he recognized Lt. Bradley, Fanny's little chum, as he thought of him. The young man was leaning on the silver-topped cane that Jake knew Fanny had bought for him. She was easily swayed by the young men in uniform. She loved having them around her. Jake was skeptical that they would live up to her dreams for them. After all, Edwin had been a huge disappointment to Jake. He found Bradley a little *too* sincere, although he'd never said as much to Fanny. She'd have jumped to the defense of any of her young men who seemed to be surrogates for her own children sometimes. Unworthy surrogates, in Jake's opinion.

"Yes, what is it?"

Bradley glanced at the waiter behind Jake. "It's about Mrs. Lee," he said. "It's somewhat private."

Jake nodded over his shoulder at the waiter and stepped outside, pulling the door shut behind him. He hoped Fanny hadn't become hysterical at the tone of his note. But he shoved the thought away. Fanny was headstrong and argumentative, but she was never hysterical. There must be something really wrong.

"It's Mrs. Lee," Bradley said. He was terribly earnest. "She's been attacked. They've taken her to the hospital. I thought you should know."

Jake's heart lurched. *No. Fanny?* He pictured Theresa Ryan in her hospital bed, all bandaged up and unconscious. But Edwin was in custody…unless they'd let him go. It couldn't happen to Fanny. Was she right after all? Had someone else attacked Theresa, not Edwin? It would be just like Fanny to run out and confront someone she thought guilty. His throat contracted, and it was hard to breathe.

"I'll come. Let me just get my coat and tell them I'm leaving." Jake turned back to the door and felt a blow to his head that smashed his forehead into the hard wood of the door. *Fanny, what's going on?* He blacked out.

Chapter Forty-Nine

I t took some time for Fanny to comprehend what Gerry Doyle was telling her. He was adamant that Matthew Bradley was dead. When she tried to argue, it was Doyle who finally made her understand. He'd figured out who the Matt Bradley she knew must be.

"That's got to be Jimmy Grover," he said. "Jimmy was the man Lt. Bradley saved when the tunnel collapsed, don't you see? He was the lieutenant's valet. He was a private. He grew up on a dairy farm in Wisconsin. He was with the lieutenant, and that was what saved him. The lieutenant saved him, sacrificed himself. We all knew Lt. Bradley got bad news from home. Right before that battle, he got a letter. It said both his parents and his fiancée died of the flu. We thought perhaps he had nothing to go home to."

"But this Lt. Bradley didn't know about the flu deaths in Chicago," Fanny said. "I had to tell him. He was devastated."

He scratched his chin. "Well, if it's Jimmy Grover, he knew Bradley's parents were dead. He was there when the lieutenant read the letter. He told the rest of us." Doyle shook snow from his hat. "Don't you see? He knew there was no family. That's why he could pretend to be Bradley. What a lousy trick."

"This man is injured. His leg is crippled."

"Sure enough, that's Jimmy. His leg was badly broke in the tunnel collapse. Eddie would have known him. We was all close. If Eddie saw him, he never told me. Eddie did say he was coming into some money. To take his girl away. But he was cagey about where he was getting it from."

Brushing snow from his shoulders, Doyle said, "We all knew Lt. Bradley came from money. His dad owned a factory in Chicago. Eddie must have figured out what Jimmy was doing, pretending to be Bradley so he could get the family money. He must've thought he could get money from Jimmy to keep quiet and leave town. It's just the kind of thing he would do. He was a sneak, that Jimmy."

"No." Fanny stared at him in surprise

"Yes. Poor Eddie. Jimmy must have killed him instead of giving him money."

Doyle was very sure of himself and seemed to relish the idea of so much villainy. Fanny was shocked. "If your friend did recognize this Jimmy, would he have told Maggie McKenna?" she asked.

"Could be."

"And if she tried to get the money...." Fanny couldn't picture the Matt Bradley she knew doing any of this. But if he did.... "I sent him to get Dr. Magrath at the boat club. Oh, my goodness. He knows the body is due to be cremated."

"He'd know I'd see it was Eddie for sure. I'd see he was Jimmy Grover, too," Doyle insisted.

"Oh, I can't believe you're right, but if there's any chance...."

"He might attack this doctor, like he did Eddie," Doyle said.

"I have to find them. The boat club is very near." She started to walk away.

"I'll come with you, ma'am." He hurried after her. He was spoiling for a fight now.

They followed Cambridge Street to the riverside. There was a scrubby park with a few small trees and a walk that ran along the river. Streetlamps illuminated a steady fall of silent snowflakes. It was like looking at the world through lace curtains. Fanny brushed accumulating snow from the brim of her hat several times.

Soon they saw the solid stone building of the Union Boat Club with lanterns lighting the doorway. Windows on the second floor blazed with light. Fanny assumed that was where the awards dinner was taking place. They could even hear a roar of laughter. It made her doubt her errand for a moment. Surely nothing could be wrong.

When Fanny had almost reached the doorway in the side of the building, something caught her right ankle, and she stumbled. Doyle put out an arm to steady her. Looking down, she saw a cane. She reached for it. It was the one she'd given to Matt and, as she held the silver wolf's head up to the light, she saw it was coated with something dark and sticky.

"Oh, no." She looked down. Drag marks on the gravel path led around the corner of the building to the riverside, where a long dock extended into the water. In the lamplight, she could see drag marks through the layer of snow on the dock. At the far end, she saw a black shape hunkered down. What was he doing? Where was Jake? "Stop!" she yelled.

The figure rose, then bent down again, and she heard a cracking sound and a splash. The black figure ducked and ran down the dock, jumping off at the shore.

"No. Help! Mr. Doyle, get help from the boat club."

Doyle tried to stop her, but she pulled away and ran to the shore. "Get help!" she yelled over her shoulder.

She couldn't see where the black figure had run, but she was much more worried about the cracking sound. Had something crashed through the thin layer of ice? "Jake, are you there?"

Should she run up the dock to the hole? But she'd never be able to pull a man out from there. She looked over her shoulder. She saw light from the boat club doorway, but she didn't see figures yet. "Jake!" No answer. "Help! Help!"

Was Jake in the river? How long would he last before he drowned, if it was him? She knew it was him. Every instinct in her body tingled with certainty. She couldn't stand here and let him drown.

"Jake." Fanny ran down the dock, all the while cursing herself for a fool, but she couldn't chance being right and not doing something. By the light of the lamps on the walk, she saw a dark hole at the end. Taking a breath, she jumped into the water. The shock of icy cold cut through her clothes, taking her breath away. Her skirts became leaden, but she fought to keep her head above water. She tried to imagine she was just testing the cold water of the lake in New Hampshire in the spring. *Come on, Fanny. It's just a little chilly.*

"Jake." Her foot stubbed against him. She plunged her arms into the cold, searching for his head and crying out with the pain of it. She grabbed onto his lapels and pulled him up with all her might, twisting to try to support his head against the dock.

Footsteps pounded, and men shouted. When Jake was pulled from her grasp, other hands clutched her arms and pulled her onto the dock, where she collapsed. Men parted to let through a man in evening clothes. He positioned Jake and, with help of the others, he began moving Jake's arms and pounding on his chest. Someone threw an overcoat around Fanny's shoulders. Watching through bleary eyes, Fanny thought at least these rowers knew what to do when someone was drowning.

She held her breath as she shivered with the cold. Peering between the men, it looked like Jake remained lifeless. She felt a wail surging up in her. Before she let it out, she heard coughing, followed by someone pounding on Jake's back. She heard him vomit out water before he sat up and uttered a swear word. She'd never been so happy to hear Jake's voice, gravelly as it might be, and she collapsed in tears.

Bells rang, and lights flashed on the shore. Police and ambulance had arrived. As Jake was bundled away, the doctor turned to examine Fanny. He had her carried to shore. She felt helpless in the cradle of arms that roughly brought her to a motorcar and shoved her into the back. The doctor crawled in the other door and did a quick examination, proclaiming her fit enough but in need of dry clothes immediately.

"Jake. Dr. Magrath," she wheezed. Her chest was tight.

"He's been taken to the hospital. He's a tough old bird. He'll be all right, I promise. I'm surprised he's not still doing his daily swim even in this weather," the doctor said, giving Fanny a handkerchief for her tears.

At her insistence, they took her to the Hancock Street house rather than the hospital. The doctor conceded that she'd probably be better off in her own home, and he called for a hot bath as they carried her in. They woke some housemaids from the other building, and the doctor remained to see her tucked into bed with a hot toddy.

He reassured her that Jake was going to be fine just before she dropped off to sleep in her warm, dry bed.

Chapter Fifty

Monday, January 27, 1919

anny woke to a sharp line of sunshine on the floor, coming from where the thick curtains didn't meet. She shivered for a minute, then fell back into the warmth of the bed. The shiver brought back the scenes from the night before. She sat up, remembering with dread. Before she could get up, the door opened. Stillman and a maid hurried in.

"You're not to get up," the young officer said. "But if you're awake, we can open the drapes." He nodded to the girl, who let in a flood of sunshine that caused Fanny to squeeze her eyes shut.

"Cook saved you some breakfast," the maid said. "I'll just get it for you." She hurried away.

"What time?" Fanny croaked.

"Ten o'clock, barely a decent hour," Stillman said. "The doctor who brought you home last night said you're not to be hurrying about. He told us what happened—as much as he knew—over a whiskey. You've had an adventure."

"Dr. Magrath?"

"He's doing fine. I called the hospital. He even ordered a breakfast of steak and eggs." Stillman pulled up a chair and sat down.

"What about Matt Bradley?" she asked. "Did he come back here?"

Stillman crossed his legs. "That's just what Detective McKenna asked. He came last night, but the doctor turned him away, wouldn't let him disturb you. We told him that Matt had been here and was gone. He rushed in, packed up, and left. Wouldn't say where he was going. When I asked what was going on, he glared bloody murder at me and left. I've no idea where he went. We still don't know what's going on."

Fanny stared at him. The man had no idea about Matt Bradley and Jimmy Grover. With some hesitation, she told Stillman about the false identity and how the man they knew as Matthew Bradley, had attacked Dr. Magrath.

Stillman's eyes opened wide. "Oh goodness. I did wonder sometimes. He seemed not to know some of the things you'd expect any officer to know. That's one reason the others avoided him. I didn't care, but some of them are quite the military snobs."

Fanny opened her mouth. The other officers had doubts about Matt? Why hadn't she noticed? She'd confided in him. It must have seemed to the others that he was teacher's pet. How could she be so blind? She was disgusted with herself. She'd not only let herself be taken in by him, she'd led him to his victims. He'd known about Theresa and the Italian workmen because of her.

The cane. She remembered how the cane with the bloody wolf's head had snagged her ankle. The thought snapped something in her brain. That's what Theresa must have remembered, too. The miniature of the bathroom had helped her to remember how she tripped over a cane. The cane Matt Bradley had lost before the molasses flood. And he'd been standing there when she mentioned it. It must have been later that Theresa realized the significance.

Detective McKenna had been right after all. Or half right. Matt (she couldn't think of him as Jimmy) had killed Maggie McKenna, but he hadn't been her lover. Her lover, Eddie, had recognized that he was *pretending* to be Lt. Bradley. Eddie had needed money to get to California with Maggie. Perhaps he'd met the fake Bradley expecting to get money and got knocked on the head instead. Maggie must have known about the meeting, and somehow Bradley had arranged to meet with her and killed her to keep her quiet. He tried to make it look like she died in an accident, falling into the tub after drinking. But the molasses flood destroyed the scene, and Theresa never believed it was an accident.

All for the money the real Matthew Bradley would inherit. Jimmy Grover knew Bradley's parents were dead. He never had any intention of returning to Chicago, where he might have been exposed as an impostor. He'd pretended ignorance of the deaths in Chicago, and she'd believed him. All the people he had harmed, and he'd almost gotten away with it. Maybe he thought he could still get away with it.

"Lt. Stillman, please get me my dressing gown from the wardrobe." Fanny sat sideways, putting her feet on the floor.

"But the doctor said you're to stay in bed."

"Lt. Stillman, please," she commanded.

He recognized the voice of authority and quickly found the plaid wool dressing gown and helped her into it.

"I must get to the telephone in the office." Stillman followed her downstairs, where she sat herself behind her desk and argued with the exchange operators until she had her brother on the line. He told her that Matt Bradley had wired him that morning, saying he had a desperate need for access to the estate. George was in the process of transferring funds for him.

With a great deal of difficulty, Fanny managed to convince George that there were serious questions about the man's identity. She had to describe how Jake had been attacked and promise she would get Jake to confirm everything she said, before her brother would agree to postpone any action on the estate. She slammed the phone down, mouthing one of Jake's swear words to the consternation of a surprised Lt. Stillman.

"I'm going back upstairs to dress," she told him in a tone to make him think twice about arguing. "And then I'm going to see Dr. Magrath and Detective McKenna."

Chapter Fifty-One

When Fanny came down the stairs, Stillman was waiting at the bottom. She could hear the men gathering in the dining room for their midday meal.

"Mrs. Lee, there's a Mrs. Thornwell on the telephone in your office. She wants to speak to you urgently."

Fanny was anxious to visit Jake, but she didn't want to worry Cornelia. "I'll see to it. Why don't you go in and have your dinner. You can take me to the hospital after you've eaten." She hurried into the office.

As she reached for the telephone receiver, Fanny's eyes fell on the heap of splinters that had been the miniature of Maggie McKenna's bathroom. Destroyed now, it had served its purpose. Theresa had remembered the cane and realized the man she knew as Lt. Bradley was with her sister when she died. Fanny shivered at the violence exhibited in the broken pieces of the little room, and something sticking out from under the desk. Stooping, she pulled out a baseball bat. Holding it away from herself, she was horrified to see rusty stains of blood. It was left from when Edwin was beaten. No one had cleaned the room in her absence, and she'd never finished tidying it. She quickly shoved the stained bat into a corner behind the desk. If only she could forget as easily. As she picked up the phone, she shivered. "Cornelia?"

"Fanny, I have good news. The board called a special meeting. They've expelled Senator Lodge, and they want to ask you to remain at Wendell House as resident manager."

Fanny lowered herself into the chair. "They want me to stay?"

"Yes. Most of them were present for the discussion at Rose's Sunday salon, and they're disgusted by Mr. Wrentham's refusal to take responsibility for the molasses flood. They're outraged by the senator's support for the man and his company. Since he was the one who demanded your dismissal, the board reversed that decision. Furthermore, they've started a relief committee. We're contacting all our male relatives who are attorneys and urging them to represent people injured by the molasses flood in suits against USIA. They won't get away with such negligence!"

Fanny wondered at the change in attitude. She knew Senator Lodge had objected to her demand that the police investigate Wrentham for the murder of Maggie McKenna. And now she knew that the Matthew Bradley imposter was guilty of the crime. She explained her misgivings haltingly to her friend.

"My goodness. You mean that nice young man we got out of jail really killed that woman? How astonishing. But no matter. The board members are furious with Mr. Wrentham and his company and furious with the senator for supporting them. So, they want your reinstatement to be a slap in the face for Wrentham and Lodge. Mr. Wrentham may not be responsible for Mrs. McKenna's death, but he's responsible for many more injuries and deaths. Just know that we want you to continue as resident manager until July, which is when we've always expected to complete the work. Can you agree to that?"

"Yes, of course."

"Fine. I'll tell them. Now you just take care of yourself and rest after your adventures. There'll be a lot more to do to make sure USIA pays for their negligence."

As she hung up, Fanny heard a click of the door closing. Jimmy Grover—the imposter, the man she'd known as Matthew Bradley—stood before her, leaning against the door. Her mouth and throat went dry, and she felt an icy flow down her spine. Goosebumps rose on her arms.

"Mrs. Lee, you must help me. Your brother refuses to send me the money from my parents' estate. I need that money!" He loomed tall above her as she sat frozen in her seat. He still wore the khaki lieutenant's uniform and boots. In one hand, he clutched a thick tree branch. It was a makeshift cane. Fanny remembered the blood-stained head of the wolf cane she'd found by the boat club. She'd given that cane to him, and he'd used it to attack Jake. Her breath came fast. What was he doing here?

He stood with a bewildered expression on his face, chewing on his lower lip. "Mrs. Lee, why is your brother delaying my money?"

Fanny was dumbstruck. Didn't he realize that she knew his real identity?

"I've got some distant relatives in San Diego, and I want to go and find them. You can see why I'd want to do that, can't you? I'm too upset to go back to Chicago now. Will you contact your brother and get him to release the funds? Please?" His eyes went to the smashed box, and they widened. He seemed surprised, as if he'd forgotten that he was the one who'd smashed it. He swallowed. "How is Mrs. Ryan?"

Fanny pictured the poor young woman all bandaged up in her hospital room, and she was afraid. Matt had kept visiting Theresa, not in hopes of her recovery but to ensure she never woke up. "Mrs. Ryan is still very sick," she told him, her voice quavering. He cringed. She was very aware that he stood between her and the door. Should she lie to him and tell him she'd get her brother to wire the money? Even if she did, would he believe her? He was still pretending to be Lt. Bradley, and she was pretending to believe him, but how long could that last? The air tingled with apprehension on both sides as the pretense between them became a thin shell of ice that would crack with the least pressure.

He stepped toward the desk and reached for the telephone. "You can telephone him in Chicago, can't you?"

Fanny stood, shoving her chair back with her knees. She could hear muffled sounds from the dining room. If she screamed, how long would it take them to come? Would they even hear her? The walls were thick.

He watched her and took another menacing step to come behind the desk. "You already talked to your brother, didn't you?" He looked hurt. "How could you betray me like that?"

Fanny stepped behind the chair to keep it between them. She was trapped. One end of the desk was flush with the wall, so she had only the corner of the room behind her. She glanced at the window to her left, but it was high and small. "You can't claim the money. You're not Matthew Bradley," she said, just trying to keep him talking. "You're Jimmy Grover." She knew Jake would be furious at her for confronting a killer, but Grover wasn't just a killer. He was one of *her* soldiers, and somehow, she'd failed him. He'd felt something for Theresa, she knew it, and he had felt something for her. But he had hidden his needs and plans from them, and when he faced exposure, he'd panicked. "You're Jimmy Grover. Lt. Matthew Bradley gave his life trying to save you. You pretended to be him, but it's over now. We know. You have to stop now and give yourself up."

His eyes widened, and he stared at her without blinking. "You don't understand. That money is mine. I *am* Bradley. When we were there in the dark, eating mud, hearing sounds of rifles and bombs for hours and hours, he gave me his life. He gave me everything. I'm Bradley now, don't you see?"

He was mad. She could see it now, too late. He was in a frenzy. Anyone who got in his way had to be eliminated. His face suffused with red, he leaned a hand on the desk and gripped his makeshift cane. She was in his way, like Eddie, Maggie, Theresa, the Italian...

She screamed, wailing it out, and saw the tree branch raised above her as he shoved the chair aside to get at her. She hunched over and felt a weight bang into her left shoulder. She screamed again as he raised the branch above his head. This stroke would crush her. The fingers of her right hand closed around the wood of the bat she'd propped against the wall. She rose up in a fit of rage and swung the bat at his body. She heard a hollow sound as the wood connected with his head. He had stooped to reach her, and the blow landed on his temple.

Unblinking, he fell backwards to the floor, then his arms and legs scrabbled against the wood in a seizure. She clutched the bat, trying to back up into the corner behind her as his body jerked.

Stillman burst through the door, followed by other men. In the confusion, she lowered the bat to the desk and drooped against the wall. Before she could collapse, they pulled Grover's body out of the way, and Stillman supported her to the chair. "I think you killed him," Stillman said in awe.

Fanny dropped her head on the desk in a flood of tears.

224

Chapter Fifty-Two

J ake Magrath pounded a fist on the bedside table of the room in Massachusetts General Hospital where he found himself that Monday afternoon. He had a knife-like pain in his head, and he could feel the pull of a bandage up there. He was sore all over, but he'd finished a plate of steak and eggs. It annoyed him that his hand shook when he raised the mug of coffee for a sip.

"Will someone tell me what the hell is going on here?" he demanded.

Frowning at him, a nurse tutted, "All right, all right. Please calm down." She then stepped aside and waved Detective McKenna into the room.

Jake was irked that she treated him like a child. He was used to ordering nurses and doctors around, not following their directives. The helplessness of lying in the bed infuriated him.

"McKenna. Good. Tell me what happened last night. What did that Lt. Bradley do? Why did he attack me? Did you get him? Is Fanny all right? Mrs. Lee? Bradley told me she'd been attacked. I was going to get my coat, and suddenly I was knocked out. I woke up, barely, in that freezing cold water, then went out again. Woke to Tommy Everett standing over me and hitting me on the back."

McKenna pulled up a chair and sat down heavily. Jake could see he must have been up all night. "I'm trying to find out," the detective said. He pulled off his bowler hat and ran a hand through his graying hair. "These doctors won't let me talk to anyone, and nobody I can talk to tells me anything worth knowing. They say you were in the water down at the river, and Mrs. Lee jumped in to save you."

"Fanny! Is she hurt?" Jake's heart pounded like a stone hammer on an iron anvil.

"She's fine. She's resting at home. You say Bradley attacked you? Why? I thought all you folks were so sure he was a fine gentleman from Chicago, and I was told to keep my mitts off him. He was gone by the time I got there last night."

The blood rose to Jake's scalp. They'd let the man get away. He was about to explode when the door was pushed open hesitantly. He let out a breath. Fanny stood in the doorway. "Fanny, are you all right?" A bruise was starting to appear on the side of her face, and she moved stiffly as she shuffled into the room. It alarmed him. He hated that he was confined to the bed, but trying to get up would just make him look ridiculous.

Fanny's anxious face fell into a smile when she heard his voice. He could tell she was even slightly amused to find him in such a helpless condition. Irritated, he looked at McKenna. "Get up, man. Give her a seat. What's the matter with you?"

McKenna rose awkwardly and moved to the other side of the bed. "They wouldn't let me see you," he said to Fanny. "They said you needed rest."

She looked quite pale to Jake. He realized he himself was probably white and drawn looking, and he hated the thought. Good thing there was no mirror. "Fanny, did you really jump in the river to save me?"

Her gaze warmed him as she looked him up and down, checking to make sure he was really all right. He felt a twinge of delight at the thought that she cared. But he was aware of McKenna at his shoulder and looked over at him. Fanny followed his glance and let out a breath as if she'd been holding it until she knew he was alive and well.

"Matt Bradley isn't really Matt Bradley," she said, then proceeded to tell them how she'd talked to Edwin, then found Gerry Doyle, and how Gerry had known the real Bradley was killed in France. The Lt. Bradley they knew was an imposter.

"Jimmy Grover?" Jake repeated.

"Yes, and I sent him to find you." He could see she regretted her action bitterly. She blamed herself that he'd been attacked.

McKenna stood by with his mouth partly open, turning his hat in his hand as she explained how it all fell into place when Doyle told her Maggie's lover would have recognized Grover and blackmailed him. "When her lover disappeared, Maggie tried to find out what happened, and Grover killed her," Fanny said.

"And Theresa Ryan realized it was him because she remembered tripping over a cane?" Jake asked. "I want to see this miniature room you made." Fanny had mentioned that the miniature had triggered Theresa's memory.

"Bradley...no, Grover destroyed it," she said.

"What about Luigi Spinelli?" Jake asked.

"Remember Luigi said he saw a soldier outside when he and Tony left Maggie that night?"

"It was this Grover pretending to be the Bradley guy?"

"Right. I think when Luigi came to Wendell House, he wasn't there to see Theresa. He was looking for Bradley to get money from him. Luigi made an appointment with him for later, and Bradley pushed him off the roof."

Jake burned when he thought of how the imposter had followed around at Fanny's heels. All the time, Grover had simply been looking to protect himself. He could have killed her. "McKenna, what're you doing here? Get out there and find this man before he tries to kill someone else. Didn't this Doyle fellow tell you all this?"

Before Fanny could speak, McKenna growled. "How was I to know? You all kept telling me to lay off that Bradley guy in no uncertain terms. Now all of a sudden, some ex-soldier says he's someone else, and we're supposed to believe him?" When Jake turned toward him, livid with rage, McKenna put on his hat. "We'll find him, we'll find him," he said.

"You'd damn well better," Jake yelled after him.

"Wait!" Fanny said. "He's here...in the hospital."

Jake gawked at her. He could see that McKenna was getting even more angry. Fanny looked at Jake and swallowed. There was something she didn't want to tell him. "What happened?"

Shivering, she described how the imposter had appeared in her office and attacked her. She hurried to assure him she was all right, sore, but whole.

He felt enraged.

"Did you kill him?"

"Oh, I hope not," she said. "Jake, it was awful. He was unconscious when they brought us here. He's in the emergency room now."

McKenna had been standing with his mouth open. Jake glared at him, and the detective rushed out, slamming the door behind him.

Fanny cringed at the noise. She collapsed back into her chair as silence descended.

"Did you really jump in the river after me?" Jake asked.

She looked down at her hands. "I was afraid help wouldn't come in time." She looked up at him with a quizzical expression. "I couldn't let you drown. Not after finding you again after all these years."

An electric thrill swept down Jake's body. *Fanny.* He laughed. "Not so easy to get rid of me." He dropped back against the pillow and closed his eyes for a moment. How strange. He should be a young man again in his twenties. And she should be young and unmarried, without children, for these feelings to rise between them. How foolish he felt.

He saw that his silence alarmed her. She bent forward and put out a gloved hand to his forearm. "Jake, are you all right? Should I get the doctor?"

He opened his eyes. "Oh, I'm just dandy. Fanny, what will you do now? Will you still move to New Hampshire?"

"No. They've asked me to stay on." She told him how the board had reversed her dismissal. Jake felt a glow of warmth sweep over him. She would stay. "Until July anyway. By then, they plan to have sent all the men to their homes. I'll move to New Hampshire then."

He let out a breath, then closed his eyes and grimaced with an unexpected pain.

Fanny pulled her hand away. "I think I'll have to." She'd told him about her financial problems. He knew he shouldn't be surprised. She seemed restrained, but then she relaxed. "You'll have to come visit. Like old times. You'll like it up in the mountains. You can get away from the city." There was a glisten of tears in her eyes, but she wasn't sad.

Of course, why not. Up in the White Mountains, away from prying eyes, away from all her relations. They could be as they were as youngsters, speaking without boundaries. Close as they wanted to be.

And maybe there was something else they could work on together. He understood that she needed a purpose to harness her restless energy. He didn't think it would be enough for her to disappear into the White Mountains to buy and sell antiques. She longed to learn and to collaborate in some task she considered useful to society. Why not work with him? He'd been thinking about it for a little while now.

"Tell me about this miniature room," he said. He watched her closely as she described how she and Theresa had worked to remember all the details of the room where Maggie had died. At first, she was humble about it, talking down the significance but, as she went on, she got more confident. Jake frowned with thought as she talked, and, eventually, she stopped. It was obvious that she worried he found her description irrelevant. That wasn't it at all.

"You have an eye for detail that I wish some of these fat-headed cops like McKenna would develop. You don't know how many times I've seen it. They walk into the scene of a crime and trample all over everything, never even seeing what's around them. I'm thinking...."

"Yes?" Fanny looked mystified.

"I think if you had a miniature scene like that, you could use it to train some of these police investigators to pay attention to the surroundings. Make them really look at the place. Only it would be so small they couldn't mess it up by trampling around." Jake's mind whirred with possibilities. "You've no idea the number of times I get to a place, and there are all sorts of clues, and these guys ignore them and jump to conclusions based on wrong assumptions. We've got to train these investigators to act like scientists, to find the truth by observing every detail and writing it down. Yes, I can see it."

"What?"

Jake glowed with enthusiasm now, and he saw her looking at him with a smile. She actually liked his brash excitement. He knew that aspect of his personality rubbed a lot of people the wrong way. But not Fanny. She enjoyed it; he could tell. "Think about it. A whole series of rooms with a whole series of clues that the police detectives would have to look at and describe what they see. Oh, yes. I can see it."

"You mean you could use miniatures to teach them?"

"I'd have to convince the authorities it's a valid course of study. Legal medicine, that's what they call it in Europe, but those stooges over in Cambridge will look down their blue-blooded noses at it, I suppose."

"At Harvard?" she asked.

"My alma mater isn't always known for its forward thinking."

"You can convince them," she said.

"And you can make the miniatures."

"Hmm." She paused, looking into space. He regretted springing his idea on her. He was too bold. It was always his major fault, and he'd done it again.

Finally, she relaxed and grinned at him with a spark in her eye. "I think I'd have to see a few of these scenes of crimes," she said. "And I'd have to see more of the various types of unnatural deaths that require investigation."

Jake looked at her. She really was lighting up at the prospect. He choked on a guffaw as he thought, *Well, it's not these old bones of mine she's lusting after. It's the bodies on my autopsy table.* That's what she wanted. She'd gotten a taste of the hunt, and she was going to be straining at the leash to track down more murderers. What would her father and brother think of that? What did he care? He didn't.

Epilogue

September 1948

Private dining room at the Ritz Carlton Hotel, Boston

"Captain Lee, the table is ready for your inspection."

Fanny followed the maître d' into the private room. Her beaded evening gown hung heavily as she moved. She wanted to make the closing dinner of the seminar a formal occasion. The long table was set for two dozen. She reached out a gloved hand to turn one of the gilt-edged serving plates, so the center design was perpendicular. She'd purchased the set the first year of these dinners and the hotel kept them for her private use.

"The centerpieces are quite nice," she told the maître d'. At the Ritz, they knew how particular she was about the flower arrangements. She'd been known to send them back at the last minute. Fanny bent her head to smell the orchid corsage pinned to her breast. Her "boys" had sent them to her room. It was a nice touch from the current crop.

She was very particular about every detail of the dinner, but the hotel staff were used to her by now. She'd stayed there off and on, ever since the Ritz Carlton opened in 1927. It was the year that had changed her life.

In the years before 1927, she'd lived at the family home in New Hampshire with her daughter Frances. They'd run an antique store in the old schoolhouse. But Fanny had spent as much time as she could in Boston, learning about unexplained deaths by following Jake Magrath to death

231

scenes, watching him perform autopsies, and working with him in the laboratory. She'd had to stay in cheap rooms or as a guest of friends in those days, but she'd learned so much.

A few times she had stayed with Theresa and Edwin O'Connell. Her housekeeper had recovered from the awful attack and found the disfigured ex-soldier at her bedside. With the help of Fanny and Jack, the humble assistant had finally admitted his passion, and Theresa had found she could love him. With Jake's help, Edwin had completed his medical studies while he continued to work in the mortuary. He finally became a medical examiner himself and was well able to support a growing family.

Jake had spent time with Fanny and her daughter in New Hampshire. Golden summer days hiking or swimming. Chill snow-buried days when the smell of wood fire filled the house.

Then, in 1926, her Uncle George died, and suddenly everything changed. Her father's partner, he had no children of his own, and he left his fortune to Fanny. No more struggles to keep within a monthly allowance. No cheap boarding houses. After that, she stayed at the Ritz for a week or a month at a time, six or seven times a year.

Fanny picked up a menu card. Eight courses were listed in flowing script. Broiled filet mignon with bordelaise sauce was the entrée. She nodded approval. Her "boys" deserved a very good meal at the end of their seminar week. The second year of the annual training sessions, she'd varied the menu by choosing turkey. But she overheard men from the first group telling men from the second year that they'd been "gypped." Now she always ordered beef.

The wine steward waited by a separate table to show her the wines that would be served. She had only one instruction. "Shut off anyone who talks in a loud voice." At the first dinner, a state police sergeant from Vermont had to be carried home when he finally passed out. Fanny wouldn't put up with that kind of exhibition again.

When she looked up, she saw a man of about sixty wearing square wire-rimmed glasses coming toward her with a big smile on his face. She'd invited the popular author, Erle Stanley Gardner, to attend this year's Seminar on

Homicide Investigation. He was the only non-law enforcement person ever invited. Fanny knew his series of mystery novels about a lawyer called Perry Mason was hugely popular. She also knew he'd been a practicing criminal lawyer before his success as an author. If she could get him to advocate for medical examiners instead of coroners across the country, he would be helpful. She was a little surprised by the cowboy hat and boots he wore, but he had behaved well enough in the classes.

"Mrs. Lee, I don't know how to thank you for letting me attend this seminar. It's been a real eye-opener for me," he said.

A tall thin man in a state trooper's uniform joined them. "It's Captain Lee to you, Gardner. She's a captain in the New Hampshire State Police," he said.

"Are you? That's amazing," Gardner said.

"I've worked with the New Hampshire State Police for a long time now," she admitted. "I'm honored to be given the recognition."

"Nonsense," said the New Hampshire man. "She singlehandedly brought our investigations into the twentieth century with scientific equipment and training." He waved to another man across the room and left them.

"How did you enjoy the Seminar in Homicide Investigations, Mr. Gardner?" Fanny asked.

"It was beyond anything I'd imagined."

"I saw you had 'The Barn' and 'The Dark Bathroom.' How did you do?" Fanny kept track of which participants were assigned which miniature rooms during the seminar.

Gardner's face reddened. "It was quite an experience having to explain my theories to the whole group. Quite a test."

Fanny could see he was less than satisfied with his performance. The investigators were given a sheet of factual information about each scene and basic witness statements to help them extrapolate from the miniature room and discuss what should happen next in an investigation. She enjoyed listening to the discussions. Critiques by other members of the seminar could be brutal, and Gardner had suffered some sharp criticisms. "You understand that you're not expected to 'solve' the crime, don't you? The exercise is meant to test and sharpen powers of observation and identify important clues, to train you to notice and remember."

"So, I learned—the hard way for 'The Dark Bathroom.' I'm afraid, as a writer, I tend to gather the details quickly and make a story to fit them. Too quickly, as it turns out."

Fanny shook her head. "You jumped to conclusions. That's exactly what we want to teach you not to do. You need to keep an open mind, gather facts, approach the scene without prejudice."

He grinned. "I had a very pretty story all worked out when I saw the doll in the bathtub and the liquor bottle. I assumed she was partly crippled because of the cane on the floor. So, I figured she'd been drinking, stumbled, hit her head, and drowned as the water filled while she was unconscious." Police detectives in the audience had quizzed him on the witness statements about men who'd been with her, the lack of any evidence she'd been lame herself, the bruise on her forehead indicating an attack, and the other signs that someone had held her down when she died. They'd poked so many holes in his theory that it had blown away in the wind.

"Bad assumptions lead to faulty investigations," she scolded him. She thought that Jake would have been proud of the way the policemen had rejected Gardner's prejudices. It was exactly what he'd wanted to teach them.

The real story behind 'The Dark Bathroom' was beside the point of the exercise. Only Fanny knew the room had been destroyed by the molasses flood, and only Fanny knew the convoluted motives of the madman who killed Maggie McKenna all those years ago.

"The details in the miniatures are just fantastic," Gardner said. "They must have taken an awful lot of work. How did you do it?"

Someone always asked. "I had the opportunity to work closely with Dr. George Magrath, who was medical examiner of Suffolk County in the twenties and thirties."

"He was the first Chair of Harvard's Department of Legal Medicine when you endowed it, right?"

"That's correct. Dr. Magrath was the Chair from 1931 until he retired. I was able to learn a great deal from him about legal medicine. He passed away in 1938. It wasn't till after the war that we began the annual seminars, but he would have approved. He believed policemen, as well as medical practitioners, needed to be aware of the varying conditions that could contribute to unexplained deaths. He wanted to give these men the tools to explain what happened accurately."

After Jake's death, she'd retreated to her home in New Hampshire. In the years just before his passing, she'd lost her brother, her parents, and even her daughter and companion, Frances, who'd died at the age of thirty-two. Then the darkness of the wars in Europe and the Pacific had descended. It was a difficult time.

As she got older, she found the world slipping away faster and faster. Memories became a blur that rushed past like a stream. Only some moments stood out like stubborn rocks against the flood. She'd wanted to capture those days of investigation with Jake—days when she had felt most alive and full of purpose. She found creation of the crime scene miniatures, detail by tiny detail, fixed those times so they couldn't be washed away as so much else was washed away. She hired a skilled carpenter to help build the scenes and furniture. She sewed clothes and created tiny utensils by herself, even knitting stockings for Maggie's legs using tiny needles. She needed to capture what she'd learned from Jake so it couldn't be lost in time.

Fanny pulled her attention back to the author in front of her. He was probably ten years younger than her. She wondered if he felt the flood of time rushing by as much as she did. If he didn't feel it at sixty, he would by seventy. Pointless to warn him.

"I'm not going to have any of your graduates appearing in my books," Gardner said, gesturing to the men filing into the room. Most carried drinks from a bar set up in the corner. They wore uniforms or their best Sunday suits for the occasion. Fanny thought Jake would have teased her about her love of surrounding herself with attentive men in uniforms.

Gardner continued, "Police detectives like these would not only solve the crime as soon as a Perry Mason, but they just might do so a hundred pages before my plot."

Fanny smiled. "It's our hope that the graduates will be able to use the skills they learned here in real investigations."

"They will. No doubt about it. I have one question, though, before we sit down." Men were beginning to find their place cards around the table. "Why are the miniature scenes referred to as 'nutshells'?"

"They're named 'Nutshell Studies of Unexplained Death' after an old police expression about the goal of investigations which is to "convict the guilty, clear the innocent, and find the truth in a nutshell," she told him. "Come along." She took his arm. "Let's sit down. I would like to start with a toast to my old friend and mentor, Jake Magrath."

Afterword

This book is fiction. For a wonderful historical account of the Great Molasses Flood, you should read Stephen Puleo's *Dark Tide*. It's a fascinating book that reads like a novel in many places because Puleo found and read through the testimony of people in the civil trial. After the USIA Company was not convicted of any criminal violations, they were sued. One hundred and nineteen individual cases against them were combined in August 1920 and heard by a special judge. Testimony went on until mid-July 1923. A verdict was not reached until April 1925. I recommend Puleo's book for a description of the outcome and also the other issues going on during the trial, especially the Sacco and Vanzetti case.

There are also many newspaper reports from the time which I used, and many pictures. There's a plaque at the site of the tank on Commercial Street, and there are annual commemorations. There are even folksongs that have been written about the flood, and you can find animations on the Internet of what actually happened.

Many of the characters in this book are fictional—including the victim, Maggie McKenna, her policeman husband, her sister Theresa, and Theresa's family. The Italian workers, Luigi and Tony, are also fictional. There was a real USIA manager, and his tale is told in Puleo's book, but I chose to invent Jeremy Wrentham, who is completely fictional.

The World War I veterans portrayed in the book are all fictional, including Matthew Bradley and Edwin O'Connell. A useful source about WWI soldiers was *The World War I Memoirs of Robert P. Patterson*. But the war stories of the men in this novel are all fictional.

Frances Glessner Lee and Dr. George "Jake" Meredith Magrath are real historical figures whose work inspired the story. A friend from my Chicago days is a docent at the beautiful historic home known as Glessner House in the South Loop, quite close to where I lived. I first learned about the daughter of the house, Frances Glessner Lee, when I attended a talk there by Corinne May Botz, the author of a book of photos *The Nutshell Studies of Unexplained Death*. With further research, I learned that these fascinating miniature rooms that reproduced crime scenes were quite famous. They were used for several decades in training sessions for police detectives. While Mrs. Lee didn't begin making the dioramas until the 1940s, I've used literary license to create a situation in which she would be inspired to create the first of her crime scene miniatures. Eventually, the rooms were moved to Maryland, and the Smithsonian recently restored the miniatures and displayed them in an exhibit. I regret that I was not able to see them during that exhibition. Bruce Goldfarb's *18 Tiny Deaths: The Untold Story of Frances Glessner Lee and the Invention of Modern Forensics* describes Mrs. Lee's work with the Harvard Department of Legal Medicine in great detail.

I was intrigued by the huge effort Mrs. Lee had put into the nutshell studies and wondered why. I learned that she even became known as the "Mother of Forensic Science." Since I was writing another historical mystery series set in the same time period, I was very curious as to how she got involved in this type of work. It seemed like an unlikely career for a society woman of the time.

This led me to Dr. Magrath, who, between 1907 and 1935, was the medical examiner in my hometown of Boston. Mrs. Lee endowed a Chair of Legal Medicine at Harvard University, and Dr. Magrath was the first person appointed to that chair. She also contributed a library of books on legal medicine to the university. When I looked into Dr. Magrath, I found articles by and about him. In particular, there were obituaries that described his vigorous and busy life.

I wanted to put the two fascinating characters together. I felt that they must have known each other. I found more information about Mrs. Lee and her family from various publications of the Glessner House. Indeed, Dr. Magrath was a friend of Frances Lee's brother. Also, I discovered, from an article on the Glessner site, that Mrs. Lee had been resident manager of a home for returning soldiers in Boston in 1919.

Dr. Magrath actually did examine the victims of the molasses flood and provided testimony at the ensuing trials. But I have no evidence that Mrs. Lee was involved, although she was in Boston at the time. I chose one of the nutshell studies as a rough model and invented the story for my book. That is the fictional part.

I have to thank William Tyre, Executive Director & Curator of Glessner House in Chicago for doing a close reading of the manuscript in an early state and offering many useful suggestions. I think I made all of the changes he suggested except for one. Bill pointed out the Frances Glessner was not called "Fanny" after she came of age at 18. And he questioned Dr. Magrath's nickname of "Jake." However, I did verify Jake as Magrath's familiar name, and in the case of Frances Glessner Lee, I was imagining that she and Jake were meeting after many years but had gotten to know each other when they were young. So, it is in a fictional re-imagining that I have my heroine think of herself as "Fanny." As we age, I think most people do continue to think of themselves as their younger selves beneath the aging skin. So, my apologies if it seems a little off to use her younger nickname, but I did it purposely to have her think of how she can reinvent herself when she wants to change her life at a midpoint. That is all fiction, thoughts of the author, so I hope Frances Glessner Lee would not be offended by the liberty.

Rose Standish Nichols is another real historical character. When I retired to Boston, I volunteered as a guide at the Nichols House Museum on Beacon Hill. From the museum staff, and research materials they provided to volunteers, I learned about Miss Nichols and wanted to include her. I have invented the sewing circle and the Sunday salon scenes at Nichols House, but I believe such debates were held in her parlor later in the next decade. I took the liberty of having a discussion of the molasses flood take place there. However, the men who appear in that scene were the real participants in the first trial that is described in Puleo's book.

Senator Henry Cabot Lodge was a historical character, but I have invented his involvement with Wendell House, my fictional characters, and the molasses flood. I have only presented some of his anti-suffrage and anti-immigrant views, but there was much more to his life. The scene where the Wendell House board dismissed Mrs. Lee is entirely fictional. She was happily employed there until July 1919, when the temporary work of returning the soldiers to their homes had always been meant to end.

Cornelia Thornwell is a fictional character. I have to confess that I borrowed her name and some of her characteristics from a character in Upton Sinclair's lengthy novel *Boston,* which is based on the Sacco and Vanzetti case. Sinclair portrays historical figures in the book, but he also invented a Brahmin widow and her fictional family as a contrast to the immigrant society of the time. I believe she is roughly based on some real women he met in Boston during the protest movement. I thought she was a good foil for some of the powerful men in my book, so I borrowed the name and created my own character.

Many of the places in the book are real historical places. Some still exist, while others have disappeared. My family has always loved going to the North End, a favorite of my FBI agent, and later police commissioner, father. I have a nephew who lived in the building that was the Florence Hotel on Fleet Street, and it was his interest in the possible history of the structure that led me to discover it had been a hotel with a café. He has a great roof deck, so that inspired the rooftop scenes.

The Charles Street Jail is now the Liberty Hotel, with one of its restaurants named "The Clink." You can still get a Negroni and oysters at the bar of Marliave, as I recently discovered with an old college friend. At first, I invented a soldier's home at the bottom of Beacon Hill, but then I found out that Fanny Lee had been at Wendell House and that the buildings still exist in the street behind the state house. They are just up Mt. Vernon Street from the Nichols House Museum, where I was volunteering as a guide before the COVID-19 pandemic shut it down. The Ritz Carlton hotel, where they held the dinners that were part of the Harvard Department of Legal Medicine seminars, has had a number of transformations over the years. I have fond memories of family outings to the Ritz for Easter breakfast, followed by a ride on the swan boats in the Boston Public Garden.

I love cities like Boston and Chicago, where my other books are set. It seems to me they are like coral reefs built up over time by the human creatures who have lived in them and left something behind when they are gone. I wanted to write a book set in my hometown of Boston, and I was intrigued by the lives and works of Frances Glessner Lee and Dr. George Magrath. The strange and fantastic incident of the molasses tank explosion offered a compelling backdrop for my story. I hope you enjoy this entirely fictional account.

Acknowledgements

Thanks to my writing group, Leslie Wheeler, Katherine Fast, Cheryl Marceau and Mark Ammons. Also, to my beta readers including my former editor Emily Victorson, Stuart Miller, and William Tyre Executive Director and Curator of Glessner House in Chicago. Thanks to Harriette Sackler and the staff of Level Best Books. Any errors are all my own.

About the Author

Frances McNamara grew up in Boston, where her father served as Police Commissioner for ten years. She has degrees from Mount Holyoke and Simmons Colleges and retired from the University of Chicago. She now divides her time between Boston and Cape Cod.

She is the author of the Emily Cabot Mystery series in addition to the Nutshell Murders series.

CPSIA information can be obtained
at www.ICGtesting.com
Printed in the USA
LVHW110820200223
739750LV00002B/9